AN

Accidental

MURDERER

BOOK ONE OF THE SYDNEY LEGAL SERIES

CHRIS TAYLOR

Books by Chris Taylor

THE MUNRO FAMILY SERIES
(In order)

The Profiler
The Investigator
The Predator
The Betrayal
The Deception
The Negotiator
The Christmas Vigil
The Ransom
The Defendant
The Shooting
The Maker
(Available in Audio)

THE SYDNEY HARBOUR HOSPITAL SERIES
(in order)

The Perfect Husband
The Body Thief
The Baby Snatchers
The Final Bullet
The Debt Collector
The Lab Test
The Stolen Identity
The Cliff-top Killer
The Likeable Fraudster

THE SYDNEY LEGAL SERIES
(in order)

An Accidental Murderer
At the Hand of her Father
A Woman Scorned
Lies and Deception
Ordinary Evil
The Ties That Bind
The Perfect Crime
Malicious Love
Toxic Inheritance

THE BARRINGTON FAMILY SERIES
(in order)

Broken Lives
Broken Promises
Broken Bonds
Broken Spirits
Broken Vows
Broken Minds
Broken Dreams
Broken Hearts
Broken Homes

THE CRAIGDON FAMILY SERIES
(in order)

Callum
Joel
Isabella
Nicholas
Sophia
Flynn
Noah
Logan
Elizabeth

Get a FREE book when you sign up for Chris Taylor's newsletter at: www.christaylorauthor.com.au

Love Audiobooks? Check out Chris Taylor Books on audio on Audible.com, Amazon.com and the iBooks store.

Join Chris Taylor's Facebook reader group/fan page and be among the first to receive news of book releases, read and review books prior to release and other amazing offers. Join Now at: www.facebook.com/groups/1758023621144744/

Find out more about all of Chris Taylor's books, by visiting her website at: www.christaylorauthor.com.au/about/books

DEDICATION

This book is dedicated to all the wonderful nurses and doctors who care for our loved ones when they are sick and ailing like they're one of their own. The world is a better place for your dedication.

And as always, to my very own sexy hero: my husband, Linden. I love you.

Acknowledgments

As usual, no book comes into being without a lot of help and support by my friends and family. A world of thanks must go to my wonderful editor, Pat Thomas. Thank you for everything that you do to make my stories even more amazing than I could ever dare to dream. To former Detective Superintendent Michael Kilfoyle, thank you for lending my story credibility. Any mistakes are wholly my own.

To Damon Freeman, Chrissy and all of the staff at damonza.com, thank you for yet another fantastic cover. To my sister, Nicole Guihot and to my friend, Ally Thomson, thank you for your excellent editorial comments, proof reading skills and suggestions. I hope you like the final result.

To Amy Atwell and her dedicated staff at Author E.M.S. who are so much more than book formatters. Amy, once again, thank you for your magic.

To the fantastic writer organizations such as Romance Writers of Australia, Romance Writers of

America and Romance Writers of New Zealand for all the help, support and encouragement they offer new and aspiring writers, including me.

To my readers, thank you for your support and love for my stories. Your encouragement and enjoyment make this journey all worthwhile.

And lastly, to my friends and family, especially my husband and children. Thank you for putting up with late dinners and even later conversations as I've emerged day after day from the sometimes scary but always enthralling world I've created on my computer.

PROLOGUE

The ward of the Lady of Lourdes Nursing Home was dark and quiet, save for the occasional snore or snuffle or groan. Nurse Jiao Zheng squinted in the dimness at the label on the medicine bottle in her hand and did her best to decipher the words. Tugging a small flashlight from the pocket of her uniform, she adjusted the beam so that it better illuminated the label and once again concentrated on the writing.

The bottle looked and felt just like the cough serum she'd administered earlier to the elderly patient who moved restlessly in the bed. From memory, the medication chart required that she administer two tablespoons of the stuff. Jiao checked the medication chart again and frowned. *Was that two tablespoons, or two teaspoons?* The words looked so much the same and it was even harder to read them in the dark.

Did it matter so much if she got it wrong? Surely a little extra couldn't hurt? It might even do some good. Poor Dulcie Eveleigh had been coughing something awful for the best part of a week. *Perhaps she needed something stronger?*

Still, it wasn't Jiao's place to question the doctor's orders. She was only a second-year nurse. Nobody would pay attention to what she might have to say. Besides, she wasn't brave enough to go suggesting alternate treatment options to members of the medical fraternity. Someone might take offense. Her job could be threatened and that was something she wouldn't jeopardize. Not for anyone.

The money she earned from the Lady of Lourdes Nursing Home wasn't as good as it would have been if she'd been employed in a busy Sydney hospital, but it was better than what she could have made back home in China. Her family were depending upon her fortnightly wage for their survival. She sent them nearly everything she made. It was never enough, but it was something and more—much more—than they would have received if she'd stayed in her hometown, undereducated and unemployed. She only wished her mother was still alive to see how successful she'd become...

Yes, she'd made the right decision to come to study in Australia. Not only had she obtained her university credentials at the reputable Richmond University and secured a job straight after graduation, she had a far better life in Sydney than she could have ever dreamed of while living in Shenzhen, a large city of more than ten million people situated in the southern part of China. Her family's life had improved, too.

Besides, she loved nursing, despite the challenges she faced. The English words were the worst, although she couldn't complain. She read better than many of her fellow students, especially those who had arrived in Australia from non-English speaking parts of the world.

Setting aside her flashlight, she poured liquid into a measuring cup. One tablespoon measured about fifteen milliliters, give or take. She remembered the conversion rate from college. She filled the cup to the fifty-milliliter mark. A little extra couldn't hurt. Leaning closer, she gently shook her patient's shoulder.

"Dulcie? Are you awake? It's Nurse Zheng. I have some medicine for you."

The woman struggled to open her eyes. She looked up at Jiao, her gaze dazed and unfocused in the dimness.

"Nurse? Is that you?" the old woman croaked.

"Yes, Mrs Eveleigh. It's time to take your medicine. Here, I'll help you sit up." Jiao moved closer and put her hand beneath the woman's head. With infinite gentleness, she raised her patient up until the woman could drink the medicine from the cup. Almost immediately, she pulled a face.

"What is that, Nurse? It tastes dreadful."

"It's cough mixture, to help your chest," Jiao replied, smiling benignly. "The doctor prescribed it."

As if on cue, her patient started coughing. The sound of it broadened Jiao's smile. She'd seen enough chest infections in the past two years to know this one had taken a strong hold. So many of their residents died from pneumonia and it always started out like this: a hacking cough that just didn't get any better. Dulcie's time was near.

"It's burning, Nurse!" the old woman said around a gasp. "Are you sure it's cough mixture?"

"Of course I'm sure. Now, lie back down and I'll get you settled. It's late. Nearly two o'clock."

"In the morning?" the patient rasped.

"Yes, Dulcie, in the morning. You try and go back to sleep."

"It's still burning, Nurse. My throat's on fire."

"It's just the medicine doing its work, my dear. You'll be fine."

"I don't feel fine."

Jiao *tut tutted* and fussed around the woman, tucking in the sheet around her and making sure she was comfortable.

"How's that now, Mrs Eveleigh?" she asked. A groan muffled against the pillow was her patient's only response.

"I'll see you in the morning," Jiao said cheerfully, ignoring the woman's discomfort. Taking care to leave the bottle of medicine on the nightstand, she collected the measuring cup and on silent, rubber-soled feet, quietly left the room.

CHAPTER 1

Six weeks later

Ben Fitzgerald's fingers moved lightning fast over the keyboard. It was always this way when he was in the home stretch of drafting his closing arguments. The witnesses had taken the stand; the evidence had been presented; documents had been tendered by both sides. As the lawyer for the plaintiff, Ben got to make his closing arguments first. It was his favorite part of any trial, especially one like this, a trial he was confident he would win.

His client had been in a motor vehicle collision with another car and had suffered permanent injuries. Samuel Anderson was barely nineteen and now, because of the accident, he'd spend the rest of his life in a wheelchair. There was no question the woman who'd caused the accident was liable. She'd been texting on the phone and had run a red light. The only thing up for discussion was the damages.

Blood taken from Sam in the emergency room right after the accident had disclosed a small amount of alcohol in his system. The defendant's lawyers were looking to pass off some of the blame and they were right to do so. The alcohol in Sam's blood was a mitigating factor. There was no getting around the fact that his impairment, however slight, had contributed to the accident. It was now a matter for the jury to decide how much of it was Sam's fault. Ben had argued long and loudly that it was a miniscule amount.

Still, even if the jury accepted that Ben's client must bear a proportion of the blame, Ben was confident their award for damages would be far more generous than the original offer put forward by the defendant's insurance company three months earlier. It was what he was betting on.

A sharp rap on his office door caught his attention. He looked up from the computer screen just as Blake Harton Junior filled the open doorway.

"What are you up to, mate?" Blake asked, closing the door behind him.

"I'm writing my closing arguments," Ben replied. "Tomorrow's the last day of the Anderson trial." He returned his attention to the words in front of him.

"How's it been going?" Blake asked and took a seat in one of the two matching leather high-backed chairs that stood opposite Ben's desk.

Ben shrugged. "Well, I think. The jury seems comfortably sympathetic. They're all still looking me in the eye. That has to be a good sign. Eight of the twelve are middle-aged women. I got lucky."

Blake chuckled. "You did, indeed. A dream jury

for an MVA. Hopefully, they all have sons around Sam's age."

"Yeah. That's what I'm aiming for and of course, I've made sure they're very aware the damages will be coming from the insurance company who owns the rather prominent building on the corner. It's not like it's coming out of the defendant's pocket." Ben typed in a few more words and then paused to look at Blake. "Are you here for any reason in particular, or are you just wanting to chew the fat?"

Blake tried to look affronted. "And here I thought you'd be pleased to see me! Didn't I agree to take that Jennings matter off your hands? By the way, the man's an asshole, just like you said. You owe me, big time."

"Yeah, right." Ben grinned, not in the least remorseful. He'd been flat out with the Anderson trial. He hadn't had a moment to give to the Jennings case. Besides, he'd done work for the man before. Brian Jennings was rude and arrogant and thought all lawyers were scum, especially those he was forced to call upon to get him out of his latest financial fix.

Ben had lost count of the number of times the man had declared his company bankrupt. It didn't seem to matter to Jennings. He'd have a new company set up before the ink was dry on the bankruptcy papers and in the blink of an eye would be back in business. Ben had no time for sharks like Jennings, but unfortunately, he didn't get to call the shots.

Despite the fact Ben billed more hours than

every other associate at Harton & Wentworth, he still hadn't made partner. That would all change when the Anderson judgment was handed down. He was sure of it. At least, he hoped things would turn out that way. He had no intention of remaining an associate for the rest of his days, even a senior one with a nice office.

It was easy for Blake. His grandfather had started the firm. Blake's father was a senior partner. Nobody was surprised when Blake was offered a junior partnership the year before last. Ben didn't begrudge him. Blake worked hard and he was one of the best criminal defense lawyers in town. Ben was proud to call him a friend. Glancing back at the man, he noticed Blake's expression had turned serious.

"So, what brings you here?" Ben asked. "It's too late in the day to invite me out to lunch."

His attempt at a joke fell flat. Blake stared at him somberly and leaned closer toward Ben's desk.

"I want to tell you about a client of mine."

Ben groaned and rolled his eyes, trying hard to suppress a grin. "I knew I'd have to do a payback somewhere. Can't it wait until after the Anderson trial? We'll finish closing arguments tomorrow. I'm sure the jury won't take more than a day or two to decide and then I'll be all yours."

"I guess it can wait a couple days," Blake replied and pushed away from Ben's desk.

Ben watched him turn and head toward the door and was flooded with guilt. Blake had helped him out more than once. Repaying the favor was the least he could do.

"Hey, Blake. I'm sorry. Sit down. Tell me about your client."

With a sigh, Blake returned to his seat and opened the file he held in his hand. Ben hadn't noticed it earlier.

"Well, this client is Miss Jiao Zheng, but her case is almost finalized. I want to talk to you about another case arising out of this."

Ben nodded. "Go on."

"First, I'll give you the background of Zheng's matter. It will help you to understand where I'm coming from. Zheng's a Chinese nurse who graduated from Richmond University two years ago. She got a job straight out of college at the Lady of Lourdes Nursing Home."

"Is that the one in Strathfield?" Ben asked.

"Yes. It has a good reputation, but six weeks ago, a patient by the name of Dulcie Eveleigh died from poisoning while under Zheng's care. Nurse Zheng was charged with murder."

"Wow. I must have missed that on the news. I've been buried deep in this Anderson trial for weeks. I haven't paid much attention to the outside world. Is there any evidence Zheng intended for the woman to die?"

Blake compressed his lips and shook his head. "No, but the police were under pressure to lay serious charges. Dulcie Eveleigh was the mother of the Minister for Immigration. George Eveleigh is complaining to anybody who'll listen that Zheng's a murderous foreigner in the guise of a nurse, intent on spreading evil across our shores. I'm sure if she were Muslim, he'd be accusing ISIS of playing a part."

Ben shook his head in disgust. "Where the hell are we going with all this and why are the media paying him any heed? I thought we were supposed to be more accepting of our international visitors, not less."

"That's the world we live in today, whether you like it or not," Blake said dryly.

Ben refrained from offering a reply and Blake continued. "Unfortunately for Zheng, she made a number of admissions during the initial police interview."

Ben frowned in disbelief. "She admitted to murder?"

"No, but she confessed to not knowing what was contained in the medicine bottle and being unable to decipher the doctor's handwriting. She wasn't sure of the correct dosage, but she administered the medicine, anyway."

Ben stared at Blake in surprise. "Hell. Who does that?"

Blake nodded. "Not only did Zheng administer the incorrect dosage, she also gave Dulcie Eveleigh more than fifty milliliters of hydrogen peroxide instead of the prescribed medicine on her chart."

Ben's body flooded with shock. "Holy shit! *Hydrogen peroxide?* Who makes a mistake like that? What did she think she was giving the poor woman?"

Blake regarded him solemnly. "She thought it was cough medicine."

"Fuck."

Blake nodded grimly. "Yeah."

"Where was the cough medicine?"

"It was found in the top drawer of the deceased's nightstand. The bottles were of a similar shape and size. In the dark, I guess it was easy enough to become confused."

"Yes, but—" Ben protested and Blake waved his hand in dismissal.

"I know what you're going to say and that's one of the reasons Zheng pleaded guilty to manslaughter."

Ben stared down at his desk, his thoughts far away from the closing arguments on his screen. He couldn't imagine how the victim's family felt. No wonder her son was screaming murder. It was a terrible mistake. A truly terrible mistake.

"How did she come to be your client?" Ben asked quietly.

"I got a call from a buddy at Legal Aid. She'd phoned his office but she didn't qualify for assistance. She works fulltime at the nursing home. At least, she did. Naturally, she's been fired." Blake sighed. "She's in a fix."

"You've got that right."

"Yeah, well, like I said, the police had no evidence of intent, but the admissions she made weren't going away. Early on, we tried to argue the language barrier and the fact that she didn't receive legal advice until after the initial interview. I came before Judge Howard and did my best to convince him she didn't understand the questions put to her by the police, but Howard didn't buy it. He quite rightly pointed out that my client was a college graduate who'd worked as a registered nurse for the past two years. He wouldn't believe her English skills were so poor as to not understand the police questions or that she wasn't bright enough to know she might need the services of a lawyer."

"Let me guess," Ben replied. "Judge Howard threw out your motion."

Blake grimaced. "You got it. So we weren't left with many options. The best I could do was get the charges reduced to manslaughter in return for a guilty plea. The prosecution's agreed to a five-year, non-parole period. With good behavior, she might be out in three. She's on bail at the moment with her passport revoked. She'll be officially sentenced the day after tomorrow."

Ben nodded. "You did as well as you could, given the circumstances. If this had gone to trial and she'd been found guilty, she would have been looking at double that and from what you've told me, the chances of being found guilty at trial sound like they were high. How did your client take the news?"

"I explained, of course, the risk she'd be taking if she went to trial. We talked about the weight of evidence the prosecution had against her. Her odds of winning weren't great. It's the reason she eventually agreed to enter a guilty plea, but even so, she wasn't overjoyed with the plea bargain. Who would be? Any time in prison has to be seen as a failure on the part of the lawyer and a criminal conviction of this nature will no doubt see her deported as soon as she does her time."

Ben frowned. "Don't tell me she's blaming you? She ought to be grateful you managed to get the sentence reduced to five years. If she'd been stuck with an overworked and underpaid lawyer from Legal Aid, she might have been facing a lot more jail time."

"Yeah, well unfortunately, most defendants don't see it that way. I think in some distant part of her brain she actually thought she might be let off with a slap on the wrist."

Ben stared at his friend, incredulous. "Are you kidding? Is she from another planet, or something?"

Blake offered a tiny smile. "No, China, actually. I'm not sure how they deal with this type of thing over there, but she was definitely taken aback when I told her she was facing jail time."

Ben shook his head in disbelief. "Some people just don't know when they're offered a good thing. I mean, this case is going to be all over the media. I'm surprised I haven't heard about it already. Then again, like I said, I've been caught up in this Anderson trial. It's taken all my focus."

"Yeah, I know how that is," Blake replied with a brief smile. "I'm glad I caught you at the end of it. I thought you might like to help."

Ben nodded. "I was wondering where the payback came in. Since you've already negotiated a great deal and the woman's about to be sentenced, it's not Zheng you want my help for. What gives?"

"You're right," Blake replied. "This doesn't involve my client, at least, not directly. I'm talking about the Lady of Lourdes Nursing Home and Richmond University."

Ben shook his head. "Okay, now I'm totally confused."

Once again, Blake leaned forward in his seat. "Zheng didn't administer the incorrect dosage and medicine to intentionally cause harm."

He paused and Ben was filled with a surge of impatience. "Okay, I get that. You've already told me the nurse was filled with remorse and the prosecution would never have agreed to drop the murder charges down to manslaughter if they thought they could prove intent. So, what's the reason? Why did she kill Dulcie Eveleigh?"

"Zheng administered a lethal dose of hydrogen peroxide to her patient because the poor nurse couldn't read."

"What?" Ben exclaimed. "I thought you just said this woman was a college graduate? And didn't you tell me the judge didn't buy your argument that your client didn't understand the questions put to her by the police? You're not making sense."

"She *is* a college graduate, hence my reference to Richmond University. Judge Howard refused to accept my arguments that she couldn't understand English, but the truth is, despite her college degree and the fact that she speaks English reasonably well, she was unable to properly read both the label on the medicine bottle and the medication chart written by the doctor. These unfortunate circumstances combined late one fateful night and led to the death of Dulcie Eveleigh."

"Bloody hell," Ben muttered, still trying to get his

head around it. "How the hell did she graduate from an Australian university without being able to read English?"

Blake smiled. "That, my friend, is the question I want you to answer. A woman is dead because her nurse was unable to read. A nurse who was apparently qualified. Someone fucked up somewhere along the way and they should be made to pay. I want you to look into it. File a lawsuit against the university on behalf of the beneficiaries to Dulcie Eveleigh's estate. Hopefully once you explain your reasons, you can get them on board...and while you're at it, add the nursing home to the claim. Someone, somewhere must have known about this, and yet they set Zheng loose on unsuspecting patients for the past two years. Frankly, I can't believe she hasn't had a hand in more deaths. We're lucky she was caught the first time."

"You can say that again," Ben murmured.

"We're lucky she was—"

"Ha! Everyone's a comedian," Ben interrupted with a roll of his eyes. He followed it with a quick smile.

Blake threw up his hands in surrender. "Hey, what can I say? I can't help it if I'm a funny guy."

"Yeah, you're real funny, Harton. But here's my word of advice for you: Don't give up your day job."

This time, Blake laughed and Ben joined him in his mirth. Finally, the two men sobered.

"So, you'll take the case?" Blake asked.

Ben thought about all that Blake had told him

and nodded solemnly. "Yeah, okay. I'll do it. Are we administering the Eveleigh estate?"

"No, but I'm sure you can persuade the beneficiaries to see it your way and put their name to a lawsuit for wrongful death. The aggrieved son has been giving sound bites to the media every opportunity he gets. He'll be only too happy to see someone pay for his mother's death. As a former lawyer, I'm betting the minister isn't afraid of being inside a courtroom."

"I guess this means we're square, then? Eveleigh for Jennings, right?"

Blake smiled. "That sounds fair. And thanks, Ben. I really appreciate you taking this on. I told Jiao Zheng that somehow, we'd make whoever's responsible pay for sending her out into the world, ill-equipped to handle the challenges of her profession." He paused and shook his head, as if overcome anew by the enormity of what had happened. "Graduating her from nursing school, knowing full well she was unable to read English… For Pete's sake, what's this world coming to?"

"That's if they knew," Ben murmured.

Blake's expression turned fierce. "I don't know who's in charge over at Richmond University, but whoever it is, they want to hope like hell they didn't." With that, he stood and headed toward the door. Before he reached it, he swung back around to face Ben.

"Oh, by the way, did you hear? The big boss is calling a meeting at five. He wants everyone to be there."

"What's that about?" Ben asked, curious. It

wasn't often the managing partner called a firm-wide meeting.

"I don't know, but if you want any chance of making junior partner, I suggest you show." With a final wave, Blake was gone.

Chapter 2

It was a couple of minutes before five when Ben exited the elevator on the fifteenth floor of the building that housed the offices of Harton & Wentworth. He'd managed to finish his closing arguments and had even had time to do a little research on Richmond University before the scheduled meeting. Blake's account of what had happened to his client intrigued Ben and he was determined to discover how such a thing had come about. *How did a nursing student graduate without being able to properly read the kind of English required for the job they'd take on?* It just didn't make sense.

Ben rounded the corner and pulled up short. The function room was nearly full to bursting. The room was noisy with chatter. Whatever the managing partner, Frederick Wentworth, had to say, it must be important. Ben spied Dimitri Gianopoulos on the far side of the room and made his way toward him.

"Dimitri! How are you doing?" he greeted his

friend and colleague with a hearty slap on the back.

"Ben! Where have you been? I've barely seen you around these past weeks."

Ben grimaced. "I've been flat out, fighting for a decent award for damages relating to a motor vehicle case."

Dimitri grinned. "Let me guess. Another sad tale of a plaintiff who's been screwed over by their big bad insurance company and who can't afford a legal bill. You're doing it *pro bono*, right?"

Ben laughed, taking the gibe in the spirit it was intended. "No, mate. This one's paying his way. Or at least, his mom and dad are. He's an Anderson from Vaucluse."

Dimitri gave a low whistle, looking impressed. "Well done! That's sure to keep the partners happy. How much are you talking?"

"The kid was T-boned by a woman who ran a red light. He's now a paraplegic. I'm going for the maximum."

"It sounds like a done deal. What's the insurance company even fighting about?"

Ben compressed his lips. "My guy's blood was tested in emergency. He was over the limit. Only a little, but he's a provisional driver. Zero tolerance."

Dimitri nodded in understanding. "Contributory negligence."

"You got it in one."

They fell silent and Ben surveyed the crowd and then glanced back toward Dimitri. "What's going on here?"

Dimitri shrugged. "Your guess is as good as mine."

Ben elbowed his friend in the ribs. "Maybe old man Wentworth's going to announce your partnership. It's about time they made that call."

Dimitri looked embarrassed. "After all that stuff that went down with my father...and my mother warming her butt in jail... I don't think so."

He looked so sad, Ben couldn't help but feel sorry for him. Dimitri's legal career had been going from strength to strength. He'd been a shoo-in for junior partner. Everyone had guessed it would happen before the end of the year. Then Dimitri's father, a senior partner at the same law firm, had come out as a gay man and his wife had been charged with a number of grisly murders. It had been a bizarre time for everyone, most especially Dimitri. Ben admired the man for holding his head high and continuing to work there. It couldn't have been easy.

"Yeah, somehow I don't think it has anything to do with my name and a partnership," Dimitri muttered.

Once again, Ben felt a stab of sympathy at the sad resignation in his friend's eyes. Ben couldn't imagine what it would feel like to sit back and watch your dreams die. He too yearned for a partnership. Every waking hour was spent working toward that goal. He was sure it would happen for him one day, and hopefully one day soon. Winning the Anderson case with a generous award for damages would go a long way to helping him achieve that partnership.

"All right, everybody, listen up."

The order for attention came from the managing partner, Frederick Wentworth. Even at seventy-four, the man stood tall and stately. He exuded calmness and authority and it was no surprise he'd been a formidable opponent in a courtroom. His thick white hair was neatly styled and framed an equally handsome face. Ben hadn't known Frederick in his younger days, but he could imagine he'd been a man to be reckoned with. Beside him, stood Blake Harton Senior, Blake's father.

Wentworth's deep baritone rumbled across the room. "Thank you for coming together on such short notice. I know you're all busy and I appreciate you giving me a little of your time."

Ben hid a wry smile. Only a fool would ignore an order that had come directly from the managing partner. Besides, like him, everyone in the room was curious as to why they were gathered there.

"I'm sure you're all wondering why we're here," Wentworth continued, as if reading Ben's mind. "Well, let me put your minds at rest." The man cleared his throat and continued.

"We've had a little excitement in the firm in recent months. I'm sure you've heard about it. Facts, rumors, half-truths—it doesn't take a genius to realize they've all done the rounds of the office, not to mention the gossip columns. Well, I'm here to set the facts straight and thereafter, it will never be referred to again.

"The truth is, one of our senior partners, Alexei Gianopoulos, has had some personal troubles. His wife was charged with several murders and is currently awaiting trial. Alexei also came forward with a...revelation." Wentworth paused and looked around the room, his gaze narrowed in a glare, as if daring anyone to contradict him. A moment later, he continued.

"Suffice it to say, the ensuing publicity has been far from positive for the firm and Alexei was only too happy to take an extended leave of absence. He remains a senior partner in this firm and we will do all we can to support him during these difficult times. He's also entitled to his privacy and I'd like to remind you that you're all under a gag order insofar as the media are concerned. No interviews, no sound bites, no opinion pieces. Period. I don't care if it's a two-bit rag or the *Sydney Morning Herald*. Those of us at Harton and Wentworth pride ourselves on taking care of our own and that includes keeping out inquisitive reporters and anyone else who is of a mind to sully our good name."

Wentworth's steely eyed glare moved around the room once again. Blake Harton Senior's followed suit. "Do I make myself clear?" Wentworth asked in a no-nonsense tone.

A low murmur of assent echoed across the floor. Ben was only too happy to join in. In his experience, loyalty was something that was often in short supply in the real world. He was all for the show of support now.

Wentworth nodded his approval. "Good. That's what I expect to hear. Now, there's something else. Though some of you might question the timing, the truth is, the senior partners and I have been thinking about this for some time. It's important to stay current in this fast-moving world of ours and one way we're going to do it is to change our name."

There was a collective gasp of disbelief. Ben was just as surprised as the rest. The name Harton & Wentworth went back several generations. It had enjoyed an outstanding reputation and was synonymous with success. Only the cream of the crop worked there. Ben had worked his butt off to secure the marks at law school before he even dreamed of applying for a job there. Six years earlier, he'd been stunned when they offered him a position. Every day since, he worked harder than the last, in his quest to be the next junior partner.

Wentworth glanced at Harton and then lifted one hand in an effort to silence the room. The murmur of voices faded away.

"I understand that this might come as a shock to some of you, but we've taken a vote and the result is unanimous. From now on, Harton and Wentworth will be known as Sydney Legal."

"Like the TV show, *Boston Legal*?" someone asked and there was a titter through the crowd.

"Exactly," Wentworth beamed. "I've always had a soft spot for James Spader and William Shatner."

Once again, a ripple of amusement filled the room. Ben glanced around him, not sure whether to join in. He caught Dimitri's eye and leaned in close, pitching his voice low.

"Is Wentworth hinting at Shatner's sexuality?"

"Who knows? The show ended with Denny and Alan getting married," Dimitri replied out of the side of his mouth. "But Wentworth's been with his wife for more than fifty years. Dad and I attended the golden anniversary bash. It was held at the Hilton." He shrugged. "Then again, look at my parents! Hell, I'm as confused as you."

Ben returned his attention to the managing partner. If the man did have a soft spot for homosexuals, it boded well for Dimitri and his father. Ben was glad. Both men were fine lawyers. They deserved to be judged for that alone, not on their personal lives and who they chose to sleep with.

"And one more thing before we go," Wentworth added, interrupting the murmur of voices. He turned slightly to one side and ushered a young woman forward. Her navy-blue suit fitted snugly, hugging her curves. Her five-inch heels made her long slim legs appear even longer. Long blond hair hung straight past her shoulders. Her face was turned away from Ben as she directed her attention to his boss.

"I'd like to welcome our latest staff member. This young lady is a fourth-year lawyer. We've snatched her away from Pearce and Kew. She has a reputation for having a fine legal mind and I'm proud to be able to say she'll be joining our team of associates. She specializes in children's court cases and will be working under Malcolm Pring. Please put your hands together and welcome Abby Brown."

The room filled with the sound of polite

applause. The woman turned to face the crowd. Ben focused on the perfect features of her face...and froze.

Abby Brown? What the hell? It couldn't be.

Seemingly unfazed by the introduction before several hundred lawyers, the woman surveyed the room calmly with a smile on her face. Her gaze drifted over to Ben and he wanted to turn away and hide. Instead, he braced himself against the impact of her eyes.

Even from this distance, he could tell the cobalt orbs were as brilliant as they'd been fifteen years earlier. He did his best to look away, but found himself snagged by her gaze. Her eyes flared in recognition and her smile faded. It felt like a sucker punch to his gut...

And then she looked away and the moment was over.

Ben sucked in a breath on a harsh gasp and tried hard to slow his racing heart. Abby Brown was a lawyer? Abby Brown was a lawyer in his firm? He couldn't believe it! How had it happened? How had Abby Brown, not only become a lawyer of some repute, but managed to snag a job in the most prestigious firm in town? It didn't seem possible, and yet it was. He shook his head in silent disbelief. The last time he'd seen Abby Brown she was a sixteen-year-old junkie living on the streets.

CHAPTER 3

Abby stared at the unmistakeable features of Ben Fitzgerald and her heart skipped a beat. Stumbling slightly from the unexpectedness of coming up close and personal with a ghost from her past, she clutched at the arm of the managing partner. He shot her a look of concern, coupled with a disapproving frown and she blushed and hurriedly dropped her hand. She'd impressed a lot of people on her way to the job at the reputable Harton & Wentworth—Sydney Legal, now—and she wasn't about to let all that hard work and effort dissolve into nothingness because of the presence of a certain man.

So what if she'd once been madly in love with him? She'd been a teenager. He was her first love. It didn't mean she still had feelings for him. No, she was a mature thirty-one-year-old, now. She knew better than to fall for a pair of smiling green eyes that hid the worst kind of betrayal. Ben Fitzgerald was her past and that's where he had to stay.

Nothing good could ever come of digging all that up again.

Despite her silent pep talk, she couldn't resist peeking at him once again. He looked good. Tall and broad shouldered, he'd filled out over the years. His chest looked as wide as Sydney Harbour, encased in an expensive tailored suit. His dark brown hair was cut shorter than he'd worn it at eighteen. Then again, he'd also been living on the streets. A barber was the last thing on his mind in those days.

Her gaze drifted over the familiar features of his face. The dark, closely cropped beard was new and it suited him. It gave him a mature, sophisticated air. Unable to help herself, she looked into his eyes. Her gaze was immediately captured by his.

The green eyes that stared back at her were wide with surprise and disbelief. He looked just as shell shocked as she felt. *Good*. At least she wasn't the only one affected by their chance encounter. Idly, she wondered at the vagaries of life and the sheer coincidence that they'd both ended up as lawyers. It was the last thing she'd have expected from him fifteen years ago. She was sure he was thinking exactly the same thing about her.

"Is everything all right, Abby?"

Abby blinked and forced her attention back to the man who continued to frown down at her.

"Yes, Mr Wentworth. I'm sorry. I guess... Being presented to such a big crowd in such a way... All those things you said... I'm a little overwhelmed."

The old man chuckled. "Don't be silly. I meant

every word. You're a real catch for our firm. Edgar Pearce used to brag about your success rate in the courtroom. If I didn't know any better, I'd have thought the old bugger was in love with you. He'd sit at the bar in the gentlemen's club night after night and sing your praises." The managing partner's voice dipped lower and his eyes filled with a possessive gleam. "I've stolen you away from him. Now, you're mine."

Abby squirmed a little under the brilliance of his regard. She wasn't anybody's, although she felt a pang of wistfulness at the mention of her old boss.

Edgar Pearce had been the kind of father she wished she'd had. He'd employed her as a legal clerk while she'd still been at college and had encouraged her every step of the way. He saw something in her that no one else had. He'd given her a chance. It was all she'd needed.

But all of that now seemed so long ago. Edgar had been involved in a car accident that left him in a semi-vegetative state and just like that, life as she knew it had irrevocably changed. It hadn't taken long for the piranhas to circle. Edgar's fellow partners had always resented the hold she had over their colleague. Abby was actually grateful when Frederick Wentworth had called her office and invited her out to lunch. She'd been taken aback at his job offer, but had barely hesitated to accept it. Moving across to Harton & Wentworth was exactly what she needed. Today, she was starting afresh—and that meant staying out of the way of Ben Fitzgerald.

Ignoring Wentworth's comment, she politely

excused herself and blended into the crowd. Moving with purpose, she deliberately strode in the opposite direction of her nemesis.

"Abby! Over here!"

Abby looked through the press of bodies and heaved a sigh of relief. Her new friend and colleague, Chinese born, Sally-Ann Li, waved to her, smiling widely.

"Congratulations!" Sally-Ann gushed, throwing her arms around Abby's waist in an enthusiastic hug. "I had no idea I was in such esteemed company. You never said a thing."

Abby felt heat rise from her neck and creep across her cheeks. She ducked her head, embarrassed by the praise. Sally-Ann was a brilliant fourth-year associate who worked on the same floor. In the three days since Abby had started, the two of them had become fast friends.

"Don't be silly," Abby responded. "Wentworth's just being kind."

"Now who's being silly?" Sally-Ann replied. "You haven't been here long enough to know Wentworth isn't kind to anyone and he certainly isn't one to offer praise. Not like that, out in the open. Trust me, he's a much more behind-closed-doors kind of guy."

Abby nodded and then changed the subject in an effort to divert the attention away from her. "What happened with Alexei Gianopoulos?"

Sally-Ann heaved an exaggerated sigh and then her lips turned up in a conspiratorial smile. Her voice lowered to a loud whisper. "He came out to everyone and his wife was sent to jail. All at the same time. You should have been here. It was hilarious!"

Abby shook her head in bemusement. It didn't sound hilarious. "Came out? As in, decided he was gay?"

Sally-Ann nodded then shrugged. "He'd been married for more than thirty years, so I guess you'd technically call him bi. Whatever. It provided good fodder around the water cooler, let me tell you."

"When did this happen?" Abby asked.

"About a month ago."

"Wow, and people are still talking about it?"

"Well, Alexei was a senior partner and his gay lover did proclaim his undying affection in the hallway outside Alexei's office to anyone who would listen. I can't remember his name, but apparently he didn't hold back when he declared to the world that Alexei was the love of his life. I wasn't there, but from all accounts, it was quite a spectacle. Factor in the bit about Alexei's wife being sent to jail for multiple murders and that his son, Dimitri, still works here..." Sally-Ann shrugged. "It's good gossip material."

"Alexei's son works here?" Abby asked in surprise.

"Yes. He's been here for years. We all expected that he'd make junior partner this year, but after what's happened with his parents... Still, you can't blame Dimitri for their mistakes. Perhaps he'll still make partner, after all. He certainly deserves it. He's a good lawyer."

Abby nodded absently and cast her gaze

around the room. About half of the occupants had wandered off, but there were still plenty of suits in the room. "Which one is he?" she asked, curious.

Sally-Ann made a show of looking around her. It wasn't until she turned right around that she spied him. "Oh, there he is. Standing against that wall. He's the short one with the dark hair, wearing the charcoal-gray suit. The guy next to him is—"

"Ben Fitzgerald," Abby interrupted. Sally-Ann turned to look at her in surprise.

"Oh, you know Ben? He's awfully cute, isn't he? He's single, you know. I've asked around. He doesn't seem to date anyone from work. I wonder if it's a conscious decision to separate work from play, or if he's gay."

As if aware that he was the topic of their conversation, Ben looked across at them and his gaze locked on Abby's. Sally-Ann's chatter receded to a mere echo in Abby's ears. Her heart pounded, her palms grew damp. She licked her lips that were now bone dry. And still Ben stared at her.

She tried to drag her gaze away and couldn't. Her chest went tight. Her breathing quickened. All of a sudden, she couldn't get enough air. With a gasp, she turned her back on him. Sally-Ann shot her a strange look and then, almost immediately, her friend's expression morphed into a wide smile.

"Oh, my God! Abby! He's coming over here!"

Abby barely had time to register the words before Ben's deep, familiar drawl sounded in her ears. He might have grown older and matured, but his voice was exactly the same. It whispered down her spine and it was all she could do not to shiver from the low, sexy sound of it.

"Abby Brown. I don't believe it. Fancy meeting you here."

Abby tensed and then forced herself to turn and face him, unwilling to make a scene. The last thing she wanted was have her colleagues wonder what was going on between the two of them. Her tight smile barely formed before it disappeared.

"Ben. It's nice to see you again. It's been awhile."

Lips that she'd kissed so many times curved up into a humorless smile. "You can say that again."

Though the words he spoke were innocuous, the expression in his eyes remained hard. Abby's stomach tightened with tension.

"Ben, is it? I don't think we've met. I'm Sally-Ann Li. I work with Abby."

To Abby's relief, Ben was forced to switch his attention to her friend. He shook the hand Sally-Ann held out to him and offered her a smile. Just like that, his features were transformed. His face relaxed into laugh lines. His teeth showed white against the tan of his skin and the darkness of his beard. Abby caught her breath at the sheer sexiness of it.

"Sally-Ann, it's nice to meet you."

He gave her a slow once-over that had Abby gritting her teeth. The petite Asian woman with the curtain of long, glossy black hair, full red lips and high cheekbones turned heads wherever she went. It irked Abby to know that, like most of the men Sally-Ann came across, Ben wasn't immune to her charms.

"How long have you worked here, Ben?" Sally-Ann tittered.

"Six years."

"I've been here four," Sally-Ann replied. "I can't believe in all that time we've never met!"

"I work in litigation," he replied, offering her a casual shrug.

"I guess that explains it," Sally-Ann giggled. "I spend all of my days in the children's court, mostly out at Parramatta. No wonder I haven't run into you before."

Desperate to bring the conversation to an end, Abby cleared her throat. "Yes, well, speaking of children's court, I'm before the judge first thing in the morning." She looked over in Ben's general direction, not feeling brave enough to meet his eyes. "It was nice talking to you again, Ben. Sally-Ann, I'll catch you in the morning."

Without waiting for their response, she turned and took a step in the direction of the exit. A warm hand grasped her firmly by the arm. Even through the thickness of her jacket, she felt his heat. She swallowed a gasp.

"Actually, Abby. I was hoping you might have a few moments. I'd like to speak with you in private."

Ben's low rumble sounded in her ears and once again, her heart took off at a gallop. She looked frantically toward Sally-Ann, but the girl merely shrugged, offered a slight wave and then disappeared into the crowd. As if sensing victory, Ben moved closer. His gaze narrowed. All of a sudden, his air of civility dissolved.

"What the hell are you doing here, Abby?" he snarled.

She took a step back, surprised at the venom in his tone. "W-what do you mean?" she stammered, hating the traitorous beat of her heart caused by his nearness.

"You know exactly what I mean. Of all the law firms to set your sights on, you chose mine. What a coincidence."

His voice dripped with sarcasm. She stared at him coldly, refusing to be intimidated. "What's your point, Ben?"

"You know exactly what my point is! You're here to stir up trouble! There's no other reason you'd target this firm."

She shook her head at him, unable to believe the extent of his arrogance. "It's always been about you, hasn't it, Ben? After all these years, nothing's changed."

His eyes glinted green steel. "Look, I don't know what game you're playing, Abby, but you can forget about it. I've worked damn hard to get where I am. I'm not having you come in and ruin it."

She stared at him, at a loss. "Why would I do that?"

"Because you can," he snarled.

Once again, Abby didn't know what to say. Ben's breath came fast. His face was flushed. He drew in a deep breath and made a visible attempt to get his temper back under control.

"How the hell did you become a lawyer, anyway?" he muttered.

"I could ask the same thing of you," she retorted, suddenly out of patience. She didn't know what Ben thought she was there for, but it was obvious he'd already made up his mind that the two of them weren't going to be friends. She ignored the shaft of disappointment that lodged itself somewhere in the vicinity of her heart and glared at him.

"You aren't the only one who's worked hard to make a success of their life," she snapped.

His gaze raked over her, taking in her hair that was cut and colored in the latest style, the expensive designer suit and the heels that had cost her a week's wages. His lips turned up in a sneer. "I'm not sure how hard you had to work at it, but I have to hand it to you, you've done a good job. I hardly recognized you."

She refrained from responding, knowing he was goading her into doing just that. She was through playing games with Ben Fitzgerald. Whatever they'd once been to each other had ended years ago. It was time to move on.

At her continued silence, Ben's gaze narrowed on hers. "I left all that crap behind me a long time ago," he said, echoing her thoughts. "Nobody knows about my past and that's the way it's going to stay. Got it?"

His voice was low and threatening. Abby held his stare. "Got it. And just so you know, I feel the same way."

He continued to eyeball her. "Good. At least we understand each other."

"Good," she replied.

With a final narrow-eyed glance, he turned on his heel and stalked away.

Abby put a trembling hand up to her chest in an effort to slow her racing heart. She felt like she'd just crossed the finish line after a five-hour marathon. *How dare he accuse her of wanting to expose his past and jeopardize his career?* She couldn't imagine why he'd think that way. They hadn't seen each other for fifteen years. She was happy for the success he'd found. He obviously didn't feel the same way about her. *But why would he think she was there to cause trouble, to take it all away?Could it have something to do with the way he'd abandoned her, all those years ago? Was it possible he felt guilty and expected her to seek revenge?*

She didn't know, but she was beyond curious to find out.

Ben pushed his way through the lawyers who remained in the function room and strode toward his office. Forcing himself to breathe slowly, he made a conscious effort to calm down, but every time he thought of Abby Brown and the threat she presented to his career, his anger reignited.

She must have known he worked at Harton &

Wentworth. It was the only explanation for her presence. If what old man Wentworth said about her was true, she could have secured a job in any number of the reputable law firms in Sydney. But no, she'd taken a position at *his* firm. He couldn't help but feel she'd deliberately sought him out for the purpose of wreaking havoc in his life, just like he'd once wreaked havoc in hers. Yes, that's what this was. Revenge. Abby Brown was seeking revenge. It was the only explanation.

Opening the door to his office, he strode in. He closed the door behind him and then threw himself down in his two-thousand-dollar ergonomic chair. The view of the city and a slice of the green and leafy Hyde Park outside his window normally soothed him, but nothing was going to calm him today. Not until he got to the bottom of why Abby Brown was now working at his firm.

A knock at the door interrupted his sour musings. "Come in."

Dimitri walked through the doorway and took a seat opposite Ben's desk. "Where did you get to? I went looking for you after the meeting and you were gone."

Ben grimaced. "Yeah, I'm sorry. I ran into..." He stopped mid-sentence, unsure about how much to say. He and Dimitri were good friends. They often came to each other for advice—both professional and personal. He completely trusted him. *But did he want his buddy knowing about Abby and the reason she'd put him on edge?*

He hadn't lied when he told her nobody

connected with the legal profession knew about his past. Not even his family—such as it was. The only person in Sydney who knew about his origins was Danielle Porter. He frowned and mentally corrected himself. She was Danielle Craigdon, now. She and Jett had married a month ago and Ben had attended their wedding.

He'd met Danielle at an AA meeting when he was twenty-two. Dani had been just seventeen. They'd hit it off right away and he'd become her sponsor. For a short time, he'd even been her lover, but they'd quickly realized they were better off as friends and they'd remained that way ever since. Ben was pleased Danielle had straightened out her life. She was a pathologist at the Sydney Harbour Hospital and had recently married the love of her life. Things had worked out for Dani. Until running into Abby Brown today, he'd hoped life would be just as kind to him.

Suppressing a sigh, he looked at Dimitri and decided to come clean. They knew each other well enough to share secrets. After all, Dimitri had entrusted him with the secret of his homosexuality. Ben had known his friend was gay a long time before the man had found the courage to come out to his family and friends.

Dimitri looked back at him, his expression filled with curiosity. "You ran into who?"

"Abby Brown," Ben said on a sigh.

Dimitri frowned. "The new girl?"

"Yeah. Except, she's not so new to me. I've known her for a long time. Since I was seventeen. We were...friends."

Dimitri's eyes widened in surprise. "Wow! Was she as hot back then as she is now?"

Ben shook his head. "You're gay, Dimitri. What do you care?"

Dimitri shrugged, smiling unrepentantly. "Just asking."

Ben thought back to all those years ago, remembering Abby's dirty, matted blond hair and the sad blue eyes. The high cheekbones in the much-too-gaunt face. Oh, yeah. Even then, Abby Brown had it all going for her. You just needed to look a little harder. Now it was all there for anyone to see.

The long, gangly limbs that had seemed so awkward and out of proportion when she was a teenager, had morphed into shapely legs that set her above the height of the average woman. She'd stood tall and poised beside Wentworth, looking every bit the successful professional. Her appearance today was a far cry from the dirty, scared, pale girl he'd fallen in love with. He had to admit, that even in those desolate days, she'd harboured a resilience and determination, an inner beauty he'd admired.

"I take it the friendship turned sour," Dimitri said, interrupting Ben's thoughts.

"Excuse me?"

"You said you were friends with Abby Brown. You've run into her looking hotter than any woman has a right to look and yet, I find you in here, hiding. I take it somewhere along the way, your friendship came to an end."

"I'm not hiding," Ben muttered irritably.

Dimitri looked at him askance. "Really? Every other available heterosexual male is still in the function room hoping for a moment with the new girl and you're in your office with the door closed. What would you call that?"

The thought of Ben's male colleagues fawning over Abby sent another surge of irritation rushing through his veins. He made a sound of frustration in the back of his throat and scrubbed at his hair. Abby had only just arrived and already she was turning his life upside down. The thought was beyond annoying.

"So," Dimitri added, leaning back in his chair and putting his hands behind his head, "are you going to tell me what's going on, or do you want me to guess?"

Ben stared at him balefully and then sighed. He might as well spill his guts, tell Dimitri everything. Well, not *everything*, but enough that his friend would understand and hopefully, lend him his support.

"I had a rough childhood. So did Abby. We met while we were both living on the streets of western Sydney. I was seventeen. She was two years younger."

Dimitri shook his head, his mouth slack with shock. "You're shitting me?"

"No. I wish I was."

"But... I don't understand. You're a brilliant lawyer. You wear thousand-dollar suits. You're well on your way to making junior partner. How did you go from being homeless to here?"

Ben compressed his lips and battled the

barrage of memories. "It's a long and tragic story, Dimitri, and one you probably don't want to hear," he replied with forced lightness. "Suffice it to say, a year and a half living rough on the streets was enough for me to realize I wanted more from life. With the help of my grandmother, I got my shit together, sat for my Higher School Certificate and went to college. And here I am."

He spread his arms wide, taking in the custom-built red cedar desk, the matching pen and pencil set that cost more than his secretary made in a week. The generous office, the view. As a senior associate at Harton & Wentworth—Sydney Legal—he had nothing to complain about—except that Abby Brown was now on the payroll.

"Come on, Ben. We're mates. You owe me more than that."

Ben regarded his friend and then nodded slowly. "You're right. The thing is, it's taken me fifteen years of hard work to get where I am today. By the age of eighteen, I was an alcoholic. I'd also dabbled in illegal drugs. Abby was my partner in crime. We weren't proud of the way we lived, but neither of us felt we had a choice. Abby had shit going down at home and me... My mother was dead. My father was in jail. As far as I was concerned, I didn't have a home."

Dimitri's face reflected his surprise. Ben nodded grimly. "Yes, Dimitri, you heard right. My father spent ten years in jail." His bark of laughter was self-deprecating. "We have more in common than you realized."

"I had no idea," Dimitri said quietly.

"Nobody does," Ben rasped.

All of a sudden, the memories of those awful times bombarded him from all sides. He squeezed his eyes shut tightly and clenched his fists in an effort to hold them at bay. When he opened his eyes again, Dimitri regarded him with understanding and compassion. Ben forged on, determined to finish it.

"Like I said, I eventually realized I was on a dead-end trip to nowhere and if I didn't do something about it, I'd die there, drunk and penniless under the bridge. I stopped taking drugs, gave up drinking and a girl I loved with all my heart. I contacted my grandmother. I was fortunate she took me in. I attended AA meetings, got sober. I haven't had a drink in fifteen years."

He stared defiantly at his friend. Dimitri's expression was filled with admiration. "I always wondered why you didn't want to come out drinking with the boys," he murmured. "Now I know."

"Now you know," Ben repeated with a grimace. He hadn't meant to spill his guts like that, but somehow, he was glad he had. He suddenly realized he felt better than he had in a long time. He'd been told a long time ago that confession was good for the soul. *Is that what this was? A confession?* The hell if he knew. All of a sudden, he was through.

"So, now you know why I'm in here hiding, as you so eloquently put it," he said brusquely. "I left that life behind a long time ago, along with Abby and all she represented. Now she's turned up here like a dish laden with garlic that lingers long after it should. I'm betting she had her pick of law firms to choose from and yet, she chose this one. She's here to cause trouble for me. I'm sure of it and I refuse to put up with it. I won't put my career—everything I've worked so hard for—at risk."

Dimitri regarded him calmly. "How do you know she's here to stir up trouble? She's obviously worked hard, too, to lift herself out of the gutter to where she is now. Perhaps she wants nothing more than to get on with her life and put the past behind her, like you?"

Ben slapped his palm against the desk. It stung. He gritted his teeth. "Because, dammit! She's *here!* At Harton—"

"Sydney Legal," Dimitri interrupted mildly.

"Sydney Legal," Ben bit out. "Why *else* would she be here, at the same firm where I work, unless it's to cause trouble?"

To his consternation, Dimitri chuckled. "Wow, I always knew you had healthy self-esteem, but isn't this taking things a bit far? The girl probably had no idea you work here. Why would she? Unless she's been following your career all these years, she might not have even known you were a lawyer. You didn't know *she* was one. Why are you jumping to such ridiculous conclusions? It could simply be coincidence. They have been known to happen every now and then."

Ben clenched his jaw in a gargantuan effort to stem his frustration. Dimitri just didn't understand. Still, Ben had no proof Abby had tracked him to Sydney Legal. It was just that in his gut, it felt likely and he wasn't prepared to set the matter aside until he knew for sure.

"Did you ask her why she took a job here?" Dimitri asked, his tone mild.

"No."

"Ah, so all this is purely conjecture?"

Once again, Ben gritted his teeth. This time, he counted to ten. "Yes."

"You know what they say about assumptions, don't you, Ben? To assume is to make an ass out of you—"

"And me," Ben finished quietly, hating that Dimitri was likely right.

Still, until he knew otherwise, he had to assume that Abby Brown was there to cause havoc in his life. If not to reveal his shameful past to his colleagues, then to cause trouble of a different kind. Fifteen years ago, he'd been head-over-heels in love with her. He'd turned his back on her in order to save his soul, perhaps even his life. He wasn't stupid enough to think he was over her, or ever would be and that made her the most dangerous person of all.

His life was finally on track. He had a nice apartment, a great job. He'd been sober for fifteen years. He refused to let Abby destroy everything he'd worked for, and worst of all, to once again possess him, heart and soul. It had been hard enough to walk away from her the first time. He'd never be able to do it again.

The buzzer on his desk phone sounded and a moment later, his secretary came on the line. "Ben, I have your next appointment."

"Thanks, Cheryl. I'll be out in a minute."

Dimitri pushed away from the desk and stood. He held his hand out to Ben. With a soft sigh, Ben shook it.

"Thanks for sharing that stuff with me, Ben. It's nice to know you trust me. If you ever want to talk about it again, I'm here."

Ben shot him a grateful smile. "Thanks, Dimitri. I appreciate it and I know my secrets are safe with you."

Dimitri nodded. "Of course. We're mates. That's the way it is."

Ben came around the desk and the two of them headed toward the door. With a wave of farewell, Dimitri disappeared down the hall. A moment later, Ben turned toward the Asian woman who sat in one of the chairs opposite his secretary's desk.

"Ms Zheng? Hi, I'm Ben Fitzgerald. Please come inside."

CHAPTER 4

The woman who had introduced herself shyly as Jiao Zheng had short, straight black hair and looked like she was in her early twenties. She took the proffered seat recently vacated by Dimitri while Ben returned to the chair behind his desk. Drawing a blank legal pad toward him, he started with the preliminaries.

"Ms Zheng, thank you for coming in so late in the day. Could you please give me your full name and address?"

In heavily accented English, the woman complied.

"Were you born in China?"

"Yes. In the city of Shenzhen. Do you know it?"

Ben nodded. "It's near Hong Kong, isn't it?"

"Yes."

"How long have you lived in Australia?"

"Five years. I came here to study."

Ben made some notes on the legal pad. "What's your date of birth?"

She stared at him in confusion, her head tilted slightly to one side. "Excuse me?"

"Your date of birth. The date you were born."

The woman nodded. "Oh. June eleventh. Nineteen ninety-three."

"So you've just turned twenty-four, correct?"

"Yes."

"I turned thirty-three last week," he offered.

Jiao continued to regard him with a bemused expression and Ben cursed silently under his breath. He didn't know why he'd offered that information. *Why would she care that their birthdays were close?* He was just trying to put the woman at ease.

She was perched on the very edge of her seat and her hands were clenched into fists in her lap. Blake had told him the woman was being sentenced to a five-year jail term that she would begin serving the day after tomorrow. He supposed having only two days of freedom left would be enough to put anyone on edge. No doubt the last place she wanted to be was in a lawyer's office. Once again, he tried to put her at ease.

"Ms Zheng, I've spoken to your lawyer, Blake Harton. He told me about your case. I'm sorry to hear what happened. It sounds like a tragic accident to me."

The woman nodded vigorously. "Accident, yes. I don't understand why I'm going to jail."

Ben bit his lip. He leaned forward and rested his elbows on his desk and clasped his hands in front of him. He wasn't familiar with the laws of China.

He didn't know how something like this was handled in her country. Unfortunately, she was in Australia and causing the death of another person through negligence was grounds for a manslaughter conviction. He was sure Blake had explained as much.

"Our laws are probably different from yours. You might not have intended to kill that patient, but the fact is, it was your fault she died. If you hadn't misread the medication label and the chart, you wouldn't have administered the incorrect dosage and I'm guessing you most certainly wouldn't have given the poor woman hydrogen peroxide."

The nurse paled and she lowered her head. Her gaze remained focused on her clenched hands.

"Did Blake explain to you why I wanted to talk with you?"

Her head remained lowered, but she gave him a brief nod. "Yes, you want to make the university responsible for my inability to read English."

"You're right," Ben said. "I must admit, I was surprised when Blake told me that was the reason this awful thing happened. You're a qualified registered nurse, aren't you?"

"Yes," came the quiet reply.

"You completed a three-year nursing degree and graduated from Richmond University, correct?"

"Yes."

Ben shook his head, trying to make sense of it. He understood Judge Howard's refusal to accept the woman couldn't properly understand English.

She was a college graduate. She'd practised her trade for two years. She mostly understood his questions...

As if aware of his thoughts, she began to fidget, but offered no further information. With a sigh, Ben dragged the legal pad closer and picked up his pen. "How about we start at the beginning?" he suggested. "You said you were born in China?"

"Yes. My parents still live there. They own a small business—a grocery shop in Shenzhen. They work hard. They want better for their only child. Between them and some members of my extended family, they got together the money needed for me to come to Australia, to study nursing."

"So, you came in on a student visa?"

"Yes."

"I thought there was some kind of English test you had to pass before you were granted entry. How did you do on that?"

She shrugged and continued to study her clenched hands. A faint blush stained her cheeks. "It was an online test."

Ben stared at her and then compressed his lips with sudden comprehension. "You had someone else sit the test. Is that what you're saying?"

The woman didn't respond. Ben didn't blame her. She'd just pleaded guilty to manslaughter. He was sure she didn't want to add fraud to her list of crimes. Still, there had to be other checks done by the university over the course of the three-year program. Assessment tasks, examinations and the like. It had been that way when he'd attended law school and that hadn't been too many years ago. He couldn't imagine the procedure had slacked off that much.

"What about afterwards, when you started your course? How did you pass the examinations?"

Once again, the woman remained silent. Ben bit back a curse of frustration. He understood her reticence, but they were getting nowhere.

"Look, Ms Zheng, you're going to jail the day after tomorrow for a considerable amount of time. I think the university and maybe even your employer have questions to answer. How they haven't been able to determine you can't read English after all this time seems incredible, but it appears to be the case. If that's true, I believe they should be held accountable for that, but I need your help. Blake led me to believe you were agreeable to helping me out, to assisting me to understand. There's certain proof I need before I can make the decision to proceed. On the surface, it appears to me we have a case against your employer and Richmond University, but I need evidence to support what and how things went wrong. Now, we can do this here or from your jail cell, but it would be a hell of a lot more convenient to do it here. Still, if you're not prepared to share information with me at the moment, there's not much I can do."

Once again, the woman stared blindly at her lap. Ben forced back a wave of frustration and tried another tack.

"Did Blake misunderstand your willingness to cooperate?"

"No! No! I... I want to help."

Ben nodded. "Very well. Let's try again. You started working at the Lady of Lourdes Nursing Home straight after graduation, right?"

"Yes. I was lucky. I got a job right away. Was able to send money home to my parents."

"That was two years ago. Do you still enjoy working there?"

This time, the woman lifted her head and he was granted a wide serene smile. "Yes. I love it. The elderly patients—residents, we call them—are so sweet and loving. They have many stories to tell. I love talking to them."

Ben thought of his grandmother and the decisions he'd soon be forced to make. Her dementia was getting worse every day. The last time he'd visited, he'd been overcome by the smell of gas. He'd discovered that she'd left the gas stove on. It was a wonder she hadn't succumbed to it. Then there were his concerns for her general health and wellbeing. These days, when he visited, it seemed like the fridge was always empty. Sometimes she couldn't tell him the last time she'd had anything to eat. He often wondered if she shopped for food at all. It was lucky he'd taken to bringing some supplies with him.

He wished he could move her in with him, but he lived in a one-bedroom apartment and even if he bought something larger, he spent so many hours at work, he was hardly home. It was becoming clear she needed close supervision. A nursing home was his only choice.

"I... I paid someone to complete my assessment tasks."

The words were softly spoken, but they broke into Ben's troubled thoughts. He blinked and focused on the woman across from him.

"What about your examinations?"

"The same."

"Aren't you issued student IDs? Did anyone at the college know it wasn't you?"

Jiao shrugged. "Nobody looked too closely. I've discovered most Caucasians think Asian people all look alike. As long as the person you're paying to take the exam looks even a little like you, it will be all right. Besides, the college doesn't care. All they care about is the money."

"How much does it cost a foreign student to enroll in a course?"

"It depends on the course, but it's a lot. Sometimes, hundreds of thousands of dollars. My family saved for many years."

Ben stared at her, aghast. No wonder the number of international students studying at Australian universities had skyrocketed. That kind of money was enough incentive for anyone to look the other way. Anger simmered low in his gut. If the university was aware that some of their students struggled with reading English, it heightened their liability and it made him even more determined to bring them to justice.

"How many foreign students can't read English?" he asked, not sure if he wanted to know.

The woman shrugged. "I don't know. Lots."

A lump of dread formed in his gut. "Hundreds?" he asked.

"Maybe."

"Tell me about your employer. You've worked at the Lady of Lourdes Nursing Home for two years, right?"

"Yes."

"And in all that time, no one ever suspected you had difficulty reading English?"

"No. I... I worked hard to hide my shortcomings."

"How?"

"I'd often use the excuse I'd left my glasses at home and ask one of the other nurses to read the words for me."

Ben stared at her. "And in two years, nobody ever got suspicious?"

"I don't think so."

Shit. How could it be so? It was even worse than he'd suspected. What the hell was going on out there?

With an effort, he kept his tumultuous thoughts hidden behind a mask of politeness and thanked the nurse for her time. She'd admitted to criminal activity, and she would be punished by serving jail time. As far as he was concerned, upon her release she'd have paid her dues.

"I appreciate you coming in to speak with me, Ms Zheng, particularly given that your time on the outside is fast running out. If I have any more questions, I'd be grateful if you'd take my call."

Pushing away from his desk, Ben stood and offered her his hand. She shook it hesitantly.

"Thank you, Ms Zheng. What you've told me will help immensely. This isn't your fault. At least, not entirely. The university and your employer must be held accountable and I won't rest until I see it done. I wish you all the best for your time in jail and if there's anything I can do, please don't hesitate to get a message to me. I'll keep you updated about this matter."

The woman nodded, her gaze directed at the floor. In silence, Ben showed her to the door.

———

Abby stared across at the young aboriginal boy who sat opposite her and tried hard to stem her irritation. She'd been quizzing him in one of the small interview rooms inside the courthouse for the past ten minutes and had received nothing more than monosyllabic answers. The boy's case was listed to be heard that morning. Court had already started. Time was running out.

"Look, Bobby. I understand that talking about what happened might make you uncomfortable, but here's the thing. Very shortly, I'm going to be asked by the judge how you want to plead and from what I've read of the police facts, it's going to be tough to plead not guilty. You were caught on CCTV cameras stealing three packets of gum and a bottle of Coke. Do you deny that it's you in the footage?"

The thirteen-year-old shook his head. Abby suppressed a sigh. "Okay, then. I don't think we have any choice but to enter a guilty plea. Now, according to the police, you only have two other minor offenses on your record. Is that correct?"

The boy nodded. Abby flicked through the

criminal record printout the police prosecutor had supplied her with upon her arrival. The two previous convictions were both for stealing. The record didn't provide any other information about the offenses, but only minimum punishments had been handed out by the court. She only hoped this judge would also be lenient. This was the third offense in as many months. Bobby might not be so lucky this time round.

She glanced at her client and noted his grubby appearance. His sweater was torn and dirty. His high-top Nikes were coming away at the seams. He'd come to court unaccompanied by any family members. Abby couldn't help but wonder if he had anyone at home who cared.

"Who do you live with, Bobby?"

"My grandmother."

"Does she know you're going to court today?"

"Yeah."

Abby's heart sank. His grandmother knew and yet she hadn't come with him, even to offer him her support. This was the third time her grandson had been before the courts. It didn't bode well for Bobby's future.

"Why did you steal the gum, Bobby? The more I can explain your behavior to the judge, the more likely he'll go easy on you. Were you hungry?"

He smirked. "It was gum. You don't steal gum because you're hungry."

Abby stemmed her irritation and tried again. "Then, why?"

The boy thrust out his bottom lip at a mutinous angle. "I was bored."

"Bored? You don't go stealing things because you're bored. That's not a reasonable excuse and if you want the judge to go easy on you, you'd better come up with something more acceptable."

"What do you want me to say?" the boy asked, his tone belligerent.

Once again, Abby swallowed her impatience. Bobby French was a child. Only a few years older than she'd been when—

No, she wouldn't go there. She'd put all that behind her a long time ago. It was a nightmare she refused to revisit. With an effort, she drew in a breath and eased it out on a quiet sigh.

"Listen, Bobby. You're thirteen. You have your whole life ahead of you. Okay, so your grandmother might not be here today, but you're lucky to have someone. I've seen plenty of kids your age and even younger who have no one. They're living on the streets. It's so much harder to get your life back on track when you've gone that far off course. Believe me, I know."

The boy's lips curled up in a sneer. "Yeah, right. Like you would know. You sit there in your fancy suit and your high-and-mighty airs and you expect me to believe you know what I'm going through. Like you know what it's like to go hungry, to stay out all night because it's safer, to feel like no one cares. You don't know shit."

Abby stared at him, her heart beating hard. She knew much more than he could imagine. "You're wrong," she surprised herself by saying. "I've been there, too. I ran away from home when

I was fifteen. I lived rough for more than a year. It wasn't easy. I was terrified most of the time. Eventually, I realized I wanted more from life. I deserved more. I got myself together, surrounded myself with people who wanted to help. I left that life behind me and here I am." She spread her arms wide. "So you see, I do understand."

Bobby stared at her with eyes as wide as saucers, but wariness still tinged his gaze. She understood his attitude. Until that morning, he'd never met her. He'd probably grown up distrusting the world. It would take more than a sad story for him to believe her, and that was fine. As long as it got him thinking about his life and what the future had in store and what he could do to change it for the better, that's all that mattered.

"How do I know you're not full of shit?" the boy demanded, still looking dubious.

"You don't," she replied. "But I'm telling you the truth." She leaned forward across the pale yellow Formica table, suddenly feeling the need to get through to him. "You're old enough to make better choices, Bobby. You know what's right and wrong. Nobody forces you to steal. If you're hungry, there's always some place you can go. A lot of the churches have soup kitchens and—"

"I already told you I didn't do it because I was hungry!" he exploded. "Don't you listen? You're just like all the rest of them! Do you know why I steal, Miss High and Mighty Lawyer who tries to pretend she's lived on the streets? I do it because I *like* it! I like the way it makes me feel! For a few moments, an hour—someone pays me attention!

I'm not invisible anymore! The store owners, the cops... They all see me, at least, they do for a while. And then, it's all over. The police charge me and send me on my way. And I go back to being invisible."

His voice had dropped to a harsh whisper. Abby's heart clenched with pain for him. She understood what it was like to be invisible. She'd spent years feeling that way. But there was nothing she could do to help him and the hundreds of other children out there who felt like that. Apart from putting him in contact with social services... It didn't seem enough, but it was all she had.

When it came time for Bobby's case to be heard, Abby stood before the judge and begged for leniency. She offered some insight into the boy's difficult background and was relieved when the judge showed mercy. After a stern warning that this would be the last time the court looked upon him so kindly, the judge handed Bobby a good behavior bond and encouraged him to clean up his act. Outside the courtroom, Abby took him aside and reiterated the judge's urgings. She hoped never to see Bobby French in such a place again.

Heading out into the midday sunshine, Abby breathed in deeply and eased the air out on a sigh. Lawyers and other professionals dressed in smart suits bustled around her, heading off on their way to lunch. She turned and walked in the direction of the deli that had been situated near the children's court for as long as she could remember. She was halfway across the street when her phone vibrated. She still had it set to silent. Pulling it out of her pocket, she glanced at the screen and smiled. It was her brother.

"Hi, Jeff. How're you doing?"

"I'm fine, Abby. How are you?"

"Great. I've just come from the children's court. Another day in the salt mines."

"I don't know how you do it. All those kids crying out for help, day in, day out. I'm sure most of them don't appreciate how hard you work for them."

Abby bit her lip and stemmed a flood of emotion. Nobody knew the real reason she did the work she did and that's how things were going to stay. She ignored his comments and changed the subject.

"How's work? Are you still churning those nurses out? I was only reading in the newspaper this morning about the chronic lack of nurses in our state hospitals. It seems like the system can't get enough. Lucky for you."

"Yes, lucky for me," he replied dryly. "The university keeps increasing the pressure on me to take in more and more students. Let's hope the nursing shortages last long enough for the newest applicants to get a job."

"You're right. It seems like we go from an undersupply to an oversupply and then back again. There never seems to be a happy medium." She sighed. "What can I do for you, anyway?"

"I just thought I'd call my sister and say hello. Is that all right?"

"Of course it is. Feel free to call me anytime. Even though we both live in the city, it seems like there's never enough time for us to get together. We need to work on that."

"You're right, and as a matter of fact, there *is* another reason for my call," he said a little sheepishly. Abby didn't bother to suppress her smile. She knew her little brother well.

"What do you need?" she asked.

"No, it's nothing like that. You wouldn't believe who just called me."

Abby frowned. She didn't have a clue who her brother might have received a call from and she didn't really care. She told him as much.

"I think you might be interested in this caller," he continued, unperturbed. "He was once a friend of yours. Ben Fitzgerald. Perhaps you don't remember him. He was—"

"I remember him."

"Yes, well, I was so surprised when he identified himself. It's been years since I saw him. I'm not sure he knew who I was. You're not going to believe it, but he's a lawyer now, like you."

At the thought of Ben and their last meeting, she compressed her lips and then forced herself to answer. "Yes. I... I ran into him yesterday afternoon. We work at the same firm."

"You have to be kidding!" Jeff exclaimed. "How about that for coincidence! I thought you said you were working for Harton and Wentworth?"

"I am."

"But I'm sure Ben said he was from Sydney Legal."

"Yes. Harton and Wentworth have voted to change their name. The change was announced yesterday. From now on, they'll be known as Sydney Legal."

"Why?"

"I don't really know for sure. I think they're trying to distance themselves from some recent embarrassements. I only started working there a few days ago. I don't know details of the history behind the change."

"Well, anyway, it doesn't matter. Ben said he wants to talk to me, but he wouldn't tell me why. I'm feeling a little apprehensive. Why would a lawyer from a big city firm want to talk to me?"

Abby's heart skipped a beat and her mouth went dry. Why *would* Ben want to speak with her brother? He'd only met Jeff once, right before Ben decided he wanted more from life than living with her on the streets. *What if he'd contacted Jeff to warn him off about opening his mouth about Ben's past, too?* Anger surged through her at the thought. The arrogance of the man. Jeff knew very little about the time Abby had lived on the streets and that's the way she'd wanted it. Not that Ben knew that, but even so nobody was going to threaten her brother.

"Jeff, I'm sorry, I don't know why Ben would call you, but yesterday he was less than pleased to see me as a new associate here. It's probably best if you stay well away from him."

"Unfortunately, I've already agreed to see him. He's due here straight after lunch. He implied it was work related. Again, I'm a little at a loss. Why would a lawyer want to speak with me?"

Abby sighed, her thoughts in turmoil. *Was Ben's visit to her brother legitimately work related, or did it have something to do with her?* She wished she knew.

CHAPTER 5

The drab, dark brick buildings that dominated the Richmond University campus looked nothing like the grand sandstone structures of Sydney University where Ben had gone to law school. Winter-yellow grass and bare branches from what appeared to be a random planting of deciduous trees along the entryway were in stark contrast to the lush green surroundings of Sydney University. It was obvious Richmond University didn't have the old money running through its veins.

Climbing the stairs that led up into the nursing department administration building, Ben looked around him. Groups of students were scattered around the vicinity, chatting to each other, eating sandwiches and talking on phones. The sight of them took him back to the time when he was a student. Attending college was something he'd never imagined when he was seventeen. Now, the recollections of his time at law school were some of his fondest memories.

Pulling out his phone, he checked the screen. It was almost two. He was right on time. He opened the door and approached a small reception desk. Behind it sat a middle-aged woman dressed head to toe in fuchsia.

"Hi, I'm Ben Fitzgerald. I'm here to see Jeff Brown."

The woman glanced down at the appointment book open on her desk and placed a tick against Ben's name.

"Take a seat, Mr Fitzgerald. I'll let him know you're here," she said with a friendly smile. Ben wondered if she'd greet him so cordially after she discovered why he was there.

"Thank you," he said and sat in one of the cheap wooden chairs that filled the modest space. Magazines that were years out of date were stacked in a neat pile on an equally dated coffee table. Ben was pulling out his phone, intent on checking his emails, when he heard footsteps coming toward him from the direction of the hall. He looked up.

Jeff Brown had only been a kid when he'd last seen him, but it was his resemblance to his sister that left Ben in no doubt as to the man's identity. Thick blond hair minus—his sister's expertly applied highlights—framed a handsome face. Jeff Brown was every bit as good looking as his sister. As the man got closer, Ben realized that unlike Abby's cobalt eyes, her brother's eyes were brown. It was the only striking difference between them.

At the thought of Abby, Ben was filled with a

surge of irritation. He'd made a conscious effort not to think about her and yet, here she was, intruding on his thoughts. It was more than annoying. At Jeff's approach, Ben stood and held out his hand.

"Jeff. It's good to see you again. It's been a long time."

"Yes, you, too, Ben. Come in."

Jeff turned and walked back in the direction he'd come from and Ben followed behind him. They passed two other offices with the doors closed before Jeff stopped and ushered Ben inside. The room was as modest as the reception area and was dominated by a cheap wooden desk. At least five filing cabinets were lined up against one wall. The only light came from two overhead fluorescents. Ben wondered how anyone could work day after day in such a suffocating box.

Jeff closed the door behind them and Ben felt even more claustrophobic. He looked around for windows, but there were none. He drew in a surreptitious breath, relieved that he wouldn't be staying long.

"What can I do for you, Ben?" Jeff asked, taking the seat behind the desk. "I must admit, I'm curious about your call."

Eager to get out of there, Ben got straight to the point. "What can you tell me about Jiao Zheng?"

Jeff frowned. "The name's not familiar. Should I know her?"

"She was a nursing student. She graduated

from Richmond University two years ago. She was recently charged with murdering one of her elderly patients."

Comprehension flooded Jeff's face. "Oh, yes. *That* Jiao Zheng. Now I remember. I saw it on the news. Terrible stuff."

"Yes, it is. What you might not know is that Zheng claims that the death was accidental. That the reason she overdosed the patient with the wrong medication was because she couldn't read English."

Ben watched Jeff's reaction. It took a moment, but the man didn't disappoint. His eyes widened in horror as the implications set in.

"I see you've connected the dots. This nurse graduated from *your* university, which presumably means she passed all minimum requirements of the course. I'd have thought that would require some degree of competence in the English language, wouldn't you?"

The color left Jeff's face. Ben almost felt sorry for him. As the head administrator of the nursing department, Jeff was going to take a lot of the heat if this went forward. Ben's thoughts zeroed back to Abby and he wondered how she'd feel about the firm they both worked for, representing the victim's estate and going after her brother. He hoped she'd see it for what it was and not take it personally, but he had a sneaking suspicion that wouldn't be the case. *Great.* Just another bug to bear between them.

"I'm afraid it's not only Jiao Zheng," Ben continued.

Jeff stared up at him in alarm. "W-what do you mean?"

"Zheng seems to think there could be hundreds of nurses gainfully employed in the New South Wales health system who struggle to read English. If she's right, it's a wonder there haven't been more deaths. The whole thing is a time bomb and you and your university are smack bang in the middle of it."

"W-what are you doing here?"

Ben shot Jeff a tight smile that was completely devoid of humor. "As of this morning, Sydney Legal is representing the estate of the late Dulcie Eveleigh. In case you don't recognize the name, she was Nurse Zheng's very unfortunate victim. I'm in the process of preparing a statement of claim against Richmond University as the first defendant. The Lady of Lourdes Nursing Home will be listed as the second. Depending upon the degree of your culpability, you could be the third."

At Ben's announcement, the color flooded back into Jeff's cheeks. His eyes blazed with fury. He pushed away from his desk and stood, almost nose to nose with Ben, who had remained standing.

Jeff's breath came fast. "You need to leave. Now."

Ben eyeballed the man a moment longer, just to make sure Jeff knew he wasn't intimidated by the man's sudden show of bravado.

"Just so you know," Ben said mildly, "this isn't over. Not by a long shot. Court documents will be served on you before the end of the week. Be sure to keep an eye out. There's a case to answer to here and you know it. If you're not directly responsible for this mess—and you want to hope to God you're not—I suggest you find out who the hell is. We need to put an end to it, and fast, before other lives are put at risk."

As the door behind Ben Fitzgerald closed, Jeff Brown eased out an unsteady breath and collapsed back into his chair. He was shaking, both from anger and fear. His stomach churned. He'd always felt uncomfortable about the university's protocol as far as their international students went. Among other things, there seemed to be a casual disregard about the student's ability to successfully complete their chosen course before receiving their credentials.

No matter what objections were made by various members of the faculties, including him, it didn't seem to concern the powers that be that a number of foreign students were totally unsuited to their course and often didn't have the academic ability or basic English skills required to even achieve a pass. More than once he'd complained about the entry standards that applied to domestic students didn't seem to apply to those who came from overseas.

Take the nursing faculty, for example. Sure, international applicants provided their high school qualifications, but the truth was, only cursory attention was paid to them and there was no follow up to verify the accuracy of the scores. Jeff knew for a fact that not a single phone call or email had been made or sent to schools in China or India or the Philippines to confirm the applicants' claims. The records presented were simply taken at face value.

The reason was simple: Foreign students paid exceptionally well for their degrees. Much more than Australian students. Sometimes it felt like anyone who could afford to buy a degree from Richmond University could get one.

Ben's revelation didn't come as a surprise. Jeff was well aware that a fair proportion of the international students couldn't properly read English. The English competency test was usually taken online and the results were attached to an online application. There were no checks to verify who'd sat the test or who completed the application.

Those that didn't sit the online test were required to complete an English language course as a prerequisite before they began their studies, but once again, nobody checked to ensure a pass was genuinely achieved. The student simply completed the required unit and then continued on their way. Jeff was as much to blame as anyone. He couldn't think of a single instance where he'd queried a student's results or checked to see that they'd passed the English literacy requirement of their course.

Student results were recorded on computer spreadsheets, of course, but who took the time to look at them, let alone to follow up on those? Nobody at the university was interested in the

English language results. It was assumed that if a student could complete three years of college education, they could read.

But now the department's casual disregard had caused a woman's death and the legal fraternity—well, one firm in particular—was out for blood. At the helm was Ben Fitzgerald, a man with a less-than-stellar past. A man not to be tampered with.

A shiver of apprehension ran down Jeff's spine. He thought fleetingly of his sister. *Had she had prior knowledge of this?* He dismissed the thought immediately. No, Abby would have told him, would have warned him. She might be a hotshot lawyer, working for the most prestigious firm in town, but she was still his sister. She had his back. He was sure of it.

Still, things weren't looking good—for him, or the university. He should call the dean. He didn't want to, but if Fitzgerald followed through with his threat to file a civil claim against them, Jeff had no choice but to warn the dean. It would come to the man's attention sooner or later. It would go better for Jeff if the news came from him. Of course, he'd do his best to minimize his culpability. He'd merely followed policy and directions. That went without saying.

With his mind made up, he steeled himself and reached over and picked up the phone.

Abby waited for the light to change and then

crossed over the busy city street, rubbing shoulders with a heavy crowd of pedestrian traffic. Court was finished for the day and like Abby, many other lawyers were making their way back to their offices. It had been a busy day filled with several cases, all depressingly familiar: young offenders with a prior criminal history, standing at the crossroads. They were young enough that there was still hope that they'd make better choices if they were given another chance. There were some she felt confident about; others, not so much.

Like Bobby French. He'd been treated leniently, but would he take advantage of the opportunity he'd been given? She didn't know. She only hoped the good people at his local juvenile justice center would be able to get through to him if she hadn't.

Picking up her pace, she lengthened her stride—as far as her calf-length, narrow skirt would allow—and walked into the grand foyer of the building that housed the offices of Sydney Legal.

Sydney Legal. The name felt strange on her lips, but she guessed she'd get used to it, like everyone else. Somehow, it suited the modern glass-and-steel building. Her high heels made a tapping sound on the highly polished marble tiles. She glanced at her feet. Not for the first time, she appreciated the beautiful floor. The intricate charcoal-gray-and-white pattern was almost a work of art. Focused as she was on her feet, she didn't notice Ben until it was too late. He materialized beside her. As he stepped forward to press the button that summoned the elevator, his sleeve brushed against hers.

Her heart skipped a beat. "Ben!" she said, startled.

He glanced in her direction before returning his gaze to the elevators. "Abby."

She tried hard to ignore him, but it was impossible. He was tall, dark and handsome and exuded sex appeal. That was a cliché, but never had it applied more aptly than to the man who stood beside her. He wore another form-fitting navy-blue suit, a crisp white shirt and a forest-green tie with tasteful navy-blue stripes. The green of the tie picked up the color in his eyes, turning them emerald.

"Have you been to court?" she asked, keeping her tone casual.

"No. I went to see your brother. He's done some growing since I saw him last. I think he was all of twelve, wasn't he? Anyway, he's done well for himself. Head administrator of the nursing department at Richmond University. Impressive."

Too late, Abby remembered the phone call she'd received earlier from Jeff. After the day she'd had, their conversation felt like a lifetime ago. Still, all of a sudden, she was acutely alert.

"Why did you visit with Jeff?" she managed, striving for casual.

"He's about to be slapped with a lawsuit. At least, his employer is."

Shock almost rendered her speechless. "*Say what?*"

Ben offered a nonchalant shrug, as if what he'd

said was of no consequence. Abby quickly regained her voice.

"What are you talking about?"

Ben folded his arms across his chest. "A nurse who graduated two years ago from Richmond University recently caused the death of a patient who resided in the Lady of Lourdes Nursing Home. Blake Harton Junior is representing the nurse. She's pleaded guilty to manslaughter."

Abby frowned as the details of the case slowly came back to her. She recalled hearing snippets on the radio as she made her way to work. It was a very sad circumstance.

"You can't possibly think Jeff had anything to do with that."

"Not directly, but you see, the nurse admitted the reason she overdosed the patient was because she couldn't read."

For the second time, Abby was stupefied. "I beg your pardon?"

"She struggles to read English. She paid people to complete her assignments and sit her exams. Apparently, she's not the only one. It's a miracle there haven't been more fatalities. Or maybe there have been and we just don't know about them. Either way, someone must be held responsible—and right now, Richmond University is firmly in my sights."

Abby shook her head, unable to believe what he was saying. "But, Jeff's the head administrator of the nursing department. If what you say is true, this will ruin his career."

"Not my problem."

She stared at him in disbelief. "What happened to you? You used to care about people. You used to have a heart."

His eyes narrowed. "I used to be a lot of things."

He stepped even closer, so close she could see the darker flecks in the green of his eyes. "And so did you," he added.

The breath caught in her throat. His gaze grew in intensity and her heart pounded. Memories of the two of them entwined, lips, kisses, skin on skin… She gasped and stepped away in a desperate effort to put some distance between them. Her face flamed. Fire danced along her nerve endings.

She was still in love with him.

The truth hit her like a Mike Tyson knockout punch to the side of the head. *Stupid! So stupid!* She couldn't be in love with him. Her love had died the day he walked out on her nearly fifteen years before. If she gave in to this, he'd only break her heart. Again. She refused to let that happen.

"Stay away from my brother," she hissed.

He lifted one perfectly shaped eyebrow in silent query. "Or what?" he said.

He was baiting her. She could see it in the expression on his face and the challenge that lit up his eyes. Making a sound of frustration, she spun on her heel and made a beeline for the exit.

Ben frowned as he watched Abby turn tail and

head back outside their building. He shouldn't have goaded her. Didn't he want her to treat the case against her brother's college in a professional manner? He'd all but thrown his pending litigation in her face. What a jerk. No wonder she'd run off.

As she disappeared through the wide glass doors, he tried not to notice her long shapely legs encased in black tights and the rounded curve of her butt. She had a figure most women would die for. He could still remember what it felt like to hold her in his arms, to love her.

He made a harsh sound of denial in the back of his throat. *No!* He refused to go there again! He didn't love her. She was dangerous and a threat to the carefully constructed life he'd built around himself, far removed from the angry young man who'd roughed it on the streets.

She'd pulled herself out of the gutter, but how did he know it wasn't all show? She'd been hooked on illegal drugs just as surely as he'd been hooked on alcohol. It had taken everything he had to walk away from her, to break the cycle of his addiction. But he *had!* He'd escaped that dead-end life and had made something of himself. He was a successful lawyer living a successful life. He couldn't go back. He *wouldn't* go back! No matter how much she appeared to have changed or how much he might want her. Besides, he had a case to focus on. Best he remember that.

Chapter 6

Abby picked up her highlighter and did her best to concentrate on the witness statement spread out on her desk. She was representing a child who'd been charged with a serious assault. A knife had been involved. The victim was hospitalized and required several stitches to his right shoulder. A little closer and it could have been life threatening. Her client was barely fourteen.

Once again, Abby tried to concentrate then sighed. She was kidding herself if she thought she could push Ben Fitzgerald and their most recent encounter out of her mind. The way he'd looked at her right before she'd hightailed it out of there had shaken her to the core. It was like he couldn't stand the sight of her and yet, once upon a time, he'd loved her. And she'd loved him. They'd been homeless, living on the streets and yet, though it should have been misery, they'd been happier than she'd ever been.

And then, it had all come crashing around her.

He'd broken up with her. He'd waited for her outside the public restrooms they used whenever they had to and told her he never wanted to see her again. She'd been coming off a meth high and hadn't fully comprehended what he'd said, but later, when she'd sobered up and had time to think about it, his words had become crystal clear.

He'd left her there, amongst the filth and degradation that had been their home for the better part of two years. They'd lived together under the bridge, with other homeless teens, craving the next drink, the next fix—like she craved a hit right now. The thought slammed into her from nowhere and fear rushed through her veins.

No!

She hadn't touched drugs since she was seventeen. The day Ben walked out on her was the last time she'd succumbed to the lure of getting high. It had been a hard-fought battle, but with the help of her aunt and uncle and a decent stint in rehab, she'd done it. She'd returned to school and left with her Higher School Certificate and she'd seen Jeff on the weekends.

She couldn't remember what had triggered her interest in law, but she did know she wanted to be an advocate for children. Going to law school seemed a viable option. She got the marks to enter and finished the course with honors. Her graduation from college and subsequent admission to the Supreme Court as a legal practitioner were the proudest days of her life.

And here she was. A successful lawyer, standing up for troubled kids, steering them back on the right path. At least, that's what she tried to do. She didn't know how many times she failed and how many times she succeeded, but she liked to believe she won more than she lost.

The fact was, she was a good person who had once gone a little off course. But she'd gotten her life together, had worked hard and every day she came to work, she did the best that she could to help other troubled kids turn their lives around.

She refused to let Ben Fitzgerald undermine her confidence and drag her back down, no matter how much her heart yearned for him. She couldn't believe the irony. Of all the law firms she could have approached, a job offer had come from Ben's firm. And now she was stuck with him.

No, not stuck with him. There were hundreds of people employed at Sydney Legal. Sally-Ann had worked there four years and hadn't run into him. That proved it was possible to avoid him. They didn't work together. It shouldn't be too hard.

She'd been right the first time. He'd hurt her once. He could hurt her again. The best thing to do was to keep away from him, and at the earliest opportunity, she'd start dating again. It was time to get Ben Fitzgerald out of her thoughts, and her life once and for all.

The phone on her desk buzzed and her secretary came on the line. "Abby, I have Jane Maxwell from Juvenile Justice on line two. Bobby French hasn't shown up for his scheduled appointment. If he misses another one, she'll have to inform the court."

Abby sighed heavily. *Damn Bobby French!*

Didn't he know she was trying to help him? Did he even care? She made a sound of despair in the back of her throat and rested her head on her desk. One step forward, two steps back. It was almost the story of her life.

———

Ben pondered the woman who sat across from him. Within the next twenty-four hours, Jiao Zheng would be taken to Long Bay Correctional Facility to be incarcerated for the next five years. He'd managed to persuade her to meet with him again in an effort to get a clearer idea of how she'd applied for an international student visa, got accepted into Richmond University, graduated and became employed by the Lady of Lourdes Nursing Home—all without anybody knowing she struggled to read English.

"I think you told me the last time that you sat the English test online, is that right?" he asked.

"Yes. Except I didn't sit it. I paid someone else to do it."

"So, let me get this right. You applied online for a student visa through the Department of Immigration. Is that correct?"

"Yes."

"And part of this procedure is proving you have sufficient competence in the English language."

"Yes."

"And you can prove this competence by completing an online assessment and the results are attached to your visa application. Is that right?"

"Yes, that's right, but you can also enroll in an English Language Intensive Course for Overseas Students to be completed before your chosen university course. If you do this, there's no need to sit the online test."

"Right." Ben scribbled a few notes on the legal pad in front of him, all the while silently shaking his head. As far as he could tell, the system was ripe for corruption. He looked up at Jiao.

"Do you know of anyone who opted to do the English language course as part of their university studies?"

"Yes, of course."

"I assume they also needed to pass this course before they could start the next one?"

"No, that's not correct. I know of at least half a dozen nurses who failed the English language course at college and still went on and completed their nursing degrees."

Ben stared at her. "So nobody at the university checked? Nobody from the Department of Immigration followed up?"

"No, not that I know of. If they did, they didn't care. Those girls graduated and are now working in the community, just like me."

Ben shuddered at the thought of what could happen. It was a wonder there hadn't been more accidental deaths. Then again, perhaps there had been and they hadn't come to the attention of the authorities. After all, who was to say an elderly patient hadn't died of natural causes if they were old and infirm and their death was anything but unexpected? The idea frightened him and he couldn't help but think of his grandmother and the very real possibility that one day in the near future, she'd be a resident of a nursing home.

"Ms Zheng, it would be very helpful if I could speak to some of these other nurses. Would you be willing to supply me with a list of names and contact details?"

"I don't know. They will get scared. They don't want to lose their jobs."

"I promise to keep their identity a secret as much as possible. It's not my intention to cause the loss of their jobs. I just want to get some idea about how extensive this problem is. I'm becoming increasingly concerned that it's far bigger than I'd imagined. We need to get to the bottom of it, for the nurses' sake, and for their patients."

Jiao stared down at her hands where they rested in her lap. After a while, she raised her head and looked up at Ben. "They won't want to talk to you, but I will tell them they must. I don't have much time, but I will tell them that if they don't want to end up like me—about to spend the next five years in jail—then they need to meet with you. Give me an hour. I will work quickly. I will give you a list."

Ben offered her a grateful smile. "Thank you, Ms Zheng. I really appreciate it. You're doing the right thing. Let's hope no more patients will die like this and no other nurses need to do jail time over an accidental murder."

Her eyes flashed. "Not murder!" she rebuked him. "No intent. Manslaughter. An accident."

Ben nodded. He didn't care what she called it. A woman had died needlessly. He was determined to make the person or persons responsible pay, and as far as he was concerned, liability for the wrongful death didn't just rest with the nurse.

All out of questions, he pushed away from his desk and once again, thanked Jiao for coming in. He couldn't imagine spending the last few hours of his freedom inside a lawyer's office, but she'd come in anyway and for that, he was grateful.

"Don't forget to email me with that list," he reminded her as he showed her to the door.

"Don't worry, Mr Fitzgerald. You will have it soon. I promise."

And with that, she turned away and disappeared down the hall. Ben was just about to close the door and return to his desk when Blake popped into view.

"Ben, how are you doing?" he asked.

"Fine. I just met with your client, Jiao Zheng. She's on her way to jail."

Blake grimaced. "I wish I could have done more for her."

"You did your best, Blake. That's all you need to remember."

"Thanks, Ben. I appreciate your vote of confidence, even if it's slightly misplaced."

"Misplaced, my ass," Ben retorted. "You're one of the best criminal lawyers in town." Ben wandered back into his office and Blake followed.

"What are you doing here, anyway?" Ben asked as he threw himself back in his chair.

"I don't know. I'm restless. I need a breath of fresh air. Got time for a bite?"

"Yeah, why not? I've been so busy I haven't had time for lunch. Let's go."

Ben and Blake made their way out of the building, crossed the road and headed to the nearest café, a place frequented by many of the staff employed by their firm. Despite the brisk breeze that blew up from Circular Quay, and with the lunch hour firmly upon them, most of the outdoor tables were full. They walked inside and perched on stools at the bar that ran the length of the counter. Within moments, a waitress appeared and took their order. Ben asked for club soda to accompany his meal. Blake ordered a Coke. The drinks arrived and Ben took a mouthful of his and sighed.

"After the morning I've had, that sure tastes good," he said.

"Yeah. Too bad we have to go back."

Ben smiled, but didn't reply. He was certain Jiao Zheng would trade places in an instant. The thought sobered him.

"Hey, isn't that the new girl? The one old man Wentworth introduced a couple of days ago?"

Ben turned to look in the direction Blake indicated. He glimpsed a flash of blond hair, a smooth cheek. And then she turned and his heart took a nosedive. It was Abby and she wasn't alone.

"Yeah, you're right," he managed, amazed

at how normal he sounded. "Who's she with?"

Blake looked across the crowd once again and then returned his gaze to Ben's. "Jeremy King. He's a senior associate. Been here for a year or so. He moved over from Maurice Cahill. He does a lot of work in the children's court. Why?"

"No reason," Ben said hurriedly before taking another mouthful of his drink. He tried hard to keep his gaze from straying in Abby's direction, but it landed there more often than he liked. He didn't realize how often until Blake drew it to his attention.

"Don't tell me you have a thing for the new girl?" Blake teased.

"No, of course not!" Ben retorted, flushing with embarrassment.

Blake grinned. "Yeah, right. You can't take your eyes off her. I don't blame you. There's plenty to like."

Ben felt a spurt of irritation and something that felt suspiciously like jealousy. He didn't want Blake or any other male taking notice of Abby's considerable attributes. A second later, he cursed silently under his breath. *Who was he kidding?* She was a beautiful woman. There wasn't a man in the room who wasn't aware of her, including her companion. Ben was being totally irrational if he thought otherwise.

Besides, what did he care if Blake or Jeremy or any of the dozen or more men who filled the café were taken with Abby Brown? Once upon a time, many years ago, he'd loved her with every fiber of his being. But that was then, before he'd turned his back on her and the life they had together. Now, she was nothing to him. He just wished to God he could believe that.

"I knew her a long time ago," he heard himself saying and then registered Blake's look of surprise.

"Wow! What a coincidence. Did you go to school together?"

"No. But we were only kids. Stay away from her. She's trouble."

Blake stared at him, as if trying to delve into his mind and work out what he meant by his comment and then he simply came out and asked the question. "What do you mean by that?"

Ben compressed his lips into a thin line, wishing he'd kept his mouth shut. For fifteen years he'd kept the facts of his childhood concealed from everyone. Now, in less than a week, he'd made two references to his past, inviting questions and speculation. *What the hell was he doing?*

It was all Abby's fault. Until she'd arrived on the scene, forcing her way into his space, his life had been going along just fine. Now he found himself remembering things from his past that he'd worked hard to forget. He refused to allow her that kind of power over his peace of mind. It had happened once, but it would never happen again.

"Just stay away from her. That's all you need to know," he muttered. He took a gulp of soda. The bubbles went up his nose and he began to cough.

Blake watched him in amusement. A grin played around his lips. He raised a single dark blond eyebrow in silent question. "Are you staking a claim?" Blake turned to look meaningfully in Abby's direction.

Unable to help himself, Ben gazed at the couple on the other side of the room. Just then, Abby reached out and touched the back of her companion's hand and smiled at him. It was a soft smile, kind and intimate. Pain burned through Ben's tortured heart.

Blake glanced at him, a sympathetic look in his eyes. "It looks like you might be too late," he said.

Ben gritted his teeth and glared down at his drink, too overwrought to answer. And here he'd been declaring, not two minutes earlier, that she was nothing to him...

Nothing, my ass.

Over the hum of the lunchtime diners that filled the café, Abby listened politely to Jeremy's recount of a sentencing hearing he'd attended earlier in the day. He'd dropped by her office right around the time she'd been silently lamenting her obsession with Ben Fitzgerald. When Jeremy invited her to lunch, she'd nearly bowled him over with her eagerness to say yes. Now she was regretting it.

It wasn't that he wasn't interesting enough: He was a lawyer of several years' experience who exhibited genuine caring and concern for his young clients. He had a good sense of humor and was physically attractive. He was tall and broad-shouldered, with nice hair and slightly crooked teeth that lent him an endearing air, but she was yet to feel anything more than the tiniest flicker of interest.

What was wrong with her? Here was a perfectly acceptable man who was smart, interesting and good-looking and yet she felt nothing. *Had she been too quick to accept his invitation? Perhaps she wasn't ready to throw herself into the dating scene again?*

She swallowed an impatient growl. *What the hell was she thinking?* It had been years since she'd dated. Her last boyfriend had been way back in college and he'd lasted barely a month. Yes, it was time to forget all about Ben Fitzgerald. It was time to put him out of her mind, out of her life, out of her heart. Once and for all.

With that thought in mind, she reached over and touched Jeremy on the back of his hand, waiting for...something. She smiled encouragingly and tightened her fingers around his, but still...nothing. Not the slightest fluttering or rush of blood or uptake in her pulse. Simply...nothing.

Dammit! What was wrong with her? Ever since she'd fallen for Ben, no man had measured up. She'd tried so hard to forget him. She'd gone a little wild in college, but nothing had lasted. No one was Ben. Finally, she'd given up. Now, she was about to embark on the futile exercise all over again. *Would she never learn?*

The waitress arrived with their food and she swallowed a grateful sigh. She'd eat quickly and then make some excuse to get the hell out of there and escape back to her office. She looked up at the waitress and murmured her thanks. She caught a movement out of the corner of her eye.

Ben.

He was there, on the other side of the room. At the bar. With another man. From the way he was dressed, it was probably another lawyer.

Her heart took off at a gallop and her mouth went sandpaper dry. She looked down at her meal and suddenly food was the last thing on her mind. Her stomach churned. She bit her lip. There was no way she could eat.

Looking up at Jeremy, she mumbled an apology. With face flaming, she excused herself, pushed away from the table and rushed from the room.

CHAPTER 7

Ben stared at the file in front of him and cursed aloud. He'd been looking at the same page for the last twenty minutes. The jury had come back with their verdict. They'd awarded the highest possible amount of damages to his client. Anderson was as pleased as he could be, short of getting his mobility back.

The end of the week had also come and gone. He'd filed and served his civil claim against Richmond University and the Lady of Lourdes Nursing Home and was in the process of drafting subpoenas, but at this rate, he wouldn't achieve anything more that day.

Damn Abby Brown for coming back into his life. It was *her* fault he couldn't concentrate. It was *her* fault his gut churned and his head spun and he could barely remember which way was up.

What the hell was she doing here, at his firm? Was it as Dimitri had suggested—a simple coincidence? Or was there something more sinister to her appearance, like Ben had initially thought? *But why hadn't she made her move?* Said something to one of the powers that be?

She'd been there a week. Plenty of time to take action. A whisper in the right ear and everything he'd worked for could come tumbling down around his ears. *What was she waiting for?* He wished he knew.

Was it possible he'd misjudged her motives? She'd looked confused and even angry when he'd accused her of being there to sabotage his career, but all that display of outrage could have been an act, part of her scheme to get him off balance, unsuspecting of her devious plan to exact revenge—to have him land on his ass.

Was he being fair? He'd barely seen her around the office. It was almost like she'd been avoiding him, just like he'd determined to avoid her.

His tumultuous thoughts continued to circle around and around in his head until he groaned from the agony of it. The truth was, he was still in love with Abby Brown and there was nothing he could do about that.

Dammit! She was all wrong! She'd always been wrong. Right from the beginning, he'd been irresistibly drawn to her beauty, her vulnerability, her air of fragile innocence. He'd wanted to protect her and keep her safe from harm, shield her from the worst life had to offer. They'd spent the better part of two years of their young lives together, living from day to day under the bridge. Loving each other, watching out for each other, supporting each other through good times and bad.

He'd never told her what brought him to the streets and she never asked, just like he never pried into her reasons. By unspoken agreement, they'd left their pasts alone and lived only in the present. It had been the best of times and the worst of times. In a matter of months, she'd become hooked on meth and he'd become a hopeless drunk. They did what they could to scrounge the money to feed their addictions.

Then one day, he'd stumbled into a church and met the kindly Father O'Leary. Ben had been raised a Catholic and had attended a Catholic school. When Father O'Leary offered to help him get off the streets and return to his family, he'd been ready to listen. By then, he was almost nineteen and realized he was throwing his life away. At the end of that chance meeting, he'd returned to the bridge determined to make changes.

But what of Abby? Had she experienced a similar kind of epiphany? Should he set aside his suspicions of her motives and just accept that she'd turned her life around, like he had? Could it be only coincidence that brought her to his firm? And if so, did she deserve a second chance?

Didn't *everyone?* Who was he to judge her? After all, not so long ago they'd been in the same situation. Was he brave enough to risk his heart— risk *everything*—to find out? The truth was, he didn't know.

With another curse of frustration, Ben pushed away from his desk and strode across the room. Grabbing his jacket from where it hung in a small cupboard used for that purpose, he pulled it on and left the office. It had been a few days since he'd visited his grandmother. Perhaps an hour or two with the woman he credited for saving his life would help him see things more clearly.

The mid-afternoon traffic was lighter than usual. He suspected it had something to do with the teachers' strike that was currently in place. It meant fewer cars on the road as parents skipped the after school run. He arrived at his grandmother's modest unit in Wollstonecraft, on Sydney's lower north shore, in a little under thirty minutes. She greeted him like she hadn't seen him in years and it saddened him to know that in her mind, it might have been that long.

"Hi, Grandma, how are you doing?" he asked, giving her a hug.

"Benjamin! How wonderful to see you! My, how you've grown!" She threw her arms around him and held on tight. The top of her head barely reached his chest. She'd shrunk in her old age. But her white hair was as thick and lustrous as ever and her makeup had been applied with an expert hand.

"Have you been out today, Grandma?" he asked, noting the nice dress and matching shoes she wore.

"No, dear. In fact, I thought I might do a spot of cooking. It's nearly Christmas, you know."

Ben bit his lip and refrained from reminding her they were only halfway through the year. Hell, if she wanted to do some Christmas cooking, who was he to argue?

He followed her into the kitchen and was immediately assailed by the smell of burnt sugar. A pot sat on the stove, blackened and charred. He hurried forward. The handle was still hot to the touch. The food burned inside the pot was beyond recognition. With a cloth, he carried it to the sink and filled it with water. Turning off the faucet, he faced his grandmother. She stood nearby, twisting her hands together.

"Grandma, what happened?" he asked gently.

"I... I was cooking toffees. You know how much you loved those as a child. I wanted to surprise you, like I used to in the days leading up to Christmas. I put the sugar and water in the pot and set it to boil, but somehow...I forgot it was there. I went to lie down for just a minute and the next thing I knew the place was filled with smoke. I'd fallen asleep and the toffee... I guess you can see what happened to the toffee."

He opened his mouth to reassure her that it didn't matter, but before he could speak, she stepped forward with a cry of anguish.

"I'm sorry, Ben! I forgot. I forgot I was cooking toffee. I wanted to surprise you. It's nearly Christmas. You love toffee at Christmas."

Ben took her in his arms and hugged her gently once again. "It's all right, Grandma," he murmured. "Don't worry about it. There's no harm done. I'll clean up the pot and in a few days the smell will be gone. You won't even know it happened."

She pulled away from him and smiled, her pale blue eyes—so much like his father's—glinting with unshed tears. "You always were such a good boy, Ben."

He grimaced. "Not always."

She shook her head and frowned at him. "Nonsense! You're too hard on yourself! The stuff that happened when you were younger—that wasn't your fault and I won't listen to anyone who tells me differently. Besides, you found your way to my doorstep and you turned your life around. You have much to be proud of, Grandson. *I'm* very proud of you!"

Ben looked at the old woman before him and his heart swelled with love. She'd taken him in when he was at his lowest and had helped him become the man he'd become. He'd never forget it.

"Would you like a cup of tea, Ben?" she asked softly. "I'll put the kettle on."

"Thanks, Grandma. That would be nice."

She shuffled over to the sink and filled the kettle before setting it to boil. Then she pulled two tea cups from the cupboard. Moving toward the pantry, she pulled up short, halfway across the room. She stood there, not moving.

Ben frowned and walked closer. "What is it, Grandma?"

She turned to him, her expression filled with consternation. "I can't remember what I was doing, Ben. I started across the kitchen, but where was I headed?"

"I think you were going to get some teabags, Grandma. We're having tea, remember? Here, let me help."

He went over to the pantry cupboard and pulled open the door. The shelves were bare of almost everything. There was an opened packet of sugar and a bag containing a few slices of bread. A jar of peanut butter, a box of teabags and nothing much else. He turned back to his grandmother.

"When did you last eat, Grandma? What did you have for lunch?"

She looked at him in surprise. "Is it lunchtime already? It feels like I only just woke up. Are you sure it's that late?"

Ben swallowed a sigh. "It's almost half-past two, Grandma. Way past lunch. Are you hungry?"

"No, Ben. I'm not hungry in the slightest, but I'll be happy to sit with you and have tea. We used to do that a lot, didn't we? Back in the old days."

She smiled like she was remembering fond times and Ben smiled, too. The years he'd spent living with her were some of the best memories of his life. The kettle boiled, and with teabags in hand, he made them each a cup. He spooned in sugar and went to the fridge for the milk.

Like the pantry, the shelves of the fridge were almost empty. A single carton of milk stood in the door. He checked the expiry date and noticed it had passed three days earlier. He emptied the contents down the sink.

Though he'd known this day would eventually arrive, it was clear the time had come. He couldn't afford to wait until his grandmother forgot to switch off some other electrical appliance and burned down the house. Neither was he certain she was eating the way she should. She was far too thin for his liking and it was obvious she'd all but given up on grocery shopping.

Normally when he visited, he brought some supplies with him, but the last time he'd been too busy and had just dropped in to say hello. The time before that, he'd picked up some fruit from a vendor with a cart outside his building, but he could still see the blackened bananas and moldy oranges in the basket on the counter. It didn't look like any of them had been touched.

He was going to have to talk to his grandmother about moving into a nursing home, where she could be properly looked after. He hated to do it to her, but he had no choice. It was the only way to guarantee she'd be safe.

He thought of Jiao Zheng who'd begun her five-year sentence, and compressed his lips. He could only hope the staff in the home he eventually chose for his grandmother were well trained and competent in English. But how could he know for sure? The truth was, he couldn't.

Thrusting the worrying thoughts aside, he brought the tea cups to the table. He set one in front of his grandmother and took the seat opposite.

She looked at his cup and her brow wrinkled into a frown. "Don't you take milk, Ben?"

He smiled. "Sometimes."

"Not today?"

"No, Grandma. Not today."

"Would you like a toffee? I cooked some, you know. It's almost Christmas. I know how much you love to eat toffees at Christmas."

Once again, he offered her a smile and tried to keep the sadness from his face. Dementia was an insidious disease. Once it took hold, it marched onwards and upwards and nothing could halt its progress. His beloved grandmother had been struck down by it well before her time and there was nothing he could do about it. Years earlier, he'd arrived on her doorstep, broken, and down and out and she'd fixed him. It pained him to know he couldn't return the favor.

"Grandma, do you ever get lonely?" he asked gently, easing himself into the topic.

She shrugged. "Sometimes. It's been a long time since you lived with me. It was awfully quiet when you left. Still, I got used to it."

"What if you could live somewhere close to other people, people your own age? Would you like that?"

She regarded him with suspicion. "What are you talking about?"

Ben sighed. This wasn't going to be easy. "I mean, perhaps it might be best to move somewhere where there are people around to look out for you."

"You look out for me, Ben."

"Yes, Grandma, you're right, but I can't be here all the time. I do my best, but sometimes I get caught up at work and it can be a few days before I find the time to drop by. I think you need someone paying closer attention to you than that.

When I arrived here, you'd been cooking, only you forgot to switch off the stove."

"I was cooking, was I?" she asked, looking surprised.

"Yes, Grandma. You were cooking. Toffees, remember? They'd burned all over the stove."

"I was cooking toffees? Really? Are you sure? I haven't cooked toffees for years. You used to love toffees, especially at Christmas time. Do you remember that?"

He smiled at her softly, his heart breaking. "Yes, Grandma. I remember. I remember everything."

He leaned across the table and took her soft, wrinkled hands in his. "Grandma, I want to see about getting you into a place where you have people looking out for you—people who can make sure you're all right. You'll have company when you want it and best of all, I'll know that you're safe. And I'll visit you there, just as often as I do here. Would you mind if I looked into that?"

She studied him with sad, pale eyes and her lips trembled with the effort to hold back tears. His heart clenched with pain. This was so much harder than he'd imagined it would be. Still, it needed to be done and he was the only one around to do it.

"All right, Ben. If you think that's what I need."

He blew out his breath on a gentle sigh of relief. "Yes, Grandma. I do. And I'll find a place closer to me so I can see you more often. How's that?"

He sat back and they finished their tea in silence. Unbidden, his thoughts returned to Abby. He wondered what she was doing. No doubt, she was still at work. He needed to get back there and make some inroads on the subpoenas that were only partially drafted. He didn't know how the claim had been received by Abby's brother and his bosses, but that was no longer his concern. Jeff would do what he had to do, just like Ben.

He wondered if Abby had told her brother anything about the life she'd led under the bridge. The one and only time he'd been introduced to Jeff they'd met him at a café at least two or three blocks away from where they lived. Ben couldn't imagine Abby had regaled her brother with too many details. It wasn't something anyone proclaimed to the world if they could help it. Hadn't she just told him that, when he'd said he wanted the past to remain in the past?

Could he trust that she'd changed for the better? That she'd given up illegal drugs for good? She certainly looked clean and there was a healthy glow to her smooth cheeks. It was a far cry from the lost and troubled teen he'd turned his back on.

Suppressing a sigh, he finished the final mouthful of tea and pushed away from the table. While he was rinsing out his cup, his grandmother spoke again.

"When would I have to move?"

He turned to face her, wiping his hands on the tea towel. "I don't know. Soon, I hope. I'll ask around and make some calls to places close to where I live. It will depend a little on availability. I'll make sure I find somewhere nice. I don't want to rush you, Grandma, but I'll feel a lot better if I know you're being looked after."

She nodded, her expression filled with sad resignation. "All right, Ben. If you think that's best. Will I still be allowed to make toffees? I know how much you love them. It's coming up for Christmas, you know."

CHAPTER 8

Abby adjusted the leather briefcase in her hand and fitted the key into her front door. A noise on the stairwell behind her caught her attention. She turned in time to see Ben coming up the stairs. She lifted her arm crossly in an effort to ward him off. Still, within seconds he was standing beside her.

"Ben Fitzgerald! What the hell are you doing here? How did you know where I live?"

He stared back at her calmly. "I followed you."

"You *followed* me? From work?"

"Yes."

She shook her head in disbelief. "Who does that? That's...creepy."

"I want to talk to you. Alone. I..." For the first time, he looked uncomfortable. "I wasn't sure you'd want to. I haven't been exactly friendly since our paths crossed again."

She continued to glare at him. "You think?" she said.

It had been a week since she'd seen him, but

the few terse words they'd exchanged since her arrival at Sydney Legal were never far from her mind.

He ducked his head and his cheeks flushed with embarrassment. The sight of it filled her with satisfaction and some of her anger eased. At least he hadn't lost touch with all common decency.

"What makes you think I want to talk to you now?" she demanded, unwilling to let him off lightly. The truth was, from the moment they'd run into each other in the function room, he'd been inexcusably rude and she was fresh from deciding to stay well away from him. She wasn't about to make this easy.

A train rattled past, shaking the glass in the window in the stairwell. Ben threw her a glance. "Doesn't that keep you awake at night?" he asked.

She shook her head. If only he knew what kept her awake at night… She cleared her throat and forced that thought from her mind. "Not that it's any of your business, but no. The last train comes through at ten and they don't start again until five. After a while, you don't even notice them."

An awkward silence fell between them. Ben nodded toward the door. "Are you going to let me in?"

Knowing she'd probably regret it, but curious to know why he was on her doorstep, Abby turned the key in the lock and opened the door. Switching on lights as she went, she set her briefcase on the hall table and walked into the living room. Crossing the floor, she closed the blinds against the oncoming night. The room was cold and she took a moment to light the gas heater that stood against the wall.

"Nice place," Ben said, looking around.

"Thank you."

"Do you live alone?"

"Yes."

He whistled, obviously impressed. "They must be paying you a whole lot better than they're paying me."

"Once again, it's not any of your business, but seeing as you asked, I was left some money by my aunt. It was enough that I was able to put down a deposit on this place." She continued on into the kitchen. He followed close behind her.

"Can I get you a drink? A soda or a coffee?" She made the offer mostly out of politeness. She didn't want him lingering in her home.

"I wish I could ask for a beer, but it's been fifteen years since I had my last drink. Still, after the day I've had, it would be nice to be able to find comfort in alcohol. It's been a rough one."

A note in his voice snagged her attention. She looked up and saw the weariness in his eyes and the fatigue that seemed to weigh down his shoulders. She wondered if there was anything in particular that had caused it, or whether it was simply just another hard day at the office and with that thought she was immediately annoyed that she cared... Then her mind snagged on something else he'd said.

"You haven't had a drink in fifteen years? That

must have been right after we..." Her voice drifted off as memories assailed her.

"Yes," he said quietly. "Right after we said goodbye. I went into rehab, cleaned up my act. Just like you."

Her belly clenched at the reference to the changes she'd made in her life since he'd walked away from her all those years ago. She wasn't ready to discuss that with him. She might never be ready.

"How's the case against the university coming along?" she asked quickly, in an effort to change the subject. She hadn't heard from Jeff since the day he'd called her and told her about Ben. She assumed there hadn't been any progress in the claim against his college.

Ben shot her an inscrutable look, but answered her question. "The statement of claim was served last Friday. I've been working on the subpoenas. The university and the nursing home have been named as defendants. They have less than a month to file and serve their defense. And then it's game on."

Abby stared at him, aghast. Fresh anger stirred. The lawyer part of her understood that he was only doing his job, but this case was personal. It involved her brother, and he knew it.

As if he could read her mind, he compressed his lips on a sigh. "I'm sorry, Abby," he said and looked like he meant it. "I'm now representing the victim's estate. From what I've been told by Jiao Zheng, there are many more nurses working in our hospitals and nursing homes who struggle to read

English. Sending Zheng to jail isn't good enough. What if it had been your grandmother who died through that nurse's negligence? Would you still think we should sit back and do nothing? That we shouldn't seek out those responsible and make them pay, make them think twice before graduating nurses and putting them into our health services, underqualified and incompetent?"

His breath came fast. His hands were on his hips. "I mean, the nurse administered hydrogen peroxide! Can you believe it? Apparently, it was on the nightstand and was a similar-looking bottle to the cough medicine she was supposed to give. Zheng couldn't read the label properly. It was dark. On top of that, she overdosed the poor woman because she couldn't decipher the medication chart!"

He shook his head. Abby could almost see the waves of frustration rolling off him. "It was one travesty after another!" he continued. "Something beyond a single nurse has to be held responsible, Abby, and I intend to pursue this claim with everything that I have."

He turned away from her and with his hands still on his hips, paced the small confines of her kitchen and then spun back to face her, his expression fierce.

"I'm sorry it affects your brother, but that's not my fault. I didn't seek his involvement. He did that all by himself. It might turn out that he had very little to do with the issuing of passes to his students and being aware of who could read English and who couldn't. I hope that's the case, but if it isn't, if there's even the slightest bit of evidence that he knew this was happening and either looked the other way—or worse, condoned it—then he has no one but himself to blame and there's nothing you or I can do about it."

"You're right," she said softly and at that moment, she truly believed it. The facts would come out, and whether or not Jeff had any liability for the tragedy that had occurred in the nursing home would also be established in due course. The die had been cast. The claim had been filed and there was nothing else to it.

Pulling open the fridge, she retrieved a bottle of Sprite and handed it to him. A six-pack of beer sat on the shelf. She'd bought it only a few nights before. She wasn't much of a drinker, but every now and then she felt like a beer. She glanced at Ben.

"Do you mind if I have a drink?"

"No. Why would I?"

She shrugged a little awkwardly. "I don't know... You are a recovering alcoholic who's been dry for fifteen years. I wouldn't want to tempt you or anything."

His bark of laughter irritated her. She glared at him. *What the hell? She was only trying to be polite.*

"It's fine, Abby. It doesn't really work that way. I conquered those demons a long time ago. Have your beer. It won't make any difference to me."

Almost defiantly, she twisted open the bottle cap and took a sip. The beer was cold and refreshing. Probably a little too cold for the early winter night, but it went down well just the same.

"Cheers," she said and clinked her bottle with his.

He gave her a small smile, as if a little unsure about whether he could trust her show of congeniality. And she understood that mistrust. After all, only a few moments earlier, she'd been angry at his intrusion. On top of that, they'd been discussing Jeff and how the court case Ben had instigated could very well ruin her brother's life.

But all of a sudden, she was tired of fighting. She spent all day fighting one way or the other—with her clients, the prosecutor, the judge...even with Ben. Her shoulders slumped on a weary sigh. "Tell me what you've been up to since you left fifteen years ago," she said softly.

His eyes widened in surprise and she didn't blame him for his reaction. She hadn't exactly been friendly the last little while.

"Are you sure you want to know?" he asked.

"Yes, I'd like to know," she replied and realized that was the truth. As much as he'd broken her heart in two when he'd abandoned her, in some ways, she had him to thank for where she was now. His leaving had provided the incentive she needed to get clean, get off the streets and make something of her life.

"Did you know I was a lawyer?" he asked.

She blinked, surprised at his sudden change in subject. "No, not until I saw you in the Sydney Legal function room."

He stared at her solemnly. "And I guess that means you didn't know I worked there."

"Of course I didn't know you worked there. I'd been employed by Pearson and Kew, but my circumstances there took a sudden change in direction and I was forced to look elsewhere for employment. Frederick Wentworth made me an offer I couldn't refuse. It came at an opportune time. That was all there was to it."

"I'm sorry," he said and a flush stained his cheeks. "I accused you of something underhanded and I was way off base. I should have known better."

"Yes," she replied. "You should have. Anyway, we're past that now. Take me back to the beginning. Tell me about the years since we parted."

"I don't know where to start," he said.

"Let's go and sit down," she suggested and led the way into the living room. Setting her beer down on the coffee table, she kicked off her high heels and loosened the buttons on her jacket. Tugging it off, she draped it over the back of a chair. Ben followed suit.

She took a seat on the sofa, collected her beer and tucked her feet beneath her. Ben took a seat in the matching armchair, opposite.

"How about you start at the beginning?" she said. "How did you become a lawyer?"

"After I left you, I went to live with my grandmother. I was too old to return to high school, so I enrolled in the local TAFE college. I got my Higher School Certificate and with the help of the head teacher's recommendation, I got accepted into law school."

"Where did you go to school?" she asked.

"Sydney University."

She smiled in surprise. "So did I."

"We always did have a lot in common," he teased.

His slow, sexy smile did weird things to her stomach. She held on desperately to her earlier promise to keep him at a distance and took a quick swallow of beer in an effort to distract herself. She cast around for something else to say. "Is your grandmother still alive?"

"Yes. She lives in a one-bedroom unit at Wollstonecraft. She moved there from Mount Druitt when I started college. I lived on campus while school was in and I spent my holidays with her. It worked well and I was able to save most of the money I earned from my part time job as a legal clerk. Once I graduated, I got a place of my own."

"She must be very proud of you," Abby murmured.

Ben smiled softly. "She is. I have a lot to be grateful for. I owe her everything." He paused and then added, "That's why it's so hard for me to contemplate uprooting her from her home."

Abby frowned in confusion. "What do you mean?"

Ben heaved a sigh. Leaning forward, he set his drink on the coffee table and then rested his elbows on his knees.

"She has dementia. It's getting worse every

day. Last week, when I visited her she'd burnt sugar on the stove. It was lucky it wasn't something more flammable..." He shook his head slowly. "I need to do something about getting her into a home. She needs someone to watch over her, and unfortunately I'm not in a position to do it. Even if I had enough room in my apartment, I still wouldn't be around enough of the time to keep an eye on her and she's only going to continue to deteriorate. Before long she'll need constant supervision and care."

Despite herself, Abby felt a stab of sympathy. It was obvious how much Ben cared for the old woman and dementia was such a debilitating disease—and so sad for those close to its victims.

"I'm so sorry, Ben," she said quietly. "That's simply awful."

"Yes," he replied. "It is."

"Do you have a particular nursing home in mind?"

He grimaced. "No. I searched online this afternoon and put in some calls to three facilities. The first one told me upfront they don't anticipate having a vacancy for at least a couple of years. I left messages at the other two. I'm still waiting to hear back."

Abby nodded in silent agreement. Finding a place in a nursing home was almost as difficult as finding an available spot in a childcare center. Not that she had any personal experience in that department, but the struggle working parents went through securing childcare was always in the news. "Are you looking in any particular area?"

"I live in Waverton, so it would be nice if she could be somewhere close enough that I could still visit regularly, even on my way home from work."

Without thinking, Abby smiled in surprise. "Waverton? You're right around the corner."

Ben's gaze captured hers and held it. "Yes," was all he said.

Butterflies swarmed in her belly. She took another gulp of beer. At this rate, she'd have to return to the fridge for another. Still, the alcohol was having an effect. She felt more relaxed in Ben's company than she had since she'd spied him in the function room at work. She tried to remember why that wasn't a good thing.

"I... I believe there's a nice place in Lane Cove," she said, pushing the thought aside. "St Patrick's, I think it's called. One of the girls I work with—Sally-Ann Li—told me about it. Her grandmother moved in there last year. She says it's nice and clean and modern and was built less than ten years ago."

Ben nodded. "It sounds good. Definitely worth a call."

Abby tugged her cell phone out of her skirt pocket and searched up the nursing home. "Here it is," she said. "St Patrick's Residential Aged Care in Lane Cove. It's close enough to Waverton. Here, take a look."

She turned the screen so that Ben could see it. To her consternation, he stood and took a seat next to her. With no other choice, she handed him the phone.

He looked at the screen and flicked through some of the pages on the nursing home website. "You're right. It looks nice. It would suit my grandmother perfectly. Let's hope they have a vacancy."

He handed the phone back to her. Their fingers touched. Her heart skipped a beat and she pulled her hand away as if it had been burned. Ben stared at the carpet, as if also trying to get his head around what had just happened.

"I-I'm sorry," she stammered, her cheeks aflame.

"It's fine," he replied, his gaze still fixed to the floor.

"Would you...? Would you like another drink?" she asked.

He glanced up at her and then lifted the bottle where it sat on the coffee table. "No, thanks, I'm good."

"Oh, all right. Do you mind if I have another one?"

He gave her a small smile. "Of course not."

"Great." Abby stood and made a beeline for the kitchen, anxious to escape. Her face still felt like it was on fire and her heart was pounding. She tugged open the fridge and stared blindly inside. With a start, she remembered why she was there and reached in and pulled out another beer. She twisted off the cap and tilted the bottle to her lips.

"Are you all right in there, Abby?"

The call came from the other room. Hurriedly swiping the back of her hand over her mouth, she walked back into the living room, beer in hand.

"Yes, of course. All good. Are you sure I can't get you another Sprite?"

"No, thanks, I haven't finished this one. But you go ahead." He indicated the open beer in her hand and she flushed and was immediately annoyed with herself. Two beers didn't make her an alcoholic. Besides, he'd said he didn't mind if she drank.

Almost defiantly, she took a couple more swallows. Two beers were almost her limit. She needed to slow things down. But she also needed to block out Ben Fitzgerald and the memory of his touch. Her fingers still tingled—which was ridiculous, but true. Because he was sitting on the couch, she took the armchair, needing to keep her distance.

"So, now it's your turn," he said.

She froze. She'd never told anyone about her past and that's the way she wanted it. She'd worked hard to block out every last second of the nightmare that had been her childhood and she wasn't about to break down those walls now. Not for Ben. Not for anyone.

"What's there to tell?" she said with forced insouciance.

He shot her a look that told her she was being facetious and he wasn't buying it for a minute.

"What?" she said, trying hard not to sound defensive but failing.

"Don't give me "what." When I left you that day, you were high on meth and looking for your next fix. It had been that way for a long time. Now you're a successful lawyer. I'd like to know how that happened."

His gaze remained steady on hers. She could tell by the expression on his face and the mutinous tilt to his chin that he wasn't going to be satisfied until she gave him an answer. With a sigh, she tilted the beer to her lips and swallowed again. The bottle was nearly empty when she set it down.

"After you left," she began quietly, "I was a mess. I'd never been there, under the bridge, alone. You were there the first night I stumbled across your hideout and you were there every day and night after that. And suddenly, you told me it was over; that you were moving on." She stared at him accusingly, the old hurts flooding her memory. "At the time, I didn't realize you meant you were done with alcohol, too. I thought you were just through with me."

She laughed, but it was devoid of humor. The sound of it fell flat in the still air. Ben didn't move.

"I look back now and it seems ridiculous how I didn't understand you were done with everything—me, our life, the way we lived. For weeks, I went from one hovel to the next, looking for you. I thought I'd find you a little further up the river or perhaps in the park behind the mall. It was a long time before it hit me that you were truly gone—not just from me, but from Mount Druitt."

"I'm sorry, Abby," he said, his voice low and ragged. "I knew you were still high the morning I told you, but it didn't occur to me that you'd think I was just moving on from our spot." Ben shook his head slowly back and forth. "I was done with it, with *all* of it. You were my only regret, but only you could fix you. I wanted to get more out of life. I knew if I stayed with you and the others there under the bridge, I'd drink myself to death. I didn't want that to happen. I didn't want it to happen to you, either, but I wasn't strong enough to help you. I could barely help myself."

She stared at him and her eyes glazed over with tears, despite her hurt and her determination to keep him at a distance. She hurriedly blinked them away and cleared her throat.

"It's all right, Ben. I understand. For a long time, I blamed you for leaving me. I was furious you abandoned me, left me to my fate. You'd done such a good job protecting me and then suddenly, you'd had enough. It took me a long time to get over it—to be honest, I'm not sure that I'm over it even now—but in the end, your leaving worked out for the best. Without you there beside me, supporting me, loving me, I didn't want to be there anymore. And I missed my family—my little brother. Jeff was only ten when I left home."

Her chest tightened with emotion, but once again, she fought for control. She wasn't going to break down in front of him. At least, not until she'd answered his question.

"It took me a few months, but finally I came to the same decision you did: If I didn't stop doing drugs and get clean, I'd be dead before I turned eighteen. Your leaving was a rude awakening. There was no bright side when I was there alone. I suddenly wanted more from life, too. So, I tracked down my aunt and uncle. They lived as far away from Mount Druitt as you could imagine—literally and metaphorically. They lived on Sydney's northern beaches, not far from Avalon. I arrived on their doorstep wearing filthy rags and barely recognizable. But they took me in without hesitation, and like your grandmother, they're the reason I'm here today."

Ben stared at her, his eyes filled with emotion. "I'm so sorry you had to go through that. But we both got lucky," he said in a husky whisper.

She nodded. She knew exactly what he meant. Every time she thought of her beloved aunt and uncle, her heart swelled with love. Over the years, looking back, she often wondered how different her life might have been if she'd gone to her aunt and uncle sooner, instead of finding her way under the bridge.

But then she wouldn't have met Ben, and despite the pain and hurt he'd caused, she wouldn't change knowing him for anything. Things might not have worked out between them, but when she'd met him years ago, it had been the first time she'd felt truly, wholly, completely loved. She wasn't certain she'd ever feel that way again. That thought saddened her.

"Why didn't you go home, Abby?"

The question was asked quietly, but the words were like fire-tipped arrows in her heart. It took everything she had not to react.

"Going home wasn't an option," she said blithely and then leaned over and picked up her beer. She tilted it to her mouth and drank until it was empty.

"You said you missed your brother... What about him?" Ben said, his voice firm. "Wasn't he still living at home?"

"Yes, of course he was," Abby snapped, wishing he'd just leave the whole subject alone.

"So it was safe enough for him there, but not for you?"

Anger boiled up inside her. She was done answering questions. Her life was none of his business; especially now. She stood and pushed away from the chair and told him as much.

He looked at her calmly. "Abby, why weren't you worried about Jeff?" he asked gently.

Her cheeks burned, her heart pounded. She crossed her arms over her chest and glared at him.

"I told you, it's none of your business! But you're right, I wasn't worried about Jeff. He wasn't at risk."

The moment the words left her mouth, she regretted them. Ben pounced.

"What do you mean?"

"Nothing. It was nothing. I shouldn't have said anything."

Ben opened his mouth as if to argue, but to her relief he closed it again. She cursed silently under her breath, angry at him, but even angrier at herself. She'd managed to keep her secrets all her life and now she'd almost told him everything. She had to learn to keep her mouth shut. It was safer that way. For both of them.

CHAPTER 9

Ben picked up his bottle of Sprite and moved to the other side of the room. Staring out the window at the darkness, he took a sip and contemplated the woman who stood a few yards away from him, looking pale and tense and...frightened. He'd noticed her getting increasingly agitated by his questions, but she'd always been cagey about her past. It hadn't mattered back when they were both hiding secrets, but all these years later, he found he really wanted to know. She'd once been an important part of his life—the most important part—and he'd barely known anything about her. Of course, she could say the same thing about him. The irony of that wasn't lost on him.

Still, she'd asked her questions and he'd answered. It wasn't his fault she hadn't asked about everything. Now she looked like she wanted to run and hide, but he was having none of it. Once and for all, he was going to get to the bottom of Abby Brown and how she'd ended up living under a bridge in Mount Druitt at the ripe old age of fifteen.

"Talk to me, Abby," he said quietly. "How do you know Jeff wasn't at risk? You'd lived in that same household—the home you fled the night we met. Was that why you left? Were *you* at risk? You never told me why you ran away from home."

Her eyes flashed fire. "Neither did you."

He nodded slowly. "You're right. And that's a fair call." Easing his breath out slowly on a sigh, he made his way back to the couch. He looked up at her.

"This isn't going to be easy to talk about and you probably won't find it easy to hear. Are you sure you don't want to take a seat?"

She shrugged, her jaw still set at a determined angle, as if she didn't want him to know she cared, but she wandered over to the chair she'd vacated and sat down. Ben leaned forward and rested his elbows on his knees, his gaze fixed on a point past the coffee table. Slowly, he began to speak.

"I grew up in a nice home on a nice street in a nice neighborhood. I had two parents who loved each other, a younger sister I liked most of the time and friends I could rely on. I guess you could say I was a happy, well-adjusted kid." He paused and then added, "The night of my sixteenth birthday, my world disintegrated."

She paled, but his announcement couldn't have come as a complete surprise. After all, by the time they'd met, he was roughing it on the streets. No teen ended up living under the bridge at Mount Druitt without some kind of trauma at home. She didn't know it, but that wasn't the worst of it.

"We'd been out to dinner, to celebrate my birthday," he continued quietly. "Dad and Mom and my sister, Jennifer. She was eleven. Anyway, we'd been to the local East Indian restaurant. It was my favorite place to eat. Dad had a few beers. Mom had a glass of wine. It was a normal family dinner, only this was the best night of my life. It was my sixteenth birthday! Finally, I was old enough to get my learner's permit. I couldn't wait to sit the test!"

Abby regarded him steadily. She reached for her beer and then seemed to remember it was empty. She sat back against her chair.

"We left the restaurant and headed for home. I was in the back, with my sister. Dad was driving pretty fast. I remember hearing Mom telling him to slow down. Dad was laughing. He loved to drive and he was behind the wheel of his almost-new car. A fire-engine red Peter Brock series Commodore."

Ben grimaced and braced himself for the next part of the story. "I'm not sure how it happened, but somehow we spun out of control. Mom was shouting at Dad. My sister and I were screaming. And then we were under the water. Somehow, he'd driven through a fence and crashed into the river. The car was sinking and we were stuck inside. I managed to unclip my seatbelt. I tried to find Jennifer, but it was dark. I couldn't see anything."

As the memories bombarded him, his breath came faster. His pulse pounded in his ears. He was back there again, under the water, his lungs burning.

"I kicked out the window and got myself out. I was moments from losing consciousness. The car was completely submerged. It seemed to take forever to break the surface, but somehow, I managed it."

"Oh, Ben! How awful! Did all of your family survive?"

Ben compressed his lips and shook his head. "No. Mom and Jennifer drowned."

This time, Abby gasped aloud and her hand went to cover her mouth. He turned his face away, unwilling to witness her shock, her pity.

"W-what about your father?" she stammered.

"He was charged with two counts of drunk driving causing death. He did ten years in jail."

Once again, Abby gasped. Ben felt an odd surge of satisfaction. She was the one who'd insisted he tell his story. She was the one who'd wanted to know.

"I still don't understand how you ended up on the streets. Weren't there any family members who were willing to take you in? Your grandmother?"

"Yes, of course. Grandma was the first to open her home, but I was in no fit state to take her up on her offer. My mother and sister were dead, at the hands of my father. I was angry at him for taking their lives. I was angry at them for dying. But most of all, I was angry at myself. I should have tried harder to save them, especially my sister. She was sitting there beside me...right there beside me... I was her big brother. I should have saved her."

His voice cracked with emotion and he clenched his jaw against a wave of pain. Even after all these years, the thought of that night still got to him. It would probably always be that way. He hadn't been near the water since. Anyone could guess why.

"Where is he now?" Abby said quietly.

"Who?"

"Your father. You said he did ten years in jail. I assume he's out now. Where is he?"

Ben bit down on a surge of anger. "Who knows? Who cares?"

"You mean, you haven't seen him since he was released?"

"No, Abby, I haven't seen him. I haven't seen him or spoken to him since the night of my sixteenth birthday and that's the way it's going to stay."

She regarded him steadily, a look of sympathy on her face. "I understand how you feel, but you need to forgive him."

His lips twisted into a sneer. "Do I now?"

"Yes! You won't be able to move on until you do!"

"Ha!" he scoffed. "Like you know all about moving on. You won't even tell me why you left home, so don't give me that crap about moving on. You don't know what you're talking about."

She stared at him and he could almost see the arguments going back and forth in her head. Well, let her argue with herself. He didn't care. What did she know? She was full of shit. Then she leaned forward and clasped her hands in her lap. She drew in a deep breath and blew it out between taut lips. She caught his gaze and held it. Her blue eyes darkened to cobalt. Her expression was filled with determination and fear.

"All right. I'll tell you."

Abby's stomach churned with nerves. She stared at Ben and prayed she wouldn't be sick. She'd promised to tell him about her childhood, about the reasons she'd left home, but now that the moment was upon her, she struggled to find the courage.

Those memories had been buried deep inside her. She never wanted to pull them out. But Ben was right. She could hardly lecture him about forgiveness and moving on when she wasn't brave enough to do those things herself. It reminded her of her young clients and their accusations that she didn't know anything about doing it rough.

Ben continued to regard her solemnly. She was sure he knew how hard this was. He knew as well as she did that no young person runs away from home to live on the street without good reason. She drew in a deep breath and steeled herself to speak. It was like ripping off an adhesive bandage. Better to do it quick.

"My father sexually abused me from the age of ten until I ran away at fifteen. My mother knew about it and did nothing to stop it. The one and only time I tried to tell her, she slapped my face and told me not to make up filthy lies."

Ben's expression barely changed but for a tic at the side of his mouth. His fists clenched where they rested on his knees. "I'm sorry," he said, his voice husky with pent-up emotion.

"Don't be," she said a little too flippantly. "It wasn't your fault."

"And it wasn't *your* fault, either, Abby." His eyes glinted with anger.

Pressure built behind her eyelids and she blinked furiously to keep the tears at bay. He'd come to her defense, like he had so many times in the past and she loved him for it. It was too bad they could never go back to the way they'd been together, to what they'd had.

She cleared her throat of the lump that had lodged there, and offered him a wobbly smile. "It's all right, Ben. My aunt paid for a lot of therapy. I don't blame myself and I've learned to overcome my feelings of bitterness and hatred toward my parents. Hate is so destructive. It eats you up inside. I learned that if I ever wanted to take back control and live life on my terms, I had to let the anger go. And I have."

As she said the words, she realized she truly meant them. Somewhere along the way, she'd set aside the nightmare of her childhood and embraced everything that was good in her life. At this point, it was working. She was a lawyer of some skill and experience. She owned a nice apartment. She had a good job—no, scrap that. She had a *great* job in a reputable firm and she really believed her work was making a difference. It was all she'd ever wanted. The only thing missing was someone to share in all that.

Her gaze flicked back to Ben. He was still staring at her, a mixture of awe and confusion on his face.

"How can you be so forgiving?" he rasped. "That man stole your innocence, your childhood, your right to grow up feeling safe and protected and loved. He took all of that from you and your mother stood by and let it happen. If anything, you should have put his ass in jail. It isn't too late, you know."

She shook her head. "I don't want to drag all that up again. What would be the point?"

His frown deepened as if he struggled to understand. "I don't get it. After what he did to you..."

"I understand what you're saying," she replied gently. "Believe me, I used to be as angry as you. Don't you remember how I was all those years ago, when you first met me? I was as prickly as a cactus. I hated the world and everything in it. I used meth to dull the pain. While I was high, I didn't think about what had happened or the awful hand I'd been dealt."

She paused, remembering those times. If it hadn't been for Ben and the care he'd shown her, she might very well have done herself in. It would have been so easy to overdose and drift away, leaving the pain, the anger, the humiliation behind her. But then she would have had to leave Ben...

He grimaced and his expression filled with pain. "And then I went and made it worse by abandoning you."

"No!" The protest burst from her mouth. He looked at her in surprise. She hurried to explain. "What I mean is, yes, you left me there and things did get worse, but like I said, things also got better. I decided I didn't want to live under the bridge without you. I also wanted more out of life. And here I am. Living proof that it's possible to turn your life around. Just like you did."

Ben's eyes were filled with admiration. "I think what you did is terrific, and I know firsthand it wasn't easy. I was only addicted to alcohol. I can't imagine what it was like coming off meth. But you did it. I'm proud of you."

She blushed at the warmth in his eyes. "Thank you. I'm proud of *you*, too." She paused and then added, "Does this mean you don't think I'm out to sabotage your career? I would never do that, Ben. Once, you were the most important person in the world to me. You still mean a great deal to me. I'd never do anything to hurt you or the successful life you've achieved and I hope you feel the same way."

She shot him a half-hearted smile. "You have the same power to ruin my career, remember? One word about how I'm a reformed drug addict and I'd never step foot in a courtroom again. Hasn't it occurred to you, the damage *you could do to me?*"

He shook his head. "No. It honestly hadn't. I'd never do anything like that to you."

She looked at him steadily. "Then do you believe me when I tell you I feel the same way?"

His chest expanded on an indrawn breath and then relaxed as he released it. "Yes, I do."

Her gaze wandered over the fine cotton of his white business shirt and the tasteful, impeccably knotted navy-and-red striped tie. His charcoal-gray suit pants stretched over muscled thighs and matched the jacket he'd draped over the back of the couch. She recalled the heat that had flooded through her at his slightest touch and rekindled need burned a path to her core. It had been so long since she'd held him, touched him, loved him. She yearned to do so again.

As if aware of the direction of her thoughts, his eyes filled with desire and his face grew taut. Slowly, he eased himself off the couch and knelt in front of her. He took her hands in his and drew her forward. Her heart took off in flight.

A thousand butterflies swarmed in her stomach, fluttering with nervous anticipation. She tried valiantly to recall all the reasons why she'd been determined to keep her distance from him, but then he leaned closer and her thoughts disintegrated like dandelion seeds on the breeze. Her lips parted on an indrawn breath.

"What about Jeremy?" he murmured, his lips mere inches from hers.

"Who's Jeremy?"

With a low growl of possession, his lips claimed hers in a fiery kiss. There was no gentle build-up, no finesse. Just Ben with a head full of passion, kissing her like he couldn't get enough.

A spark ignited deep inside her and she kissed him back for all she was worth. The old hurts from her past dissolved into nothingness. All she could think of was how good it felt to be with him like this again. For so long, she'd been merely existing, going through the motions. She needed Ben to bring everything back to life. Burying her fingers in his hair, she held his head still while she took all that he gave. His beard was soft. He tasted warm and sweet with the Sprite still on his lips.

He broke away and his breath came fast, just as fast as hers. With eyes that were dark with desire, he held out his hand in wordless invitation. With her hand in his, he helped her to her feet. She shook with nerves and need.

Scooping her into his arms, he kneeled back on the floor and lay her gently on the thick rug in front of the heater.

She stared up at him and her heart raced. She'd dreamed of this moment forever. Though she hadn't seen him since she was a teenager, her heart hadn't forgotten him. And neither did her body. He traced a finger across her cheek and then lower, down her breastbone. A trail of fire followed in his wake. Her nipples puckered with desire.

Loosening the buttons of her blouse, he gently spread the fabric open. She was grateful she'd worn matching white lace underwear. His gaze drifted over her breasts and then his hands continued their exploration. Cupping each breast, he rubbed the pads of his thumbs over her sensitive nipples.

"You're so beautiful," he whispered. "As beautiful as you were at sixteen."

"Fifteen," she corrected. "When we met, I hadn't yet turned sixteen."

"It doesn't matter. It never did. I loved you then like I love you now. You're perfect, so absolutely perfect." He buried his face in her neck.

Abby reveled in the sensations he caused as he nibbled and suckled her ear. Her mind kept going back to the words he'd said.

He loved her! At least, that's what he'd said. Perhaps it was just passion talk, and would be meaningless in the cold light of day. She didn't know, but right there, right then, she believed he meant it. She wasn't going to let anything spoil the moment she'd waited for more than half her life.

He pulled away and stared down at her, his eyes glittering emerald with his need. Almost shyly, she reached up and loosened his tie and then worked her fingers over his buttons. When she was done, she spread his shirt wide.

His chest was broad and liberally sprinkled with soft, curly brown hair. She ran her fingers through it. As a teenager, he'd had a nice body, but years had passed and he was a man. There was still a lot to like. His chest was broader, his arms were more muscular and he now sported a moustache and a trim beard. It tickled her skin when he kissed her, but she was surprised at how silky it felt. It was nothing like the rough whiskers he grew as a teen.

Ben reached behind her and unclasped her bra, freeing her breasts. Almost impatiently, he tugged at her blouse and removed it. The bra quickly followed suit. Once again, his hands went to her breasts, but they were quickly replaced by his mouth. She gasped at the feel of his warm lips on her nipples and she moved restlessly beneath him.

"Hey, what's the hurry? Do you have other plans?" he murmured lazily and swiped her nipple again.

"I'm hungry," she said, her gaze roving over him, leaving him in no doubt as to what she meant.

He groaned and undid his belt and in short order shucked off his pants. His underwear quickly followed. She had no more than a moment to admire the sheer length and breadth of him before he was once again kneeling by her side.

His hands went to her skirt and she rolled to one side so he could reach the zipper. It slid down with barely a whisper and within moments, she was as naked as he was. They stared at each other in wonder. Their breath came fast.

"You're so beautiful," Ben whispered again.

"So are you."

With a groan, they came together, rolling across the floor. The carpet was soft beneath their skin, cushioning them, protecting them. Ben's hands skimmed over her ribcage, her hips and then lower, to her core. Her legs fell open of their own accord and his fingers delved into her warmth. She burned everywhere he touched her. She burned from the inside out. She needed to feel him inside her, filling her, loving her.

"I want you, Ben." Her voice was husky with desire.

His eyes flared with emotion and he captured her mouth in another soul-searching kiss. He kissed her like he couldn't get enough of her, tasting her lips, her nose, her chin. He nibbled her ears and nuzzled her neck and all the while, his fingers played with her moist softness. He stroked with first one finger, then added two. He plunged in all the way. It was madness, it was mind-blowing... But it wasn't enough.

"Fuck me, Ben."

The coarse words fell out of her mouth, but she wasn't sorry. She was filled with a raw, animal-like need. She yearned for his cock to fill her, stretch her, claim her. To drive her wild with need.

He pulled away and fumbled in his pants and came up with a condom. Sheathing himself, he lay back down beside her and pressed against her. His cock was hard and throbbing. Even through the condom, she felt his heat.

"Turn over," he demanded, his voice rough.

With a surge of excitement, she did as he said and came up on all fours. He maneuvered himself behind her. A moment later, his cock pressed at her entrance. She leaned back against him and made small murmurs of encouragement. She was burning up with desire.

"Please, Ben. Give me your cock," she begged and pressed against him again.

With a groan, he thrust into her and she gasped from the impact. He filled her and stretched her and claimed her, just like she wanted him to. Over and over, he plunged in and drew out, holding her hips firmly with his hands. Unfettered, her breasts bounced and jiggled in time with the movement of his hips.

Desire built inside her, a roaring flame, a building pressure until she couldn't bear it another moment. With her hands fisted in the carpet, she reached her crescendo and toppled over the other side. She bucked and screamed against him and finally went limp.

His thrusts came faster, harder. His fingers dug into her hips. He groaned and then cried out his release...

Awhile later, his grip loosened and he collapsed against her back. She lowered herself to the floor and he followed her down. Spooning against her, he reached around and put an arm across her breasts. Too spent to bother with the light, she fell asleep.

CHAPTER 10

Ben woke with a start, squinting into the light. Unfamiliar furnishings surrounded him. He rolled over and realized he was lying on the floor and with a rush, everything came back to him.

Abby.

She lay asleep beside him in the warm space, her breath coming deep and even. Still naked, she slept like she didn't have a care in the world. He wished he could say the same. Her revelations about her childhood still shook him to the core. Every time he thought about it, he was filled with renewed anger. Still, it wasn't his place to demand retribution and right now, he was feeling guilty for even being in her space, and worse still, for making love to her. He certainly hadn't planned on it happening, and now that it had, he wasn't sure what to do about it.

He glanced at his watch. It was a little past midnight. He needed to get home. The last thing he wanted was to have her wake beside him in the morning, full of expectations. He'd said the 'L' word, for Pete's sake! *Had he been that stupid?*

So what if he was still in love with her? He shouldn't have gone and *told* her! They hadn't seen each other for fifteen years. *What did he really know about who she'd become?* She was an ex-junkie. She said she'd changed. She looked like she'd changed, but how could he be sure? She threw back two beers like they were nothing. Okay, so she'd never had a problem with alcohol—that had been all him—but still, could he be with someone who was once an addict? Could *she?*

Moving away from her, he stood and pulled on his clothes. His stomach rumbled, reminding him it had been hours since he'd last eaten. When he'd followed Abby home, his only thought had been to talk to her, away from the office. He'd intended to say his piece and go home. Things hadn't quite gone as planned.

He grimaced. That was an understatement. He'd ravished her. The stupid thing was, he wanted to do it all over again. He looked down at her, still sleeping peacefully. She was even more beautiful in repose. Her mouth was relaxed and her lips slightly parted. The little lines that marred the smoothness of her forehead had disappeared. She murmured something in her sleep and then smiled and his breath caught in his throat.

His heart stilled and then beat a frantic tattoo against his chest. He wasn't exactly spying on her, but still... Her eyes remained closed and her breathing deepened and he swallowed a sigh of relief.

Tugging on his jacket, he picked up his shoes

and socks and sat on the couch to put them on. Once again, he looked over toward Abby. Was he going to leave her lying there all night? Though the heater had kept the room cozy, the floor wasn't exactly comfortable. Already, he felt a crick in his neck.

But he couldn't just move her, could he? What if she woke? He didn't want to have to explain why he was leaving. Not right there, when he hadn't had time to think things through properly. He'd probably end up saying something he regretted and that wouldn't be good for either of them. No, better to leave now.

With his mind made up, he turned away but only made it halfway across the room before his conscience got the better of him. He swung back toward her, bent down and lifted her in his arms. She weighed next to nothing.

Stumbling down the hallway in the dimness, he passed the bathroom on his left. The bedroom on his right was being used as a wardrobe, with clothes and shoes lying all around. He stifled a grin and kept walking.

Abby mumbled again in her sleep and turned her face into his chest. The feel of her in his arms brought back a rush of memories and his cock hardened in response. He cursed under his breath.

Quickening his steps, he walked through the open doorway of the room at the very end. A large four-poster bed complete with lacy white canopy and too many cushions to count filled the room. Despite himself, he smiled. It was so girly, so frilly, so feminine. So Abby.

Keeping his mind firmly above his waistband, he settled her gently against the mattress. She sighed softly and curled into the pillows. Her eyelashes fluttered open and all of a sudden, she was reaching for him.

"Ben? Where are you going? Come back to bed."

"*Shh*, honey. Go back to sleep. It's late. I'll see you in the morning."

He leaned over to peck her cheek, but she turned her head at the last minute and wrapped her arms around his neck. Dragging him closer, she kissed him with her lips and her tongue. By the time she released him, he was rock hard and it was all he could do to remember why he wasn't throwing himself down beside her and taking all that she so freely offered.

Reluctantly, he stepped away from her. With his footsteps silenced by the thick carpet, he left the room, closing the door and taking his tumultuous thoughts with him.

———————

Abby twirled a loose lock of hair around her fingers and did her best to concentrate on the brief that lay open on her desk. She'd been staring at the same page for more than ten minutes, reading the same lines over and over again. Her lack of concentration was all Ben's fault. He'd left sometime during the night without saying goodbye. At least, she didn't think he'd said goodbye. She vaguely remembered him carrying her to bed, but her memories were a little hazy. The beers she'd had on an empty stomach hadn't helped matters.

She'd never been much of a drinker, but she enjoyed a beer every now and then. They helped her relax and unwind after a long day. She thought about Ben and the fact that he was a reformed alcoholic. He said he didn't mind that she drank, but was it fair to him to tempt him? For all she knew, he'd tasted the alcohol on her lips. *Could even that small amount cause a relapse?*

She didn't know much about an addiction to alcohol, but if it was anything like a drug addiction, it was best to stay well clear of the stuff. There was no way she would put herself in the situation where she was around people using drugs. She was strong enough in her conviction that she'd beaten her addiction, but there was no need to tempt fate. That would be plain stupid. She hadn't worked this hard and come this far to throw it all away and she was sure Ben felt the same way.

Ben.

Try as she might, her thoughts circled back to him and with it, all the reasons why she'd vowed to stay away from him. He'd hurt her badly when they were younger. He'd walked away from her without a second glance, abandoned her to her uncertain fate. Oh, she understood his reasons. She'd come to the same conclusion: Leave the safety and security of the bridge and clean up her act or risk succumbing to the darkness forever. In the end, there hadn't been a decision to make, but she wished it hadn't also entailed the heartbreak Ben had inflicted upon her when he left.

Did she want to risk her heart all over again? What if it happened a second time? What if he decided she reminded him too much of the past, of the life he'd left behind? What if she fell hard for him a second time and he walked away again? Could she handle the devastation a second time? Would it toss her back into the shadowy world where she needed narcotics to get through the pain?

That thought terrified her. She'd worked too hard and had come too far to throw it all away on a man. Even a man like Ben.

Tears pricked her eyes and she bit down on a sob. She loved him with everything that she was, but what if it wasn't enough? What if he took all she had and still turned his back on her, leaving her desolate once again?

She shook her head, filled with doubt and confusion. She wondered where he was and what he was thinking. *Was he in court or in his office?* Perhaps he'd gone downstairs to grab a coffee or a bite to eat. It was almost half-past twelve. Court broke for lunch at one. Did she dare take the elevator downstairs and leave the building on the pretext of going out to buy something to eat and just casually saunter past the courthouse? What if he wasn't in court? She'd have gone to all that effort for nothing. Still, she had to eat some time. Why not now? Did she *want* to see him again?

The thoughts chased themselves around in her

head and she groaned. They hadn't even had the talk to sort out their feelings and where things might be headed, if anywhere, and already, Ben Fitzgerald was taking over her life. *What hope was there for her?* After all these years, she prided herself on having a clear direction. Turning down Ben's suggestion that she go to the police about her father was just another example of how far she'd come.

She hadn't been lying when she told him she was at peace with her childhood, including the part her father played in its destruction. She'd heard from Jeff that their father was dying from bowel cancer and only had weeks to live. *Good riddance.* She didn't care. Her love for Wallace Brown had died on the night of her tenth birthday. But that didn't mean she wanted to dredge up the nightmares from her past and go public, expose her and her brother to the horror of what had been her childhood home. She couldn't think of anything worse.

At the thought of her brother, she reached for her phone and dialed his number. Ben had told her the claim against the university and the nursing home had been served. She wondered how Jeff was holding up.

"Richmond University. This is Jeff Brown."

"Jeff, it's Abby. How are you doing?"

"Abby. Hi. I'm fine." He sounded distracted.

"Are you busy?" she asked.

"Yes. Thanks to your buddy, Ben Fitzgerald. I'm flat out preparing an affidavit for our lawyers so that they can prepare a defense to the civil claim he served on us last week. You don't happen to know anything about that, do you?" His tone sounded almost accusatory.

Abby bit her lip. "I didn't know anything about it when you called me last week, but I've spoken to Ben about it since. I'm sorry, Jeff. Is it bad?"

He sighed on the other end of the phone. "Yes, it's bad! Of course it's bad! I'm in the firing line, Abby! I'm the one officially responsible for graduating all our nursing students. Me. It's my fault those nurses graduated without being able to properly read English. The bosses are in a panic. They don't have a clue how many other nurses might come out of the woodwork and make similar admissions. There's talk of shredding records."

Abby gasped. "They can't do that! That's illegal! They could be destroying evidence."

"That's what I told them, but who knows if they'll listen. Besides, most records are stored on a hard drive these days. Even the English language test is mostly completed online. Destroying paper records will hardly put out the fire."

"What are you going to do?"

"I'm going to round up all the underlings and try and find out how far this goes and how many people are involved. I'm not sure how much luck I'll have. The nurses that graduated with less than average English skills are hardly going to come forward and confess to fraud. At this stage, all I can do is cross my fingers and hope for the best."

"I think you should get a lawyer," she said.

"The university has already engaged someone from Harris Botham and Marshall."

"Yes, but they're representing your employer. I think you should have a lawyer who's looking out for *you*."

Jeff fell silent and Abby could only guess he was trying to come to terms with the implications of her statement.

"Is your job threatened?" she asked quietly.

"Not just my job. My whole career's on the line. I'm the head administrator of the nursing department. The fact that I had nothing to do with grading the papers or handing out marks is beside the point. It was my job to know that we were graduating incompetent nurses. I'm the boss. The buck stops with me."

"It seems so unfair!" Abby cried.

"No, Abby, that's where you're wrong. Like I said, I'm the boss. I should have kept a closer eye on my staff. I haven't been happy about the application process at this university since I took over the job from Ellen King. It's been all about churning out the numbers and making money. There's never any follow-up on who has or hasn't passed the English language course and we don't pay much attention to who sits the exams. At least before now, as long as the money kept rolling in, the powers that be were happy. I had concerns about the way things worked, but I kept quiet and toed the party line. The truth is, I was a coward. Now I'm paying the price."

"You aren't a coward, Jeff!" Abby protested.

"Yes, I am," he said quietly. "In more ways than

one."

Abby's heart skipped a beat at the graveness of his tone. "What are you talking about?"

"You know what I'm talking about."

"No, Jeff. I don't."

"Bullshit."

Abby started in surprise. She'd never heard her brother swear. "Jeff, what's this all about?"

"It's about you, Abby. You and Dad."

Dread pooled in Abby's belly. Her hands turned clammy on the phone. "W-what are you saying, Jeff?"

"Oh, for fuck's sake, Abby! Why are you still pretending? Why are you still protecting him? After all these years! *Fuck!* He doesn't deserve it!"

Abby sat frozen in shock, unable to believe what she was hearing. Her chest went tight. She couldn't breathe. *Did Jeff know about what her father did to her? How could he?* Until last night and the early failed attempt to tell her mother, she hadn't told a soul.

"I know that Dad raped you, okay?" Jeff said in a calmer tone. "I woke up one night and heard a noise. I came into your room. I saw him, Abby. I saw what he was doing to you."

Abby's heart pounded like it was going to burst out of her chest. All these years her little brother had carried that secret. She couldn't imagine how he felt. *Oh, yes she could.* She'd carried the secret, too.

"Jeff, I'm so sorry!" she cried. "I didn't know you were there! I didn't know!"

"It's all right, Abby. It wasn't your fault. It was

never your fault. I was eight when I found out about it and for seventeen years I've kept my mouth shut. At the time, I didn't know what was happening, but when I finally worked it out, I forced it to the far recesses of my mind. I kept telling myself that if I didn't think about it, it wasn't really happening and then there was the fact I didn't know what to do. I was just a stupid kid... Who was I going to tell? I was too embarrassed to say anything to you. But that was no excuse, Abby and I'm sorry. I'm sorry for keeping quiet. I should have said something, told someone. I should have made him stop."

"No! Jeff! No! You were a little boy. You were too young to do anything. I was five years older and *I* didn't have the courage to talk. Please, don't blame yourself. I've put it all behind me. I'm at peace with it and I refuse to let what happened ruin the rest of my life. Please be happy for me, Jeff. I've come a long way. I've made a life for myself, a very good life. I'm happy. Do you believe me?"

"How can you be happy when he got away with what he did? It's the reason you ran away from home, isn't it?"

"Yes, it is. By the time I turned fifteen, I thought I was old enough to survive on my own out on the streets. And I did. I'm proud of the person I am today and I hope you're proud of me, too."

"Of course I'm proud of you!" Jeff exclaimed, his voice choked. "I look at everything you've achieved after all that happened to you and I can't believe you're my sister! It doesn't mean I don't still lie awake at night eaten away by guilt."

Abby felt a wave of sadness. "Oh, Jeff. Honey, hearing you say that makes me feel so sad. It had nothing to do with you, little brother. Not then, not ever. Please believe me. I want you to let this go. It isn't healthy and it isn't true. The only person responsible for what happened to me is our father and I hope he repents in hell."

"Me, too," came the soft reply.

There was a lull in their conversation while they were both caught up in their thoughts. Abby was the first to break it.

"How many nurses graduated without being able to properly read English?" she asked quietly.

Jeff sighed. "I don't know. Even Jaio Zheng is one too many."

"I guess we can be thankful there's only been one death."

"Yeah, that we know of."

"I'm sorry, Jeff," she said a second time, knowing how ineffectual it sounded. All he'd worked for was coming crashing around his ears and there was nothing anybody could do about it.

"Listen, Abby, thanks for calling, but I'm going to have to go. I have a heap to do."

"Yes, of course. I'll let you go. Hey, why don't you come over for dinner one night this week? I could cook tacos. Your favorite."

"Sure," he replied, sounding far from enthusiastic.

"I'll even whip up a chocolate mousse for after. What do you think?"

"Yeah, okay."

"Great. I'll call you later and we can work out when we're both free."

Abby hung up the phone and stared blindly at the papers spread before her. She couldn't believe that for all these years Jeff had known what happened to her and hadn't said anything. She didn't blame him for not going to the police or even a trusted adult. He was a child! He was only ten when she'd left! He was in no position to report such an awful crime. But her heart ached over the secret he'd carried and the anguish in his voice when he spoke of it. She determined to have him over for dinner as soon as possible and reassure him once again that there was no reason for his guilt.

Her thoughts turned to Ben and she sighed. When compared to the problems her brother faced, the question of Ben and where to go from here hardly mattered. He'd told her last night he still loved her, but did that still hold true today? She didn't know and now wasn't really the time to find out.

Her brother needed her. She'd best focus all her energy on him. No, as far as Ben Fitzgerald was concerned, she'd take her cue from him. Let him be the one to make the next move. Then she'd know where she stood.

CHAPTER 11

Ben stared down at the legal pad in front of him and tried his best to concentrate on what Wang Xiu Ying was saying. She was the third name on the list of nurses Jiao Zheng had provided right before her incarceration and Wang Xiu Ying was the third nurse to shamefully admit she struggled with the English language.

Ben had made notes throughout each interview, but the story was depressingly the same. The nurses either had arranged for someone else to sit the online English test required by the Department of Immigration, or they had someone else sit the examination at the university. Either way, they were granted student visas to study in Australia and ultimately graduated with a degree.

The first two women he interviewed had studied at Richmond University, but Wang Xiu Ying had attended Nepean. The implications of this case were so much bigger than he'd thought. It was becoming more and more obvious he was barely scratching the surface. *How many other universities turned a blind eye to their international students and their failures?*

He could only hope there were no more accidental deaths, but after listening to the three women he'd interviewed, he was afraid it was only a matter of time. The system was in freefall. How had the universities gotten away with allowing this to go on for so long? They were dealing with people's lives!

Ben's stomach rumbled loudly enough for the woman seated across from him to hear. She stopped mid-sentence and stared at him. Heat crept across his cheeks.

"I'm sorry, Ms Xiu Ying, perhaps we could finish this after lunch? Would that be all right?"

"Lunch. Yes. I will come back after lunch."

"Thank you." Ben pushed away from his desk and escorted the young woman to the door. Closing it behind her, he took his jacket from the cupboard and tugged it on.

After he'd snuck out of Abby's apartment, he'd walked down to the end of her street and was fortunate enough to find a cab. He only lived around the corner, but it was a little too far to walk, especially at that time of night. By the time he'd showered and crawled into bed, it was half-past two. He'd set the alarm, but had slept through it and there had been no time for breakfast. Cheryl had booked back-to-back appointments and he hadn't even had time to get a coffee. Now it was going on for one and he was starving.

But that wasn't the real reason he hadn't

ventured out. The truth was, he was hiding. He wasn't ready to face Abby and answer her questions and if he went outside, he risked running into her. It could be in the elevator or the foyer or out near the coffee vendor. It could be anywhere.

Then again, she might be in court. *Court.* He should have thought of that earlier. Court was in session from ten until one. They took an hour for lunch and then resumed. If she were in court, he could have snuck out and been back in his office by now, sated.

He shook his head and cursed. *What the hell was he doing?* Hiding, sneaking, conniving... It was ridiculous. He was an adult. He didn't hide out. He didn't sneak. He went where he wanted, when he wanted and that was the way it had always been. He wasn't going to let something—whatever it was with Abby—change the way he did things. Besides, if he was man enough to sleep with her and take all she offered, he was man enough to face her in the morning...or lunchtime. Whatever.

At the thought of their night together, he remembered what she'd told him about her father. He cursed again more viciously. Another crime gone unpunished. Still, it wasn't his fight, no matter how much he wished it were.

Knowing what her father had done to her made him furious. He wished he could get in a room with the man for five minutes. Only one of them would walk out in one piece. The man didn't deserve to breathe the same air as the rest of them. Ben thought he was angry at *his* father, but that had nothing on the way he felt about Wallace Brown.

Knowing what Abby had been through helped him understand why she'd turned to drugs. She'd been fifteen and dealing with something unimaginable. He knew all about using substances to dull the pain, block the nightmare, to forget—even for just a little while. He was just lucky he got himself out of the quagmire before it destroyed him. Now he was an AA sponsor and he was proud of it. He helped others recover, reclaim their lives. His friend, Danielle Craigdon, was a prime example.

Perhaps Dani could help him sort out his feelings for Abby? They still called each other regularly and often caught up for lunch. He could see if she was free now. He could tell her about what was going on in his life and get her advice. It was a good plan.

Tugging his cell phone out of his pocket, he dialed Dani's number and was relieved when she answered.

"Hi, Ben, how are you doing?"

"Great, Dani. Actually… I'm not so great. I was wondering if you had time for lunch."

"Now?"

"Yes."

"I guess so. We're pretty quiet here today, thank goodness. It's nice to get a day like that every now and then."

"So you can make it?" He tried not to sound too eager.

"Sure. The usual place?"

"See you in fifteen."

Ben made it outside his building without seeing Abby and he quickly made a beeline for the bus. It was difficult to get parking around the Sydney Harbour Hospital were Dani worked and it was often just as fast on public transit.

Dani was already waiting at their usual park bench beneath a tree on the edge of No.1 Oval at the University of Sydney. The college was within walking distance of the hospital and not only was it leafy and green and pleasant, it was a convenient place to meet. They greeted each other with a hug.

"Hey, you," Dani said, punching him lightly on the arm.

"Hello to you," he replied and looked her up and down.

She was dressed in a bright yellow, fitted dress that hugged her curves. "You look good, Dani. Married life must agree with you."

She smiled and it lit up her face. Even her eyes glowed. "It's great. You ought to try it sometime."

"Yeah, yeah, yeah," he said and immediately thought of Abby.

"So, what's up?" Dani asked, pulling a sandwich from her bag.

In an effort to buy time, he pulled out the banana he'd bought on his way to their meeting place and began to peel it. He'd taken two bites before he found the courage to speak.

"I've met a girl."

Dani's face split into a wide grin. "About time!"

"Yeah, well you might not think it's so great after you hear what I have to say."

Dani raised her eyebrows, the smile still playing around her lips. "Sounds ominous," she teased.

He didn't share her mirth. Slowly, her smile faded. "Talk to me, Ben. What's going on?"

With a sigh, he told her everything, even about last night when he'd spent a few blissful hours in her arms. When he finished, he looked over at Dani.

"So, I'm hoping you have some advice because I don't know what to do. I love her. I've always loved her, but I'm scared, Dani. I'm scared that she might relapse, or maybe I will. She's a drug addict. I'm an alcoholic. We both know it's a struggle we'll battle the rest of our lives. I don't know if I need to complicate things by getting into a relationship with someone who also had a dependency problem. It's hard enough keeping my own demons at bay."

"You're overthinking this, Benjamin. People can change, and they can change for ever. You did. So did I. Why not Abby? From what you've said, she's done amazing things to turn her life around. She deserves a second chance. We all do."

He stared at Dani for a long moment, his thoughts in turmoil and then he looked away and sighed.

"You're right," he admitted quietly, meeting her gaze once again. "I guess I'm just scared that things might not work out. We're not teenagers this time. A broken heart won't mend so fast. Even though I was the one to break things off last time, it was still a hard thing to do. I loved her. I wanted to be with her, to protect her and keep her safe. Leaving her was an act of survival. I bore the burden of guilt when I knew she might not survive without me after I left. That I might never see her again if she did survive because she would continue her decline into addiction. I never imagined she would also dig herself out, that she could do that without my love and support... I had to get away from her and that scene or it would have been the death of me. Literally. But I was always in love with her. I still am."

Dani regarded him in silence, her eyes filled with compassion. "I don't have all the answers, Ben, but what I do know is that sometimes we have to take a risk. Sometimes we get hurt, but at other times we don't. We find that perfect someone; we find that magical place. We get to understand what true love feels like and it's like nothing anyone can consciously replace. Nothing truly worth having is easy, Ben. Didn't you once tell me that? Remember? I was down and depressed and doubting Jett and the way he felt about me. You were the one who made me see that what he and I had was worth fighting for. Remember?"

He nodded. "Yes, I remember." And he did. Matters of the heart always seemed so much more clearer when it was someone else's heart at stake.

"So, I say, go for it. What do you have to lose?"

His lips twisted into a semblance of a smile. "Ha! It's easy for you to say! You took a leap of faith and it paid dividends. You couldn't look happier.

But we both know it doesn't always work out like that and Jett didn't have a history of drug or alcohol dependence. And I have a great deal to lose..."

"You're right," she said. "But Jett had his hang-ups, believe me. None of us go through life without collecting a little baggage along the way. It's just the way it is. The trick is knowing whether you can live with that person's baggage, or not."

She smiled softly. "For me, I hit the jackpot. Jett's my soulmate and he feels that way, too. It was meant to be. But who's to say it won't be that way for you Abby? You're both so strong, have overcome so many demons. Jett and I don't have a monopoly on happy-ever-afters. This woman has held your heart from the time you were seventeen. That has to count for something." Dani paused and then cocked her head at an angle and regarded him solemnly. "How does Abby feel?"

Ben was suddenly inundated with images of him and Abby making love the night before. She was as wild and passionate and giving as he had been. "She still cares. At least, I think she does."

"There you go!" Dani declared, breaking into a grin. "What are you waiting for?"

Ben's lips tugged upwards until he was grinning, too. "Okay," he said, arriving at a decision. "You're right. I'm going to go for it!"

"Yay!" Dani cheered. "Good for you!"

Ben glanced at his watch and noted the time. "I'm sorry, Dani, but I have to go. I'm in the middle of deposing a witness."

"That's okay. I need to go, too."

They stood and disposed of their trash in a nearby garbage bin and then hugged each other goodbye.

"Thanks for listening and…everything," Ben said.

"Anytime," Dani replied softly. She turned away in the direction of the hospital and then turned back. "Hey, how's your grandmother?"

Ben grimaced and remembered he still had to call the aged care facility Abby had told him about. He made a mental note to do it on the way back to the office. "She's not so good," he replied.

"Dementia is a cruel disease," Dani commented quietly.

"Yes. That it is. I'm going to have to put her in a home."

"Oh, Ben!" Dani cried. She knew how much his grandmother meant to him.

Ben swallowed the lump in his throat. "Yeah."

"Well, let me know if there's anything Jett and I can do to help."

He gave Dani a grateful smile. "Thanks, Dani. I really appreciate it."

"Like I said, anytime."

On the bus, heading back to his office, Ben found the number of the nursing home in Lane Cove and dialed. He inquired about the availability of spaces.

"I'm sorry, Mr Fitzgerald. We have quite a substantial waiting list. As I'm sure you can appreciate, rooms only become available when one of our residents passes away. We have no way of knowing how many or how often. I'm sure you understand."

"Of course," Ben agreed, his heart sinking. It had been the same for the others. And then he had a sudden thought. "How much would it cost to go to the top of the list?"

The woman on the other end of the phone blustered. "We don't usually operate that way, Mr Fitzgerald. The board—"

"How much?" Ben interrupted. He'd never come across a business that didn't like the sound of money.

The woman named a sum that had Ben's eyes rolling back in his head, but he made sure his surprise didn't color the tone of his voice. "All right. You'll have the check on your desk before the day is over. How soon can my grandmother move in?"

The woman *ummed* and *ahhed* a few more times, but eventually gave him a date a fortnight hence. He nodded, satisfied. It would have to do. He thought of all the work ahead of him, packing up his grandmother's things, putting her unit on the market, moving her into the home. In addition to all the things he had on his plate at work, it would be a struggle, but he had no choice. He refused to put his grandmother at risk—and right now, she needed a whole lot more care than he could provide.

Somehow, he'd juggle his caseload and make it happen. Perhaps Abby might even give him a hand. The thought filled him with wary anticipation. His decision to throw himself into a relationship with her was still so new and daunting. *Was he doing the right thing?*

It had sounded so easy when he was with Dani. Now, he wasn't so sure. But what he was sure of was that he wasn't a coward. He loved Abby and he hoped she might still feel something for him. She wouldn't have made love to him with so much passion if she didn't, right? He would find the courage from somewhere to make it work—or die trying. He was certain it wouldn't come to that.

Decision made, he got off the bus just down the street from his building and with a bounce in his step, headed back to work.

CHAPTER 12

With her head down, Abby stared at the pavement beneath her feet and took care to avoid stepping on the cracks that lined the sidewalk. She'd escaped the office for an hour and was now returning to her desk. The time she'd enjoyed outside was just what she'd needed. The day was pleasantly warm. She'd kicked off her shoes and walked barefoot across the thick, soft carpet of grass in nearby Hyde Park and relished the sun on her face. For just a little while, she'd been able to forget about Ben.

Ben.

The very thought of him sent her pulse leaping. Memories of their night together flooded her brain. Even as a teenager, he'd been a passionate and considerate lover, but as a man full grown... The night had been nothing less than magical. She hoped—

"Oh! I'm so sorry! I didn't see you! Are you—?"

Flustered, she looked up into Ben's eyes. He looked almost as startled as she felt. She realized she'd stumbled right into him while she'd been lost in her daydreams. Daydreams about *him*... Heat crept across her cheeks.

"Abby. How are you?" he asked in a casual voice that gave no indication that he even remembered their night together.

"I-I'm fine. Thanks. Sorry again for running into you. I wasn't looking where I was going..." He smiled and her stomach flip-flopped. "No harm done."

She swallowed and tried to think of something to say. Anything. "You've been to lunch." She cringed. The previous evening, she'd been rolling around naked with this man. *Is that all she could think of to say? Apparently so.*

"Yes," he replied, seemingly unfazed by her question. "I'm on my way back inside."

"Oh."

He moved a little closer. She could see the darker flecks in his green eyes. "Why don't we talk?" he suggested. "Do you have a minute?"

Her heart skipped a beat and then galloped away. *Was he going to talk about last night? About the "L" word?* Or was he going to tell her it had all been a mistake; that it should never have happened and wouldn't happen again. Oh, God, she couldn't bear it if he said that. She was already halfway back in love with him.

Ha! What was she talking about? She'd never stopped loving him.

"Abby?"

He looked at her with a curious expression on his face and she realized she hadn't answered him. "Oh, I'm sorry. Yes, of course. Where would you—?"

"Over here," he interrupted and took her by the arm. He led her away from the crowd of lunch goers that filled the sidewalk until they were sheltered by the side of their building. He released his hold on her arm, but she continued to feel the heat from his fingers. He looked at her apologetically.

"I'm sorry I left in such a hurry last night."

She shrugged as if it was no consequence and waited for him to say more.

"The truth is, my head was all over the place," he continued. "I didn't know what to think, what to say, what it all meant. The only thing I know is that last night was amazing."

Her head snapped up and she searched his eyes, looking for the truth. "Really?" She couldn't keep the hope from her voice.

He smiled back at her. "Yes. Really."

"It was amazing for me, too," she admitted a little shyly. She wasn't used to discussing her sexual interludes with her partner the next day.

"I'm glad," he said and smiled again.

He reached out and took her hand and laced her fingers with his. Her heart catapulted into the next universe. She couldn't stop grinning. And then he spoiled everything.

"I'm not going to lie and pretend the thought of being with you doesn't terrify me."

She frowned in surprise and opened her mouth to speak, but he beat her to it.

"Please, let me finish." He looked away and his voice became distant. "I remember how it used to be, back when we were living under the bridge and how I knew if I didn't get away, I'd die there amongst the filth and squalor. You were a part of that scene and you were battling demons, just like me."

"You're right," she replied. "But I've changed. Just like you. And I'm glad," she said softly, knowing it was true.

He looked into her eyes and squeezed her hand. "So am I."

Their gazes locked. Abby's chest tightened so much she couldn't breathe. Ben's green eyes darkened with emotion. His fingers tightened around hers. She swallowed a lump of nerves and hoped her hands weren't damp. Her pulse pounded in her ears.

"You're so damned beautiful," Ben muttered and reached out to cup her cheek.

She lay her head against his palm, loving the feel of his touch. She wanted to run her fingers through his hair, like she had last night, pressing kisses all over his face. She wanted to—

No, they were out in public. Standing right outside their building. There were people everywhere. She couldn't do any of the things she wanted to do. And then, as if Ben read her mind, his hand slipped from her cheek to her butt and he pulled her close against him.

"To hell with it," he muttered and his mouth descended, crushing her lips beneath his.

He kissed her with all the passion he'd shown her the night before and she loved it. Her arms came around his neck and her fingers twined in his hair. His hands cupped her ass and he pulled her in even closer until she could feel the solid, hard length of him through his suit pants.

"Can you feel how much I want you?" His voice was husky with need.

She nodded, almost beyond words. "I want you, too."

He kissed her again and then reluctantly set her away. "Dammit! I just remembered. I have a witness waiting upstairs. I have to go."

"That's okay," she managed. "I... I have work waiting, too." In unison, they walked together toward the entrance.

"Would you like to come over tonight?" she asked, still a little unsure of how this was supposed to work.

"I'd like that, but I'm afraid I can't. Remember my grandmother? I managed to find her a place at that aged care facility you told me about. The one in Lane Cove. She can move in two weeks. I need to go and see her and make sure she's still okay about it and to make a start packing up her house. She's a bit of a hoarder and she's lived there long enough to gather quite a collection."

His smile was soft and tender. Abby's heart clenched. This man was a keeper. "Perhaps I could come with you and help?" she offered.

He looked at her, his expression filled with eagerness. "Would you?"

"Yes, of course."

He grinned and his eyes lit up with pleasure. "All right, then. Let's do it. I'll pick you up around seven, okay?"

"That sounds good. Here, take my number in case you get delayed." After asking for his number, she texted her contact details to his phone. "There."

"We might have time to do dinner after," he suggested.

She smiled softly and squeezed his hand. "That would be nice."

———

Ben stepped out of the elevator on his floor and felt like he was walking on air. Wang Xiu Ying sat on the small leather couch in the waiting area opposite his secretary's desk. Cheryl looked at him with a frown.

"What are you so happy about?" she grumbled.

"Nothing in particular," he quipped. "It's a beautiful day out there. You ought to go and see."

"I'm quite happy in here, thank you. Where the heating is."

"Oh, come on, Cheryl, it isn't that cold out there. In fact, the sun is positively warm. I almost took off my jacket."

She rolled her eyes and smothered a grin. He grinned back at her. She was well into her fifties, but she still had a trim figure. Her hair was cut and colored in the latest style and she always dressed with flair. She'd been his secretary for all the years he'd been there and the two of them got on well.

"Wang Xia Ying is waiting," Cheryl said.

"Right." He turned to the woman perched on the edge of the couch. "Follow me, please. Let's get this over with."

It was more than an hour later that Ben finally stopped quizzing the nurse and saw her out of his office. It still shocked him how easily international students could con the system and no one seemed to notice or care. Not the universities, the immigration department and certainly not the students. They were aware of the potential for danger when they weren't competent in English, but they still went ahead and took on jobs where people's lives were in their hands. They needed the money that badly that they were willing to take the risk.

He thought of his grandmother and how he was about to place her in one of those very nursing homes. It seemed that the students with the worst English skills tended to go for the jobs in the aged care facilities. Ben guessed that the occasional death in such places was expected and if a patient just happened to die accidentally...well, the person who caused it might very well get away with it. Who knew? There was a real possibility such a thing might have already happened.

Thoughts of his grandmother reminded him of the need to call her. These days, she didn't go very far from home, but he still wanted to make sure she'd be there when he dropped by later. He reached over and picked up the phone on his desk and dialed her number. She answered on the third ring.

"Grandma, it's Ben. How are you?"

"I'm fine, Ben. What are you up to?"

He paused and hoped that she was still receptive to the idea of moving out. "Remember when we talked about living somewhere where there were people close by, people who could look out for you?"

"No, Ben. I don't remember. What are you talking about?"

Ben suppressed a groan. This was going to be harder than he thought. He was suddenly pleased all over again that Abby had agreed to go with him when he broke the news.

"It's all right, Grandma. We'll talk about it later. I just wanted to call and see if you were home tonight."

"Of course I'll be home. Where else would I be?"

"I don't know, Grandma. I thought I'd come over and visit for a while. I—" Ben broke off, suddenly unsure what to say. He'd invited Abby to meet his grandmother. He wanted to give the old woman a little warning.

"What is it, Ben?"

"I'd like to bring someone to meet you. Someone special. A girl."

"A girl?"

Ben heard the surprise in his grandmother's voice. He laughed nervously. "Yes, Grandma. A girl. Don't sound so shocked."

"Well, what do you expect? You've never brought a girl home to meet me before. At least, I don't remember you bringing a girl home. She must be very special."

An image of Abby crowded Ben's mind. He smiled reflexively. "Yes, Grandma. She is."

A knock sounded on the door. Ben looked up and held his hand over the mouth of the receiver. "Come in."

He watched Blake walk in through the open doorway and head toward the vacant chair opposite Ben's desk. Ben pointed to the phone and Blake nodded before throwing himself down on the seat.

"I'm sorry, Grandma, but I have to go. I'll see you later. Probably around half-past seven. Is that all right?"

"Of course it is, Ben. You're welcome anytime."

"Great. I'll see you then." He hung up the phone and turned his attention to Blake. "To what do I owe this pleasure?"

Blake merely scowled. "I just keep thinking about Jiao Zheng. She got five years. Five years, Ben!"

"That's what you expected, wasn't it?"

"Yes, but the more I think about it, the more I think it's bullshit. She didn't mean to do it. She confessed right away." He paused for a minute. His fists clenched and unclenched. "We ought to appeal."

"Does she want to?" Ben asked.

"I haven't spoken to her about it, yet. She wasn't happy about the sentence, but at the time, I genuinely thought she'd been given a good deal. Now I'm not so sure. Especially after what the judge said at the sentence hearing. He was scathing about a system that allowed a fully qualified registered nurse to work in the health system with a minimal grasp of the English language in its written form. He seemed to sympathize with my client."

"Good," Ben replied. "Those kind of comments will only help my civil suit."

"Do you have a court date yet?" Blake asked.

"No, but subpoenas will be issued next week. They have another twenty days to file and serve their defense and thereafter, the case will be listed for mention."

"When's the return date for the subpoenas?"

"I made sure it coincided with the last date they have to file their defense. Twenty days from today," Ben said.

Blake nodded. "Good. That means you'll get everything at once. You'll be in a better position to know how strong your case is. How did your defendants react when they were served with the claim?"

"I'm not sure," Ben replied. "I haven't heard from anyone. Anthony McDougall of Harris Botham and Marshall filed a notice of appearance on behalf of the university two days ago and I believe Richard Halliwell Senior from Halliwell and Westman is representing the nursing home."

Blake whistled. "They've brought in the big guns."

"Wouldn't you? You heard the judge. The deans of that university must be in a panic and the nursing home—well, they can't simply shrug and declare they had no idea one of their nurses struggled to decipher the written word. They must be in a scramble trying to work out where to turn, who to point the finger at."

Blake chuckled. "I wouldn't like to be the person responsible for graduating those nurses, that's for sure."

Ben thought of Jeff Brown and then Abby. He frowned. Not for the first time, he hoped the lawsuit wouldn't affect their relationship. They had enough to negotiate without adding that conflict to their difficulties. He tried to take comfort in the knowledge that Abby was a lawyer. She knew how these things worked. It wasn't personal. It was his job. He only hoped she'd see it that way when it came time for her brother to take the stand.

CHAPTER 13

Abby smoothed her hair back into a sleek ponytail and fixed it in place with a band. She wore a plain white T-shirt and Levis, coupled with an array of her favourite colored wooden bangles. She swiped on some pale pink lip gloss and pursed her lips together. All in all, she was satisfied with the way she looked. Her hair was clean and shiny. Her makeup had been applied with an expert hand. Her clothes were simple, but fashionable. There wasn't a shred of evidence she'd once spent nearly two years of her life homeless and living under a bridge.

The sound of her doorbell sent a flurry of nerves rushing through her veins. They settled in her stomach and made her feel a little sick. Meeting Ben's grandmother was a big deal. She didn't want to read too much into his invitation, but it was obvious the woman was an important part of his life and Abby could tell how much he cared about her. She didn't want to mess things up.

She was falling head over heels in love with him

and the ferocity of her feelings scared her. She'd fallen hard and fast for him once before and things hadn't ended well. After Ben left, she'd gone into a downward spiral, depressed and sadder than she'd ever been. It had taken her more than a month to pull herself together and realize she needed to clean up her act and do something more with her life.

And she'd done it. With the help of her uncle and aunt, she'd gone to rehab, kicked her addiction to meth, gone back to school and eventually graduated as a lawyer. It had been the hardest times of her life, but she'd managed it and she was proud of the woman she'd become. The only sad part was that her aunt and uncle hadn't lived long enough to see it. Uncle Albert had died from lung cancer. He'd been a heavy smoker for most of his life. Aunt Irene died a few weeks later from pneumonia. That had been a tough winter.

The doorbell sounded again and she quickly gathered her makeup together and dropped it into the bottom drawer of the vanity. With a last glance in the bathroom mirror, she turned and hurried down the hall.

Ben looked delicious dressed in casual dark chinos and an emerald-colored, open-neck polo shirt that made his eyes look even greener. His dark hair was damp and curled slightly over his ears. His smile was slow and sexy and the butterflies in her belly took flight and multiplied.

"Hello, there," he murmured. His gaze traveled from her head to her toes and back up again.

When his eyes met hers, his were filled with warmth and appreciation. Her heart skipped a beat and her nipples went taut. She hoped he wouldn't notice.

"You look lovely," he said and leaned in and kissed her, brushing her cheek with his beard.

She blushed, flustered by his nearness. "Th-thank you. So do you. Look nice, that is." The blush climbed further across her cheeks and she turned away in an effort to hide her face.

"I'll just get my bag," she said and headed back down the hall, grateful when he made no attempt to follow her. In the privacy of her bedroom, she took a few moments to get her herself under control. Drawing a deep breath, she smoothed her hands down the denim of her jeans, collected her handbag from the dresser and left the room.

Ben waited where she'd left him, although his gaze was fixed on a framed photograph that hung on the wall. It was a black-and-white picture of her and Jeff, taken when they were children. She wore a short, frilly white dress that ended just below her knees. It was teamed up with short white socks. Her hair was done up in ringlets and bows. Jeff was in a suit. At five, he was beyond cute. She knew the picture well. It had been taken right before her tenth birthday. There was a party, with balloons, sweets, candles and cake. Although she didn't know it at the time, that was the last day of her innocence.

"Ready?" she asked, injecting a light note in her voice. She refused to let the nightmare of her childhood interfere with her night. She was going on a date with Ben. She'd make sure it was a night to remember.

He looked at her and smiled another slow, intimate smile that made her feel like she was the most desirable woman in the world. Her pulse jumped and then began to hammer a rapid staccato in her chest.

"Let's go," he murmured and held out his arm.

She touched his arm lightly with her fingers and relished the feel of his warm skin. His biceps bulged under the short sleeves of his shirt. She knew firsthand how powerfully he was built and the strength in his broad chest. She guessed he must be a regular at the gym. No one came by muscles like that by just sitting behind a desk.

She pulled the door to her apartment closed behind them, locked it and then walked arm in arm with him down the short corridor to the stairwell. Once outside, he pointed to a shiny red sports car. She'd never been good with cars—one looked pretty much like the other—so it wasn't until they got up close and she recognized the badge at the front that she realized what kind it was.

"A Ferrari. Very nice," she said and grinned. She was going out with the hottest guy in town and riding in a red Ferrari. She almost pinched herself to make sure this wasn't all a dream.

Ben shrugged unapologetically. "I earn good money. I live modestly and save hard. I don't have an ex-wife or kids to support. I spend my money on things I like. I like fast cars."

Her grin widened. "Fair enough." It pleased her to hear he had no ex-spouse or children. That simplified things.

Ben wove the Ferrari in and out of the early evening traffic with a confidence that had Abby relaxing back against the soft leather of her seat. The purr of the engine was almost hypnotic. She could feel the unleashed power of it. For the first time in her life, she understood the appeal of a powerful motor car and why people all over yearned to own one.

The traffic had thinned and it seemed no time at all that Ben pulled over to the curb outside an older style block of units. Though the brickwork had faded and the front retaining wall had a distinct lean, the place was neat and tidy. A row of garbage bins with numbers painted on them stood in a line down one side of the boundary fence. Opposite were the garages that belonged to each unit.

"Does your grandmother still drive?" Abby asked, curious.

"Yes, she does, believe it or not. Her eyesight's as good as ever and she seems to get around town all right. Lately I've worried that she might forget how to get back home, or where she's left the car. She's done that a couple of times."

"Oh, no," Abby said gently. "What happened?"

Ben sighed quietly. "She told me she'd been going to the mall to do some shopping. She wanted pantyhose."

Abby cocked a single eyebrow and fought to keep the smile off her face. "All right."

"Yes, anyway, apparently she needed pantyhose and it couldn't possibly wait. She drove to the mall and parked the car and then couldn't remember where she'd left it. She walked up and down rows and rows of vehicles and still couldn't find hers. Eventually, she called me and I called security at the mall. She gave them a description of the car and they found it on the other side of the parking lot—nowhere near where she'd been looking." He smiled sadly and shook his head.

Abby sympathized with him. She couldn't imagine loving someone with such an awful illness. She reached over and squeezed his arm. "Did she get the pantyhose?"

Ben laughed. "I never asked! I guess so. That's what she went there for."

Abby noticed the tenderness in his eyes every time he mentioned his grandmother. "You love her a lot, don't you?" she murmured.

His laughter faded and his gaze held hers. "I do and I owe her everything."

All of a sudden, Abby's nerves returned. "Do you think she'll like me?" she asked a little anxiously.

Ben reached out and stroked his fingers down her cheek. "She'll love you. Just like I do."

It was the second time he'd said it and this time they weren't naked together. Abby stared at him, her heart pounding.

"You love me? You really love me?" she asked, hardly daring to believe it.

"Yes, Abby," he said quietly. "I really love you. I never stopped loving you."

They sat in silence, then as if in slow motion, his face drew nearer and a second or two later, his lips touched hers. Feather light, they whispered over her mouth, the softest, sweetest kiss she'd ever had in her life. After it was over, she gazed at him in wonder.

"I love you, too," she whispered. "I always have and I always will."

He smiled and his eyes filled with warmth. "I'm glad." He drew back and unclipped his seatbelt. "Come on, let's go and meet my grandma. I can't wait to introduce you."

Ben held her hand as they walked up the short path that led to the entry of the building.

"Grandma's on the third floor of a four-storey walk-up. I hope you don't mind."

She smiled. "Are you forgetting I also live in a four-storey walk-up?"

He grinned. "Right. But at least you're only on the second floor. Are you up for this?"

She winked. "I'm game if you are."

They were both lightly puffing by the time they reached the landing outside his grandmother's unit. Ben knocked on the door and a short time later, it was opened by a woman with a halo of white hair who barely stood five feet tall.

"Ben! Honey! It's lovely to see you! I didn't know you'd be stopping by!"

"I called you earlier, Grandma. Remember?"

The old woman frowned. "Was that today? Oh, silly me. I forgot. The days all seem the same." She suddenly noticed Abby and her expression filled with curiosity. "And who do we have here?"

Abby stuck out her hand. "I'm Abby Brown. I'm a...friend of Ben's. It's very nice to meet you."

Ben's grandmother shook her hand and then threw a look in his direction. "Have I met Abby before?" she asked. "I can't remember."

"No, Grandma," Ben responded, leading the older woman inside. "I've brought Abby over to meet you."

Evelyn Fitzgerald nodded slowly. "That's nice, Ben. You've never brought a girl home before, that I remember. This one must be special."

Ben's gaze rested on Abby. When he responded, his voice was husky with emotion. "She is, Grandma. She's very special."

Abby looked at him and her heart swelled with love. For a moment, it seemed like they were the only two people in the room.

"Would you like a cup of tea, Abby?"

Evelyn's question broke the spell. Abby blinked and tried hard to stem the blush that threatened to climb across her face. "Yes, thank you, Mrs Fitzgerald. That would be lovely."

"Call me Evie," the old woman insisted and turned and shuffled toward the small kitchen.

Abby looked around her. Though the furniture was mostly new and stylish, there was a disheveled air about the place. Abby guessed it had something to do with the hundreds of collectibles that crammed every surface of the room. In addition to the knick-knacks there were the piles of magazines and newspapers that sat on chairs and tables and even on the floor. Evie was a reader. That knowledge brought a smile to Abby's lips.

"How do you take your tea, Abby?" Evie called from the kitchen.

"With cream and sugar, thank you," Abby responded and moved closer to where the woman stood, pouring boiling water from a kettle into a tea cup.

"Can you get the cream out of the fridge for me, Ben?" Evie asked.

Ben went over to the fridge and opened the door. He peered inside. A moment later, he closed the door, emptyhanded.

"It looks like you're out of cream, Grandma."

She looked crestfallen. "Oh, dear! Don't tell me I've forgotten again! I was down at the store only yesterday. I was sure I had cream on my list."

"It's all right," Abby hurried to reassure her. "I'll take it without. It's fine."

The woman frowned. "Are you sure?"

"Yes, of course. I take it black all the time," she lied.

Ben shot her a look of gratitude and mouthed the words *thank you*. Abby acknowledged him with a smile.

Evie brought over a tray with three tea cups and a bowl of sugar and set it on the table. "At least I have sugar!" she chuckled. She turned to Abby. "I always have sugar on hand. I need it to make toffees. Ben loves toffees, don't you, Ben?"

"Yes, Grandma. I love toffees."

His grandmother smiled tenderly. "It was one of our favorite things to do in the weeks leading up to Christmas. We'd make toffees and wrap them in clear cellophane and tie them with pretty ribbons. We'd go around the neighborhood and hand them out to everyone. It was so nice, wasn't it, Ben?"

"Yes, Grandma, it was," he replied and Abby could tell he meant it. She was pleased he had some pleasant memories of his youth to replace the other, not so pleasant ones.

Abby was touched when Ben pulled out her seat and then sat in the chair next to her. Evie sat across from them and leaned over to pour the tea.

"I'll do that, Grandma," Ben offered and filled each cup to the brim.

Evie looked at the cups and smiled. "Everyone here likes black tea!" She clapped her hands together and laughed. "Fancy that!"

"What a coincidence." Ben grinned and Abby's heart contracted with love. How had she gotten so lucky to have this wonderful man back in her life? It didn't seem real, and yet here they were—sharing tea and conversation at his grandmother's.

Evie took a sip from her cup and then set it back down. Her gaze fell on Abby. "So, Abby, how long have you known Ben?"

Abby risked a glance in Ben's direction. His expression remained calm. "Um, we met a long time ago, but we...lost touch. We only recently ran into each other again when we discovered we both worked for the same law firm in the city."

"I see. You work for Harton and Wentworth—?"

"They've actually changed their name," Ben interjected. "They're called Sydney Legal, now."

Evie frowned. "Sydney Legal? That's an odd name. What happened to Harton and Wentworth?"

Ben shrugged. "I'm not sure the reasoning behind it. They had some bad press a little while back. I think they just wanted a change."

"I like it," Abby said. "It sounds modern and hip and happening. It's sure to draw a younger crowd."

Evie nodded, but looked unconvinced. She took another sip from her tea. "So, Abby. You're a lawyer. You must be smart."

"Of course she's smart. And beautiful," Ben responded.

Abby glanced at him and blushed. Evie looked from one to the other, a calculating look in her eyes. All of a sudden, she turned to Ben.

"Grandson, would you mind checking to see if I've locked the windows? I'm not sure that I remembered them all. I'll be going to bed soon and I want to make sure everything's secure."

Ben looked at her in surprise but pushed away from the table. "Of course, Grandma. I'll go and check right away."

"Thank you, Ben," Evie said and gave him a beatific smile.

Abby watched the exchange with interest and wasn't surprised when Evie leaned closer over the table the moment Ben disappeared.

"There. Now I can talk to you properly. What designs do you have on my grandson?"

Abby blinked in surprise. "I'm sorry?"

The old woman dismissed her question with a wave of her hand. "Don't give me that nonsense.

He likes you a lot. Any fool can see it. But my grandson has done it tough over the years and although he's worked hard to get where he is, he's still vulnerable. From the time his mother and sister died, he didn't have a whole lot of love in his life. He was nearly nineteen when he knocked on my door. An adult. I did my best to help him and I like to think I played a part in the man he is today, but I know my grandson. He yearns to love and be loved. It's been missing for a long time."

Ben's grandmother lifted her tea cup and took a sip and then returned it to the saucer again. Abby watched her in silence. A moment later, Evie continued.

"You're the first girl he's ever brought home, as far as I can remember. I see the way he looks at you and I can tell he's falling hard and fast. You say you met a long time ago, but how well do you really know him?"

CHAPTER 14

Abby squirmed under the intensity of Evie's gaze. "I... I think I know him pretty well," she replied, not sure if she wanted to reveal her own sordid past to his grandmother.

"Pretty well isn't good enough. Ben has a lot of secrets. A relationship with someone who is oblivious to those secrets will never work."

"I know about the car accident," Abby said.

Evie's gaze widened. "So, he told you about that. Well, that's a start."

"I also know about the time he spent homeless, living on the streets. I know that he was an alcoholic before he turned eighteen and I know that, with your help, he's done everything he can to turn his life around."

Evie sat back. Her face was flooded with happiness. "You don't know how wonderful it is to hear you say those things, Abby," Evie said quietly.

Abby frowned. "I don't understand."

"Ben loves you even more than I suspected and I think you must love him, too. For you to know all about those darkest moments, he must trust you like nobody else. It makes my poor old heart sing to know he's found the woman he deserves. Someone who loves him, despite his mistakes and imperfections."

Abby held her gaze solemnly. "None of us are perfect, Evie."

The old woman waved her comment away a little impatiently. "I'm eighty-two years old, honey. Do you think I don't know that?"

Abby bit her lip and then came to a decision. "What I mean is, *I'm* not perfect. The reason I know that stuff about Ben is because I was there. I met him under the bridge."

Evie frowned and her eyes narrowed on Abby's face. "You mean the bridge in Mount Druitt?"

"Yes. I was born in Mount Druitt. When I was fifteen, I ran away from home. I ended up under the bridge. Ben was already living there..."

The woman stared at her curiously. "How long did you stay?"

"Close to two years."

"Were you an alcoholic, too?"

Abby compressed her lips into a thin line and shook her head sadly. "No. I was worse. I was a drug addict."

Evie's eyes widened in shock and then her expression filled with compassion. "Oh, my goodness! You poor child! I can't imagine what brought you to that state. And yet, look at you! You obviously managed to get back on your feet."

Abby nodded. "Yes. Like Ben, I realized one

day that I was on a highway to nowhere and if I didn't do something about it, I'd die there under that bridge. Ben told me recently he felt the same way. That was why he left. He went to you and I... I went to an aunt and uncle. They helped me, just like you helped Ben."

She paused and a moment of silence fell between them as the two of them became lost in their thoughts. Evie was the first one to break it.

"It's funny, I always thought it was ironic that Ben had ended up living beneath the Mount Druitt bridge."

Abby looked at her questioningly and Evie explained. "He hates the water. He won't go near the stuff and yet, he lived under a bridge. I guess he really thought he was without options."

Abby absorbed the surprising news. "There was never much water in the river," she said. "Barely enough to wash in every now and then, unless there was a real downpour." And then she added, "I didn't know Ben hated the water. Can he swim?"

"Yes, of course. It's one of the reasons he survived the accident. He had to swim across a strong current and ended up on a riverbank on the other side. His little sister was held tight by her seatbelt. She had no chance." Evie heaved a ragged sigh. "Ben's mom died on impact. The autopsy report showed there was no water in her lungs. My son, Ben's father, got out with just a few scratches. I was relieved he was alive, but, oh, dear, the fact that he'd been driving drunk was difficult to take. Still, it was a long time ago. I learned to forgive him. He was my son. What else could I do?" She stared off wistfully, then continued, "As far as I know, Ben hasn't been near the water since. I guess it brings back bad memories of nearly drowning."

"I understand his reluctance," Abby murmured, filled with sympathy at what Ben had endured. It's funny, I hate the water, too."

Evie's expression turned curious. "Did you have something bad happen to you, too?"

"Nothing like Ben," she said hurriedly. "But when I was four, I fell into a neighbor's pool. Of course, I couldn't swim. All I remember is the water covering my head and my feet flailing about. I couldn't reach the bottom. Every time I opened my mouth to scream, I swallowed mouthfuls of water. I thought I was going to die."

The memories of that awful time came rushing back to her. All of a sudden, she was under the water again, desperately trying to breathe. Her heart pounded. Her palms grew damp. With an effort, she filled her lungs with air and forced herself to slow her breathing. She glanced at Evie. The woman looked at her with a sympathetic expression.

"After that, I was terrified of the water. So much so, that I never learned to swim. I look back now and regret that my parents didn't force me to get lessons. Now I think I'm too scared to give it a go." Her fleeting smile was filled with regret.

"It's never too late for anything, Abby," Evie said gently. "Don't let opportunities pass you by. You never know how long you have left. Look at me.

I'm eighty-two and it feels like just yesterday when I was a young woman, a wife, a mother. Now my time's almost over. Don't look back with regret."

Again she was silent, and this time she looked like she had a regret. "Pay attention. I know what I'm talking about. I told you I'd forgiven my son, but it took me a long time. By the time I realized my anger had left me, he was already locked up in jail. I tried to visit him a couple of times, but he refused to see me. He's been out now for years and I haven't been able to find him. Either that, or he doesn't want to be found." She patted Abby's hand. "Don't leave it too late, Abby, that's all I want to say. Just look toward the future and embrace the time that you have."

Abby nodded. She reached over and squeezed the old woman's hand. "You're right and thank you for telling me about Ben's reluctance to go near the water. The whole time we lived under the bridge, I never asked him why he didn't go in the water, even to cool off. Mostly we washed ourselves using a garden tap at the edge of the park. I remember being curious about that when the river was right there, but in those days I was too self-absorbed and concerned about my own troubles to give it much thought. Now I know why he didn't swim or wash there. It helps me to understand him better and makes me want to share myself even more with him." She paused and then said, "How did you ever forgive your son for doing what he did?"

Evie sighed again, her expression filled with sadness. "I don't know. I guess the good Lord helped me through it. I couldn't have gotten there on my own. Now, when my memory's failing and you'd think I'd forget, I remember everything about that terrible time. It doesn't seem fair, does it? Our family's been torn apart too long... He's my son."

She looked up and Abby saw the tears that sparkled in the old woman's eyes. Abby swallowed the lump that had lodged itself in her throat. She cleared her throat. "You're right. It doesn't seem fair."

"Ben wants me to go into a nursing home."

Abby started in surprise at the change in subject. "He worries about you, Evie. Living here all on your own. If it makes you feel any better, I have a friend whose grandmother lives in an aged care facility in Lane Cove. At first, her grandmother was reluctant to move there, but now she loves it. She has friends and companionship whenever she wants it. There are organized games and outings. Her meals come prepared straight from the kitchen. She doesn't even have to wash the dishes! How good would that be?" Abby grinned.

Evie regarded her thoughtfully. "I guess I could get used to something like that. It would nice to have someone to talk to every now and then. Ben's been an angel, but there are some things I'd like to talk about with a friend. Do you know what I mean?"

Abby held the old woman's gaze. "Yes, I do."

Just then, Ben stepped back into the room. She wasn't sure how much of their conversation he'd heard, but from the look on his face, he'd heard enough. Returning to his seat, he reached over and took both of his grandmother's hands in his own.

"I'm glad you're coming around to the idea of moving, Grandma. Just so you know, I'm not doing this to punish you. I just need to be sure you're safe; that someone's looking out for you at any given time of the day. I want to know that you're eating well and that if you fall, there'll be someone on hand to help you. I'm doing this because I care, Grandma. I care a lot."

Evie's expression softened and once again, tears welled up in her eyes. "I know you do, Grandson. I love you just as much."

"I only want what's best for you, Grandma. Please try and remember that."

Evie laughed and the sound of it was lovely to hear. "Oh, Ben! You're so funny! You of all people know how bad my memory is!"

Ben smiled softly back at her. When Evie's laughter had faded, she gazed steadily at her grandson.

"You always were the best of boys, Ben. I've been so proud of you. I'm still proud of you and no matter what happens, don't you forget it!"

"Thank you, Grandma. You don't know how much that means to me." Ben's voice was husky with emotion.

This time, it was Abby's turn to tear up.

"How soon would I have to move?" Evie asked.

"I've managed to secure you a spot at the same place Abby was telling you about. The one in Lane Cove. It's not too far away from here. You'll still be on the north shore and closer to my work, so I can see you more often. They said you can move in a fortnight. Is that all right with you?"

Evie's eyebrows flew up in surprise. "A fortnight? That's not very long."

"No," Ben said. "But I'm sure we can get you packed up and in by then. Abby will help, won't you?"

He looked at her and the hope on his face had her heart turning over in her chest. "Of course." She smiled. "I'd love to help."

"But there's so much stuff to sort through," Evie protested. "We couldn't possibly get through it in two weeks."

"Between the three of us, I'm sure we can do it," Ben replied. "But if not, we'll finish clearing this place after we have you settled. Right, Abby?"

She grinned and winked at Evie. "Right."

Ben's answering smile warmed her. Their eyes met and held and it seemed like an eon of time before he dropped his gaze and cleared his throat.

"I'm going to duck out to the corner store and buy a few supplies. Would you like me to get some of those honey snaps, Grandma? I know how much you like them."

Evie looked up at him and smiled. "That would be lovely, Ben. Thank you."

He smiled again and nodded. "No problem. I won't be long."

———

After packing the groceries away in his

grandmother's cupboard and restocking the fridge with microwavable dinners, Ben took care to remove the fuses from the stove before he and Abby bid his grandmother goodnight. She kissed them both on their way out the door and with tears glinting in her eyes, begged them both to return soon. Ben assured her he'd see her soon. Taking Abby's hand, together they walked down the stairs. He held the door of the Ferrari open for her and she murmured her thanks and slid into the seat.

"I hope you like East Indian food," he said, as he switched on the ignition. The engine sprang to life.

"I love East Indian food," she replied.

"Good, because I took the liberty of ordering some takeout while I was grocery shopping. It should be just about ready to collect."

"Sounds perfect."

With a quick smile, he put the car into gear and pulled onto the road. A few minutes later, he arrived at their destination and brought the car to a halt. He opened the door and then turned to her.

"It's gotten a little cool out. Why don't you stay here, where it's warm?"

Abby rubbed her bare arms and shivered. "You're right. I forgot to bring a jacket."

"I won't be long," he promised and headed toward the restaurant to collect their order.

After paying for the food and with bags of takeout containers in hand, he paused outside the shop. A liquor store was situated right next door. *Should he buy her some beer?* She'd had beer in her fridge. It was obvious she liked to drink. *Could he risk going into a liquor store?* Though he'd been sober for the better part of fifteen years, he hadn't tempted fate by going into bars or wandering around liquor stores. *Could he trust himself to go in and buy the six-pack and leave? Would it be that simple?*

"Ben? Are you all right?"

Abby's voice cut through the noise in his head and he blinked hard to clear it. She'd climbed out of the car and now stood a few feet away, a concerned expression on her face.

"Ben?" she asked again.

"I'm fine," he answered hurriedly and turned toward the car.

"You were just standing there," she said. "I wasn't sure what you were doing."

He stopped and turned to face her. "I'm sorry. I was going to buy you some beer. I noticed you like to drink. I... I just wasn't sure if I was up to heading inside the liquor store."

Understanding and compassion filled her eyes. "Oh, Ben. How sweet you are and so very thoughtful. But please, don't worry. I'm only a very occasional drinker. I rarely touch the stuff, to tell the truth. The other night... I was nervous and I thought the alcohol would calm me down. That's all it was. I'm not a regular drinker at all. I hope you believe me."

He stared at her and saw the sincerity in her face. He nodded. "I do." Without thinking, he leaned over and kissed her.

Her lips were warm and giving, and immediately

opened beneath his. Fire ripped through his veins and sent his blood pounding to his groin. His cock hardened and his body tensed. Need thumped through every pore. He didn't know what it was about this woman, but she turned him on like no other woman ever had.

By the time they broke apart, they were both breathing fast. They stared at each other a moment, dumbfounded and then they both began to laugh. First Abby and then Ben. They laughed so hard it hurt. The passion between them was mind blowing, and it felt so damned good. He was so glad he'd taken a chance on her, like Dani had urged him to. Life was all about second chances. He knew that firsthand. He was head over heels in love with her again. He couldn't wait to get her home.

Abby set foot in Ben's apartment and took the time to appreciate the clean, sleek lines. Unlike her place which was full of comfortable furniture and homey works of art, his place was all modern black, white and chrome. The only concession to color was a large oil painting that took up half of one wall. The reds and oranges and yellows and purples came together to form a magnificent sunset. She didn't recognize the artist, but the picture was truly breathtaking.

"I picked that up at the markets one time," Ben said, noticing her interest.

"It's beautiful," she said.

"Yes, I agree."

"I like your place," she said, looking around the open concept kitchen and living room. It's..." She paused, searching for the right word.

"Austere. Clinical. Passionless." He laughed. "Plenty of my friends have labeled it even worse."

"I wasn't going to say that at all!" she protested. "You're not at all passionless and they're wrong, it's lovely. Okay, it's far from over furnished, but I guess if I'd lived any length of time with your grandmother, I'd be going for the minimalist look, too."

Ben laughed again and reached for her. She walked into his arms without hesitation, as if she belonged there. She sighed when he hugged her tight. It felt so good to be pressed up against him, being held close to his heart again.

She could feel its steady thump against her breastbone, strong and reassuring. In recent years she had almost forgotten how much she'd missed him and the feeling of security he'd always given her.

As if privy to her thoughts, he tilted her chin up and feathered kisses over her lips, her nose, her ears. Desire kindled quickly and she lifted her arms and draped them around his neck. Opening her mouth, she ran her tongue over his lips and dared to delve inside. His tongue tangled with hers, sending a surge of desperate need to her core. On the drive home, with the smell of Indian takeout wafting through the air, she'd been starving, but now, with Ben's arms around her, with his hard body pressed against hers, she could only think about getting naked and loving him.

Determined to put her thoughts into action, she let go of him and pushed away. With hands that weren't quite steady, she tugged at her T-shirt and pulled it out of her jeans. She kept her gaze fixed on his while she did a little striptease. Inch by inch, she revealed more skin until finally, she pulled the shirt over her head and tossed it away.

Next, came her jeans. She sat down on his sofa—all soft white leather and chrome—and pulled off her ankle boots and socks. Coming upright, she released the top button of her Levis and slowly eased down the zip. Ben stood still, his gaze fixed on her. The only thing that moved was his chest as it rose and fell with each breath. Swiveling her hips and wriggling her butt, she lowered the denim, all the while watching his reaction. Kicking the jeans off her feet, she stood in front of him wearing nothing but her underwear.

She grinned and sauntered closer. "Your turn."

Sliding her fingers under his waistband, she loosened his polo shirt from his pants and eased it up. With her hands splayed wide on his skin, she reveled in the touch of his washboard abs and well-defined pecs, all the time raising his shirt until he ducked his head and helped her pull it off.

With a sigh, she ran her fingers through his brown chest hair, loving its soft, springy feel. With a cheeky grin, she tilted her head and flicked her tongue over one of his nipples. It hardened instantly and she felt him shiver. A growl came from deep inside his throat. She smiled, loving the feeling of being in control, of being able to bring this wonderful man to his knees. It was intoxicating, almost as intoxicating as the taste of his skin beneath her lips. And his expression revealed he was not opposed...

Impatient now, she reached for his belt and made short work of his pants. He helped her by pulling off his boots. He stood before her, half-naked, tall and proud. Through the pale blue cotton of his underwear, she could clearly see the outline of his cock. With a possessive smile, she encircled his hardness with her hand, through the fabric of his boxers. His mouth parted on a gasp and her smile widened. She could get used to feeling like this.

With her gaze fixed on his, she lowered herself to her knees. The thick carpet provided a luxurious cushion. She reached up and tugged at his waistband and slid his underwear over his hips. His cock sprang free, thick and impressive amidst a nest of dark curls. She tossed the boxers over her shoulder and went to work.

Her mouth opened over the head of his shaft and slowly moved along its length. With long slow licks, she worked her way from top to bottom, side to side, and repeated it all over again. He stood still, at attention, his head thrown back, his hands on either side of her head. She reached in between his legs and fondled his balls.

"Abby!" He gasped. "You're a witch!"

She let go and looked back up at him, one eyebrow raised in question. "You don't like?"

"Of course I like," he said roughly. "I like too much."

"Never too much," she said and went back to work on his cock.

Sucking and licking and stroking, she also worked her hand up and down his erection. Fluid gathered on the tip and she swiped it with her tongue. It tasted slightly salty and she sucked even harder.

"I'm going to come if you keep that up."

She grinned up at him cheekily. "So, come."

He made a noise of impatience in the back of his throat and reached for her. "You little minx. Come here. This isn't over. Not by a long shot. Now it's my turn to drive you wild."

His words went through her like a surge of electricity. Her heart pounded with anticipation and blood rushed through her ears. Her center burned and tingled. She had to feel him there.

As if reading her mind, he picked her up and carried her to the sofa. It was big enough for two. He pushed her down until she lay on her back and her legs fell open wide. He chuckled. "And I thought I was the impatient one."

Quickly, he removed her bra and slid her panties down. She lay spread-eagled before him, completely naked and didn't feel an ounce of shame. This was Ben, the man who had her heart. The man she'd always loved. She burned with a need so great, she couldn't wait to have him inside her.

"I want you, Ben."

He eyes gleamed. "*Mm*, I can see that." He leaned forward and ran a finger across her slit and then brought it up to his lips. "You're so wet. Are you sure you haven't come already? Perhaps you took advantage of yourself while you were waiting for me in the car. Have you fucked yourself already, Abby? Am I too late?"

His teasing words should have shocked her, but they filled her with excitement instead. Desire raged like a bushfire out of control. She squirmed on the couch and reached for him. To her consternation, he pulled away.

"Oh, no! You're not going to get away with it that easily. If it was good enough for me, it's good enough for you."

"W-what do you mean?" she managed, her breath coming fast.

"I mean, I'm going to drive you as wild as you drove me. Now, quit talking. I'm busy."

And with that, he kneeled on the floor beside her and spread her legs as wide as they would go. He lowered his head and tasted her. Long, slow licks from top to bottom and all the way back up again, just like she'd done to him. Just when she thought she couldn't bear it any longer, he changed tack and nuzzled her with his mouth. His beard was soft and ticklish and added an extra depth of sensation. His tongue probed her entrance and a moment later slipped inside her warmth.

Her hands clenched into fists as she rode out the waves of pleasure. His finger replaced his tongue and then two fingers. She ground herself against his hand, needing more, wanting him to fill her and stretch her wide.

"I need you. I need you inside me. Your cock. Please. I need your cock."

With a wicked smile, he came up from the floor and straddled her hips. His cock was hard and proudly jutting from the juncture of his thighs. He rubbed its thick length along her stomach, back and forth until she was wild with need. She bucked her hips against him, trying to dislodge him, trying to get him where she wanted him.

"Easy, honey. We have all night. I'm going to make this spectacular. Believe me, it will be worth the wait."

"I don't want to wait," she whined and reached up to pull him down on her.

He didn't resist and a moment later he lay full against her. Skin to skin, heartbeat to heartbeat, she was in heaven and hell all at once. His cock, huge and hard, pressed against her mound, but not far enough that she could manoeuvre him where she wanted him. Biting down on her frustration, she wiggled beneath him. He chuckled in her ear.

"Relax. It's not all about the destination. The journey's just as important. Trust me. Sit back. Enjoy it."

Abby gazed up at him and blew her breath out on a sigh. Ben was right. The journey was just as important and if he was willing to take her on the trip of a lifetime, who was she to complain? With that thought, she relaxed and offered him a teasing smile.

"All right. Just remember though, we take turns about. It's only fair, after all."

His eyes gleamed with amusement. "Who said anything about playing fair?"

CHAPTER 15

en's cock was so hard, he thought he might explode. He used to feel that way when he was a teenager and would wake, hot and hard, after a particularly lurid dream. But now he was a grown man, a man of thirty-three. He'd learned to control his body's responses and keep his desire in check. But Abby Brown was driving him over the edge. With her, it had always been like that. A smile, a kiss, a soft hand in his and he was burning all over. Now, years later, it was no different.

She'd blown him away with her striptease and then going down on him... He'd repaid the favor by using his lips, his mouth, his tongue to drive her wild, but somehow, it still felt like she was the one in control. Though she lay sprawled across his couch, naked as the day she was born, there was a light of confidence—almost arrogance— gleaming in her eyes that made his stomach clench with need.

"Are you finished?" she drawled in that low,

husky voice that turned his insides upside down.

"For now. What did you have in mind?"

She laughed, a "wait and see" kind of chuckle and pulled herself upright. She sauntered over to the fridge and opened it. He followed her progress with a mixture of enjoyment and anticipation. Tall and curvy in all the right places, she was a more than pleasing sight.

And then she bent over at the waist and exposed her wet slit to his hungry gaze. His body jerked and his cock twitched. She really was a minx. Unable to help himself, his hand went to his rigid shaft and he stroked away some of the pressure. At last, she stood and with a triumphant grin, held up a can of whipping cream.

Once again, his insides flipped over and anticipation flooded through his veins. She walked back to where he sat on the couch and with a casual air, came to stand between his legs.

"You're looking mighty tasty, Mr Fitzgerald." She practically purred, scraping the fingernails of one hand across his chest. "But there's always room for improvement. Don't you think?"

Before he could answer, she pressed her palm against his pectorals and pushed him back against the couch. Then she depressed the nozzle on the can and a curl of whipped cream spurted out. It landed just above one of his nipples. With her gaze on his, she slowly leaned forward and with long swipes of her tongue, licked it off.

"*Mm*, very tasty," she murmured and licked him once again.

His body went hard and blood rushed to his groin.

His cock jerked reflexively in his hand. He'd never had a woman do anything like what Abby was doing. It was like a teenage boy's fantasy, only this was happening for real. He trembled with desire, but held back. All he wanted to do was flip her onto the couch and bury his cock in her warmth.

Another spurt of cream curled on the other side of his chest and that nipple was treated to the same sensuous attention. With his hands clenched into fists and held stiffly by his sides, he didn't know how much more he could endure.

Abby glanced up at him as if to gage the effect her actions were having on him. He managed a tight smile and reached for her free hand. He drew it down until she encircled his engorged cock.

"*Mm*," she murmured again. "You're right. I'm sure that will taste divine." And with that, she spurted cream all over his shaft, with an extra dollop curled over the head for good measure.

The cream was cold on his cock. Before he could draw breath, she bent over and took him in her mouth. Licking and sucking and swiping, her tongue, so warm and wet, she spent agonizing moments driving him wild. When he finally got control of his faculties, he reached for the can of cream and pulled it out of her hand.

"Hey!" she protested with a laugh. "I was having fun with that."

"My turn." His voice was rough with need. His body burned for release, but he'd promised her a night to remember. He was determined to see it through.

Pulling her close, he switched their positions until she was once again lying on her back on the couch. Bending her knees, he settled himself between her legs and then leaned over and squirted a swirly decoration of cream around both of her nipples. She gasped and giggled and then cried out in surprise and delight when he suckled the cream off her breasts.

"*Mm*, you definitely weren't exaggerating," he said, his mouth covered in whipped cream. "That does taste good." He licked his lips. Her eyes followed the movement of his tongue. Her eyes darkened with desire.

His cock throbbed.

Not done yet, Ben ignored his body's urgings and squirted cream all over the sensitive flesh between her legs and then lowered his head and lapped. It was even more erotic than the last time. The cream was sweet. Her lips were sweeter. He licked and suckled until he couldn't stand it a moment more. And neither could she.

Writhing above him, her eyes were closed and little gasps of desire escaped her mouth. Her fingers were buried in his hair, tugging and holding and squeezing, all at once. As if sensing his gaze, she opened her eyes and stared at him. Her gaze was a tumult of emotion.

"I want you, Ben. Please. I want you *now*."

Pushed beyond his endurance, Ben was just as eager as she was to bury himself inside her and climb with her to the peak. Moving so that he was positioned between her thighs, he sheathed his cock and then probed her entrance. She watched him with eyes that glowed with desire and it made the act of entering her even more sensual.

With a control he didn't know he possessed, he eased inside her an inch at a time. She moved restlessly beneath him, grasping his hips and urging him on. Sweat broke out on his brow at the effort it took to resist her silent encouragement. He wanted this to be excruciating, exhilarating, unforgettable for both of them.

"Ben!" she gasped and he knew exactly how she felt.

Blood pounded in his cock, through his chest, in his ears. Every nerve ending was on edge, poised for the moment they were completely one, joined in the most intimate way possible. He gritted his teeth and eased inside her another inch. She twisted her hips and then tightened her internal muscles around his cock. That was the beginning of the end.

With a groan, he plunged all the way inside her, unable to hold back a minute longer. Her hands came up and she clung to his shoulders, her hips meeting his, thrust for thrust. Her breath came fast, melding with his. Their gasps and groans chorused together. The pressure inside him continued to build and then she was there before him.

Crying out, she convulsed around his cock, her fingernails digging into his skin. The feel of her orgasm sent him over the edge and he tensed and then let out a shout of fulfilment. He shuddered and emptied himself inside her. Feeling replete and utterly spent, he collapsed against her and buried his face against her neck. Her perfume, sweet and exotic, filled his head.

He didn't know how long he lay there in heaven, but he slowly became aware of his weight on top of her and moved to roll on his side. Her stomach grumbled. Ben laughed.

"Is that your not-too-subtle way of telling me you're hungry?"

A faint blush stole across her cheeks, making her look even more adorable. "I'm sorry. We skipped dinner and it's been a long time since lunch."

"You're right and I'm sorry for getting distracted." He slapped her lightly on the butt. "You know, it's all your fault. You shouldn't have taken off your clothes. I completely forgot what I was supposed to be doing."

She grinned. "But it was worth it, wasn't it? Hunger pains notwithstanding?"

He pressed a kiss against her lips. "It was entirely worth it. In fact, I can't wait to do it all over again."

She groaned and he laughed. "Just kidding. Why don't you go and have a shower and I'll heat up our dinner. There are clean towels in the cupboard below the sink. Help yourself."

She wriggled off the sofa and stood. "Thank you. A shower sounds great."

She disappeared down the hall and Ben tugged on his underwear and headed toward the kitchen. Pulling takeout containers from the bag, he set the food out on two plates and then proceeded to heat them in the microwave. He hummed under his breath, feeling better than he ever had in his life. He was in love with the most beautiful woman in the world and the best thing was, she felt the same way. He didn't know how he'd gotten so lucky, but he wasn't going to mess things up this time. They'd both learned from their past and were now in a much better place. This time, things were going to work.

He thought of the lawsuit he'd instigated against her brother and her brother's employer and frowned. The heat was being turned up on the case. In a few short weeks, they'd be squaring off in a courtroom. Him and Jeff. Him and Abby's brother. His anticipated happiness of just a few moments ago, dimmed. Once again, he wondered if it would cause a problem between them and could only hope like hell that it wouldn't.

Jeff Brown tilted the scotch glass to his lips and emptied the contents. The alcohol burned a fiery path down his throat, almost snatching his breath. It was only mid-afternoon, but he needed the courage the alcohol gave him to face what was to come. A copy of the statement of claim that he'd received a fortnight earlier and the handful of subpoenas that had been served upon him that morning lay on the coffee table. The innocuous pieces of paper seemed to mock him. The words printed on the plain paper made demands for all of his files, dating back five years.

For three of those years, he wasn't even in the job, but like his lawyer had said, the court wouldn't care about that. The relatives of Dulcie Eveleigh were baying for blood and Ben Fitzgerald was making sure he earned his money. That was all there was to it.

Leaning forward, Jeff poured another shot into his glass and then added a bit more for good measure. The fact was, for the past two years he'd pretty much turned a blind eye to the decided lack of professionalism he'd witnessed in his department. International students brought in considerable money for the university—for any university. Richmond was no different.

Early on, Jeff had expressed his concerns about the way they graduated students without proper checks and balances, but the bigwigs didn't seem to care and they were paying him considerable money to go along with their policies and keep his mouth shut. And so he had.

Anyone knowing what they were looking for would soon determine that the records showed a decided lack of attention to exam marks and even less concern over whether the student who was enrolled in the course was the same one who sat the exam. Photo IDs were issued at the commencement of the course and were supposed to be shown prior to entry into the exam room, but who looked closely at the photos and who cared if they didn't exactly match? It was a practise that happened all the time, not only in his department. It was just that nurses were responsible for other peoples' lives and in the case of Jiao Zheng, a patient under her care had died.

It was a tragic set of circumstances and he felt incredibly guilty, but should he be forced to pay for someone else's mistake with his career? He wasn't the one who wrote the policies, who laughed over his concerns. He wasn't the one who put profit above everything else, to the detriment of innocent people. And yet, by all accounts he would be the scapegoat. The dean had already indicated as much.

"This is your problem, Jeff," the man had said to him less than twelve hours earlier. "You need to deal with it."

"But—"

The dean had cut him off with a sharp rebuke and had leveled him with a glare. "This is your problem, Jeff," he repeated. "This deals directly with the nursing department, the very department of which you are in control. Am I right?"

"Yes," Jeff admitted, downcast.

"And this Zheng woman was a nurse from your department. She graduated under your watch. Am I right?"

"Yes, but the subpoenas require files from up to five years ago. I wasn't even—"

"The only reported death this case refers to happened under your supervision. You're the only one in the firing line, Jeff. And even if these bloodsucking lawyers dig up evidence of wrongdoing that goes further back, your predecessor is no longer around to defend herself. Ellen King was killed in a car accident twelve months ago. I won't hear you speak ill of the dead."

Jeff lowered his gaze and stared at the rich Aubusson carpet that covered the floor of the dean's office.

"Do you understand, Jeff?"

The harsh words hammered into his brain. *Oh, yes, he understood.* He understood that he was on his own. There would be no help from the university. They were hanging him out to dry. The previous head administrator of the nursing department was deceased. There would be no supporting evidence coming from her. Ben Fitzgerald and his team of lawyers could pore over her files, but without the witness who created them, the evidence they found would be hearsay at best. No, it was Jeff who was squarely in their sights. Jeff who'd be forced to answer their questions…

The records would show a number of formal complaints made by some of the teachers about the way things were being done, but they would also show that he did nothing about those complaints. He might not have been the one to write the policies, but he sure as hell had done everything he could to implement them—just like he'd been ordered. He'd even managed to ignore his own conscience.

The thought sent a shaft of pain stabbing through his head. *Was he responsible for the death of Dulcie Eveleigh? Had his decision to look the other way brought about the loss of her life?* He couldn't bear the thought.

He emptied the second glass of scotch, but the alcohol didn't deaden the pain. A familiar urge overtook him. He breathed hard, trying to fight it. He hadn't resorted to the oblivion of heroin for more than two years. He'd promised Abby if he managed to score the job as head administrator of the department of nursing he'd give it up for good. The job had come through and he'd kept his promise. He hadn't touched the stuff since. But now, with the feeling of impending disaster pressing upon him, he couldn't seem to find the strength to keep up the fight.

The temptation to disappear from the world for a few welcome hours got stronger. Sweat popped out on his brow. With a trembling hand, he tugged the phone out of his pocket, scrolled through his contacts and found the familiar name.

The call connected and a gruff voice answered with a single word. "Yes?"

"I... I need some gear."

"How much?"

"I have five hundred dollars."

"See you soon."

The line went dead.

Jeff pushed the phone back in his pocket and leaned back against the couch. His chest was tight with despair and anticipation. He didn't want to go down that road again. *But what choice did he have?* He needed the relief of getting high, if only for a few hours. He didn't think he was strong enough to get through the next few weeks without it. He thought of his sister and how far she'd come and how hard she'd had to work to get there. If anyone understood what he was going through, it was Abby. With a helpless cry, he pulled out his phone again and dialed her number.

———————

The sound of Abby's cell phone ringing snagged her attention. She glanced at the screen and recognized her brother's number. She hadn't heard from him since their conversation earlier in the week. She was supposed to have called him about catching up for dinner, but work and Ben Fitzgerald had gotten in the way.

She grimaced. Not so long ago, she'd vowed to give Jeff her priority. Barely a week later and she'd already broken her promise. *What kind of sister was she?* He was going through a terrible time with the lawsuit and she'd barely spoken to him about it.

He would have received the subpoenas by now. She hoped he'd called one of lawyers she'd suggested and had sought their advice. She wondered how he was coping with the stress of being involved in this lawsuit. As a lawyer who dealt with the courts every day, it was easy to forget how traumatic they could be to the average person. She picked up her phone and answered it.

"Jeff, how are you? I'm sorry I haven't called. I've been snowed under and—"

"It's all right, Abby. I know how it is with you lawyers. Ben Fitzgerald's been every bit as busy as you."

His tone was low and sarcastic and Abby bit her tongue. Ben was just doing his job, but it wouldn't help Jeff for her to point that out. Better to offer him the sympathetic ear he needed.

"Is there anything I can do to help?" she asked quietly and then closed her eyes against her brother's scornful laugh.

"Help? How can you do that? Can you make this lawsuit go away? Wave a wand and have the pile of subpoenas demanding access to my files disappear? Can you do either of those things, Abby? That would be a big help."

She remained silent, refusing to rise to the bait. He was upset and stressed over the litigation. She understood.

"What? Nothing to say? No suggestions?" he scoffed again. "Some help you are."

"That's not fair, Jeff," she replied sharply. She bit her lip and drew in a deep breath. Getting cross with him wouldn't help. "I'm sorry," she added. "I didn't mean to snap. This lawsuit isn't your fault. Stop taking all the blame. You were only following orders. You said you tried to have discussions about policy and were shut down. Other than resign, there wasn't much else you could do. The court will see it that way. It's those in charge of the university, the people who pay your salary, who create the policies, who are in the plaintiffs' sights."

"Yeah, right," Jeff replied, his tone churlish. "Just try telling the bigwigs that. I've been named as one of the defendants. The dean's already wiped his hands of me. They're throwing me to the wolves. Even my own lawyer has expressed serious concerns about my chances of getting out of this unscathed."

His voice cracked and Abby's heart clenched with pain. She was relieved he'd secured his own legal counsel, but she hated knowing her brother was so distraught. She was filled with anger at the thought of the heads of the university who had made her brother almost accept that he, and he alone, was responsible. It wasn't fair and it wasn't right and she was upset at Ben for naming her brother as a party to the suit. *Why had he done that?* It hadn't been necessary. It was the university and perhaps the nursing home who were responsible, who he should have in his sights.

She sighed. There was nothing she could do about it. She wasn't even involved in the case. She could probably talk to Ben about it, but would he listen? He was on the other side. It was in his interests to have the defendants at each other's throats.

"Can I come over tonight, sis? I need to see a friendly face."

Jeff's words broke into her thoughts. She cleared her throat. "Of course. I'll make tacos, like I promised."

"And chocolate mousse?" Jeff teased.

Abby laughed. "We'll see. I'm not sure what time I'll finish here. It might have to be store-bought this time."

"Store-bought sounds just fine," Jeff said.

"Great. If you get home before me, the key's in its usual place."

"Under the mat, right?"

"Yes."

"You do know that every burglar in town will look there first, don't you?"

Abby smiled and rolled her eyes. "Probably."

Jeff chuckled. "I'll see you tonight."

Abby ended the call, pleased her brother sounded better than he had when their conversation had commenced. She decided to go and speak to Ben after all. Who knows? She might be able to persuade him to drop the case against her brother. She and Ben had spent the night wrapped in each other's arms, declaring their love for each other. That had to mean something, didn't it? She was about to find out.

CHAPTER 16

Ben pushed away from his chair and showed Li Min out of his office. She was the seventh nurse he'd interviewed from Jiao Zheng's list and her story was depressingly the same: She scraped through the compulsory English language test required by the immigration department in order to qualify for a student visa and then had paid someone to complete her assessment tasks and written examinations.

When Ben had asked what kind of checks the university made to ensure it was the enrolled student sitting the exam, Li Min had shrugged and told him she was required to flash her student ID badge and have her name marked off on a list, but that was all. Nobody looked too closely at the photos, and besides, hers had been taken when she'd first enrolled. The IDs weren't renewed every year. It was easy enough to pass off a photo that might not look quite the same when it was two or three years old, or longer. He couldn't believe there hadn't been more accidental deaths.

A brisk knock on the door caught his attention. He looked up briefly from the papers scattered all over his desk. "Come in."

He returned his attention to Li Min's statement and didn't become aware of Abby until she stood right in front of his desk. He looked up at her and was immediately bombarded with erotic images of the two of them wrapped in each other's arms. Naked skin, warm wet lips, lashings of whipped cream. His pulse leaped in anticipation. His body surged with need. She cleared her throat and he blinked, forcing the images from his mind.

"Abby. H-hi. It's good to see you."

She stared at him and her expression remained somber. His desire dwindled almost as quickly as it had arrived.

"I've just gotten off the phone with my brother. He's upset about the lawsuit, feels he's being hung out to dry."

Ben held her gaze. "I'm just doing my job, Abby. Representing my clients."

She shook her head. "I don't understand why you had to name him as one of the defendants. He's an employee! He's just doing his job. He has nothing to do with writing of policies. That's the university's job. All Jeff is guilty of is implementing them. He can't be held responsible for that."

Ben continued to regard her calmly. "I understand, Abby, but until the university complies with my subpoenas and provides me with the material I need to determine who is culpable, I need to keep my options open. That includes naming Jeff in the claim."

"I already told you!" she cried and threw her arms up in the air. "He was only following orders. He didn't make up the rules. Go after the real bad guys here, the university bigwigs who formulated the policies about these things, or the nursing home administrators who should have kept a closer eye on their staff. They're the real criminals. Not my brother."

Ben forced himself to hold on to his temper. He didn't want this to turn into a fight. He loved her and she loved him. *Surely they were mature enough to keep work out of their relationship?* He tried again.

"Look, Abby, it's like I said. Until I have a chance to go through the files, I don't know where I'm at. The university's policies and procedures on this might be squeaky clean. They might set out all the procedures for ensuring their students can not only all read English, but that they're the same students who sit the exams. I've had the opportunity to interview a few ex-students and I'm not convinced that's the case, but until I have the proof in front of me, I have to cover all the bases and that means bringing in Jeff. I mean, how do we know that the policies don't all say the right things and he's simply chosen to ignore them? To cut corners?"

Her expression remained mutinous. "Jeff wouldn't do that."

He held her gaze. "How do you know?"

He said it softly, without rancor, but she tensed in anger all the same. He swallowed a sigh and braced himself for another outburst. She didn't disappoint.

Twin spots of color reddened her cheeks. Her eyes flashed fire. "I just *know*, dammit!" she cried and swung away. She began pacing his office. "He's my brother! He follows the rules! He always has. I know he isn't responsible for this. I just know it!"

Her voice cracked on the final words and Ben felt the pain of them in his heart. He wished he could do something to help her, but he couldn't. He owed it to his clients and to the deceased to do the best he could—and that meant covering all the bases. It was as simple as that.

"I'm sorry, Abby. I wish there was something I could do."

She spun on her heel to face him. "Of *course* there's something you can do! You can take him off the proceedings! Go after the university! Grill the nursing home executives! They should be the ones in your sights. Not my brother."

Ben drew in a deep breath and eased it slowly out. "It's not that easy, Abby. Your brother's the head administrator of the nursing department. He's directly responsible for his department and everything that goes on in it. I need to find out what he knew and what he didn't. What he still knows."

"He's my *brother*, Ben!" she cried. "Don't you understand? He's been through some rough times. His childhood wasn't the best."

Ben frowned. "I thought you said he was safe."

She growled with irritation and glared at him. "He wasn't abused by my father, if that's what you mean, but it doesn't mean he wasn't abused in other ways. They never showed him an iota of love. At least, not while I lived there. The truth is, my parents were wicked. They didn't want either of us. I don't know why they even chose to have kids. God only knows, we would have been better off not born at all. But we were and somehow, we made it through that nightmare and came out the other side."

She moved closer and her eyes pleaded with his. "Please, Ben. This job means the world to Jeff. It's everything he has. Don't take it away from him. Please."

Ben's chest went tight. It was everything he'd dreaded. He wished she could see it from his point of view—a lawyer employed to do a job to the best of his ability. He sighed, knowing she wasn't going to like his next words.

"I'm sorry, Abby. I'll say it again. I wish there was something I could do."

"You could drop the lawsuit," she said quietly.

He regarded her steadily. "We both know I can't do that." He sighed and looked away, hating the disappointment that shadowed her eyes. "Would you rather I have someone else from the firm take over and run the case? Would that make you feel any better?"

Her eyes widened in shock. Her reaction didn't surprise him. This was a big case. It would garner plenty of media attention. It would be a fantastic boost to his career. He might even be named partner.

The tension went out of her body and the heat went out of her eyes. "You'd do that for me?" she asked quietly, almost disbelievingly.

He stared at her and nodded. "Yes."

Tears sprang to her eyes, but she blinked them away. Coming around to his side of the desk, she framed his face with her hands. Leaning down, she pressed her lips up against his. It was a sweet and soulful kiss and he felt it all the way to his toes.

"Thank you," she said, gently pulling away.

He looked at her. He might have just kissed his chance at a partnership goodbye, but Abby mattered far more. "It won't help your brother, though," he murmured, wanting her to be clear on where things stood. "Whether it's me or someone else..."

She sighed quietly. "I know."

He compressed his lips and stared at the statements spread out before him. He needed to get them together in preparation for handing them on to some other lucky attorney.

"Would you like to go for a drink after work?" she asked. "I promise I'll stick to soda."

He smiled, recognizing her offer for the olive branch that it was. "Sure. That would be nice."

"In fact, come over for dinner. I promised Jeff I'd cook his favorite meal. He's... He's been a little down."

Ben was shaking his head before she'd even finished. "I don't think that's such a good idea, Abby. Your brother's seen enough of me lately."

"Don't be silly! It will give you a chance to tell him you're off the case. It will make breaking the news of us a little easier, too."

He stared at her dubiously and she lowered her gaze.

"There is an us, isn't there, Ben?"

The uncertainty in her voice did his head in. No matter what happened between him and the lawsuit he'd instigated against her brother, there was nothing and no one more important than Abby and the way he felt about her.

"Of course there is!" he hastened to reassure her and pushed away from his chair. He took her in his arms and hugged her tightly, inhaling the sweet scent of her hair. She felt so good, so right, so his.

He'd made the right decision. His career meant nothing if it meant he couldn't have Abby. There was no argument to be had.

Laden with shopping bags, Abby made her way up the stairs to her condo. Ben followed behind her, also carrying bags. She'd promised Jeff tacos and chocolate mousse and that's exactly what he was going to get. She'd also picked up some crusty bread, a tub of vanilla ice cream and a couple of bottles of non-alcoholic wine.

She still couldn't believe Ben had agreed to remove himself from the case. It just went to show how much he cared. She almost had to pinch herself every time she thought about it. She didn't deserve this good man. Ben was right when he said it wouldn't make the case go away, but at least she could take comfort in the knowledge that it wasn't Ben who was inflicting the grief on her brother.

Juggling the shopping bags full of food, she reached for her key and inserted it into the lock. She opened the door and then stood back for Ben to enter. He walked in ahead of her and then came to a halt a few steps into the hall. She frowned as he turned, wondering what had caused the look of shock on his face.

"Ben? What is it?" She closed the door behind her with her foot and came up beside him. He stood in the doorway that led to the living room and stared at something across the room. Abby looked in the direction of his gaze and froze.

———————

Ben's gaze locked on the drug paraphernalia that was spread out on the coffee table. A syringe, a box of matches, a teaspoon and remnants of white powder were on display for all to see. He stared at them, numb with shock. He could barely process what they meant. Abby had sworn to him she hadn't touched drugs since she'd cleaned up her act as a teenager. *Had she been lying to him all this time?* He turned to face her, filled with dread.

"What the hell is going on here, Abby?" he snarled.

She was pale and her eyes were wide. She shook her head back and forth. "I don't know,

Ben! I swear! It's not mine! I don't know anything about all this."

He stared at her in disgust. To think he'd fallen for her innocent charm. He'd fallen for her beautiful body and the promise in her eyes. He was a fool! He had nobody to blame but himself. He'd changed for the better. He wanted to believe Abby had changed, too. But she hadn't. She hadn't changed one bit! She'd only gotten better at hiding it.

Spinning on his heel, he put the groceries down next to where he stood. Shooting her a look filled with disgust, he left without another word.

———

Abby fell to her knees and stared at the drug equipment in horror. It must be Jeff's. It had to be. It was the only thing that made sense. Still, she recalled the look of loathing Ben had thrown at her on his way out and cried out with the pain of it. He hadn't believed her protestations of innocence and now everything they'd found together was lost. She cried like her heart was broken—and it was. She'd thought she'd had a broken heart when he left her years before, but that was nothing compared to the pain she felt now.

She didn't know how long she lay curled in a fetal position on the floor, but gradually she became aware of the sound of snoring coming from the spare room. Wiping her nose with the back of her hand, she dragged herself to her feet and made her way down the hall. The door to the spare room was open and Jeff lay sprawled out across the bed. Fully clothed and sound asleep, his mouth gaped open.

Anger surged through her, followed immediately by remorse. She knew of Jeff's weakness for heroin. She'd been the one to help him break his addiction. It had been at least two years since he'd last used the drug. At least, that's what she'd thought. Perhaps he'd been lying to her all this time? Perhaps he wasn't clean at all, but merely had gotten better at pretending? She didn't know and right there and then, she didn't have the energy to think about it a moment longer.

CHAPTER 17

The traffic lights turned green and Ben pressed his foot against the accelerator. Just the slightest pressure and the Ferrari surged forward. It could go from zero to one hundred miles per hour in less than seven seconds. Its top speed was over two hundred miles an hour.

Not that he ever got to drive it that fast. Australia wasn't like Europe, with its Autobahn. There were a few roads in the outback where the speed wasn't limited but they weren't the kind of places he'd take his Ferrari. Though the roads were sealed, there were other dangers, like kangaroos, emus and other wildlife. They could do some real damage to a Ferrari, not to mention its driver.

A car pulled out in front of him and Ben slammed on the brakes, barely avoiding a collision. "Dammit!" he cursed and thumped the steering wheel. The streets were full of idiots and he'd let his attention drift. He should have been more focused on the road instead of having his head full of Abby and his recent discovery at her house.

Was she still doing drugs? After everything she'd said? After everything they'd shared? How could he have trusted her again? Had she lied to him, or was there some other explanation? Some other reason for the heroin, syringes, matches on her coffee table? What other explanation could there be?

The questions hammered around and around in his head until he wanted to scream out loud, but worse than the pain in his head was the pain in his heart. He'd been right to be wary of the new and improved Abby and yet, he'd wanted so much for her to have changed. He loved her, he'd always loved her. If he'd had any choice fifteen years ago, he'd have never abandoned her.

But he knew all those years ago that she was poison and that no matter how much he loved her, he needed to cut her off, clean her out of his system, get the hell away from her and never think about her again. And for a decade and a half, he'd managed to do just that and his life had been just fine. He had a nice apartment, a good job, great friends. It had been enough.

Until it wasn't.

He cursed again and wondered what the hell he was going to do. He couldn't drive around all night. He was tired. He'd been working hard and most nights he spent with Abby. He couldn't remember the last time he'd had a full night's sleep without the interruption of lengthy lovemaking sessions. Not that he'd complained, but he was feeling the effects and right now, it was time to call it a night.

He looked around him and for the first time, took notice of his surroundings. He recognized the tall fig trees and wide streets of Dani Craigdon's suburb. Somehow, his subconscious had brought him here, to Dani's door. He'd once helped her through a crisis of confidence that involved an affair of the heart and now it was her turn to repay the favor.

He glanced at the clock on his console. It was a little past nine. Late, but not too late. Parking at the curb outside her house, he cut the lights and climbed out. A nearby streetlight illuminated the neatly kept garden beds and the lawn that was freshly mown. The house was surrounded by other similar stately homes. Dani had done well for herself. Jett was not only a good provider, he was also a good man.

Ben used the brass ring knocker centered on the front door. A moment later, the wooden panel opened.

"Ben! What are you doing here?" Dani asked in surprise.

He shrugged, not knowing what to say. "I... I..."

Dani's expression filled with understanding. Without another word, she stepped back and ushered him inside. The lights had been dimmed in the living room and the yellow glow gave a soft illumination to the room. The night was cool, but a gas faux fireplace kept the chill out of the air. Dani took his coat and in a daze, Ben made his way to the sofa and sat down.

"Where's Jett?" he asked quietly.

"He's upstairs taking a shower."

Ben nodded. Dani moved further into the room and then perched on the edge of the sofa. "What's the matter, Ben? What happened?"

Ben leaned forward and rested his hands on his knees. He blew out his breath on a heavy sigh. "I'm in trouble, Dani. Big trouble."

Her forehead creased into a frown. "What's the matter? Did something happen at work?"

"No, nothing like that. It's...Abby."

Dani sighed quietly and moved closer to him on the couch. She reached out and squeezed his shoulder in a sign of comfort. "Talk to me, Ben. Tell me what happened."

In stilted sentences, Ben relayed to Dani what had happened. He talked about the drugs, the syringe, the obvious signs that Abby had been using. Dani listened without interrupting. Eventually, Ben fell silent.

"Are you sure it was hers?"

The question was asked quietly, without inflection. Ben looked at Dani and told her the truth.

"No, but who else's could it have been? She lives alone."

Dani eyed him steadily and asked another question of her own. "Do you trust her?"

Ben rubbed his hands across his face and groaned. "I don't know! I used to. Back when we were living on the streets, but—we were living on the streets. All we had was each other."

"What about now?"

Ben raised his face to stare at Dani. She stared back at him. "I don't know."

"Then I guess you have some thinking to do."

———

Abby leaned up against the kitchen counter in her pajamas and sipped her morning coffee. She stared off into space. Her eyes were gritty from lack of sleep. It was barely seven and already she had a headache. It was going to be a long day.

She'd gone to bed sometime after Ben had left and had spent the night tossing and turning. She vacillated between desolation that he'd been so quick to jump to such a terrible conclusion and anger that he could think for a moment that she could have deceived him all this time.

A sound in the hallway caught her attention. She looked up in time to see Jeff stumble into the room. Her anger immediately ignited and she forced herself to take a deep breath. Unaware of her tension, Jeff helped himself to coffee and then took a seat at the small breakfast table. His eyes were red and puffy. He looked awful, like someone coming down off a high. Abby couldn't stay quiet a moment longer.

"Do you mind telling me about the stuff on the coffee table?"

A red flush stained Jeff's cheeks. "I'm sorry, sis. I really am. I shouldn't have. It's the first time in more than two years. I swear! It's just... With this court case and the pressure from work...and you...and Dad... I just couldn't take it anymore."

With that simple admission, Abby's anger dissolved. She knew better than anyone how living with such an awful secret could eat away at you and turn you mad. She'd run away from home to escape the nightmare and if it hadn't been for Ben, and later, her uncle and aunt, she might never have found her way back to the light.

"There hasn't been a day since I found out about what Dad did to you that I haven't blamed myself for keeping quiet," Jeff confessed softly. "I should have said something, done something! I should have gone to the police! It went on for years and I let it!"

Abby was horrified. "No, Jeff! No! It wasn't you! It was nothing to do with you! Please don't blame yourself. It's so wrong of you to do that. You weren't responsible! You were a little boy! Just a little boy..."

Her voice faded away. Tears rolled down her cheeks. She was overwrought with the knowledge that Jeff had been carrying around so much guilt all these years. It was just another agony her father had inflicted on his innocent children.

"The guilt has eaten away at me, all the way to my soul," Jeff admitted, his voice ragged with emotion. "It was the reason I first turned to drugs. I never told you that."

Abby was horrified all over again. She couldn't believe the destruction her father's actions had wrought. "Oh, no! Jeff! You poor thing! I'm so sorry! I wish you'd never been subjected to that."

"It's all right," Jeff assured her, though his voice

caught on a sob. "I'm okay. Most of the time I can control it. It's true what I told you. I'd been clean for more than two years." He looked up at her. "Do you believe me?"

She reached over and squeezed his hand. "Yes, honey. I do."

Jeff offered her an apologetic smile. "Thank you. That means a lot to me."

Silence fell between them and they both sipped their coffee. Abby looked across at her brother and decided to trust him with another one of her secrets.

"I haven't told you this before, but I met Ben on the streets."

Jeff frowned. "Ben Fitzgerald?"

"Yes."

Jeff's frown deepened. "He lived on the *streets*?"

"Yes."

Jeff shook his head in confusion. "I don't understand. That day you introduced me in the coffee shop—he looked a little down and out, but I just thought that's the way he was. You told me he was your friend."

"Yes, and he was. But we met under the bridge at Mount Druitt. We shared space there for the better part of two years."

"What happened to him? How did he find himself in a place like that?"

Abby drew in a deep breath and eased it out. "Let's just say he's had his fair share of challenges. Life hasn't always been easy for Ben either, and it hasn't always been kind. But it's not my place to tell his story. Maybe one day, he'll tell you about it himself."

"Not likely," Jeff scoffed. "The man's suing me."

Abby regarded her brother steadily and decided to come clean. "I... I know. But... We're... We're seeing each other. At least, we were until last night."

Jeff's expression filled with surprise. "You're seeing each other? As in...*dating?*"

"Yes. Well, we were."

Jeff shook his head in bewilderment and stared off into the distance. A long moment later, he sighed quietly and then looked back at her. "What happened last night?"

Abby grimaced and told him about Ben finding the drug paraphernalia.

"Oh, hell, Abby, I'm so sorry."

She shrugged. "Yeah."

Jeff wasn't fooled by her casual tone. "Let me call him, Abby. Let me call him and explain."

She shook her head. "It's probably best if you don't. Don't worry, we'll work it out."

"But it's my fault he misunderstood!" Jeff protested. "*I'm* the reason he left. I want to make it right. I *need* to make it right. Please."

Abby stared at him for a long moment. Eventually, she lowered her gaze. "I'm not sure it will do any good, but if you really want to try, it's okay with me."

———

Ben rubbed the sleep from his eyes and blinked hard to focus on the traffic ahead of him. He was on his way to work, but he was far from looking forward to it. It had been late when he'd left Dani's and had driven home, no closer to a resolution. He'd spent the night pacing his apartment and had watched the sunrise with a heavy heart.

But now, after a shave and a quick shower, he'd come to a decision. He'd call Abby and ask if they could meet. He'd give her the opportunity to explain. He should have done that right from the start. At the time of his discovery, she'd denied knowing anything about the drugs, but he hadn't been in the mood to listen. In the clear light of day, he felt differently. If he truly loved her, he needed to give her the benefit of the doubt, or at least be prepared to hear her out. With that thought in mind, he reached over to where his cell phone sat in the hands-free cradle.

The phone rang before he had a chance to dial her number. He glanced at the screen and frowned. The number had no Caller ID. He hesitated for a few seconds and then answered it.

"Ben Fitzgerald."

"Ben, it's Jeff Brown."

"Jeff. I'm sorry, I should have told you already. I've taken myself off your case. It's been assigned to one of the other lawyers. I'll find out who—"

"I'm not calling about the case, Ben," Jeff interrupted.

Ben frowned in surprise. "You're not?"

"No. I'm calling about Abby. She told me you came over last night and found... You know what you found."

"What does it have to do with you?" Ben asked warily. He applauded Jeff coming to his sister's defense, but it really wasn't any of Jeff's business.

"The thing is, Ben, those drugs were mine. I was there last night. I was feeling depressed. I called Abby. She invited me over. I got there early in the afternoon, long before Abby arrived home. I was sad and depressed and anxious. I got high."

Ben's head was spinning. *The drugs were Jeff's. They weren't Abby's at all.* He suddenly remembered her mentioning Jeff and how she'd invited him over for dinner. With the shock of discovering the drugs on her coffee table, he'd forgotten. Dread burned a hole in his gut and a wave of nausea rolled through him.

He should have trusted her! He should never have walked out! He'd ruined everything! Oh, God! What had he done?

There was no question that he believed Jeff. It didn't make sense the man would lie about such a thing for his sister. Jeff was in the middle of a huge lawsuit. Owning up to being a drug user was the last thing he'd want to do. He had no way of knowing what Ben might do with the information. And yet, he *had* owned up. Ben felt a surge of admiration. A moment later, he was filled with panic. *What if Abby wouldn't talk to him? Accept his apology? What if he was too late?* The thoughts turned his blood cold.

He had to call her right away. He had to beg her forgiveness. With that thought in mind, he ended the call from Jeff and dialed her number. The phone rang out for an eternity and eventually went through to voicemail. His heart sank like a stone. He left a message simply asking her to call him. Now all he could do was wait.

CHAPTER 18

Abby stepped out of the shower and reached for a towel. After drying off, she wrapped it around her and used another one to twist around her freshly shampooed hair. She'd lost some time talking with Jeff and was now going to be late for work. She needed to call her secretary and let her know.

Padding into her bedroom, she went to the nightstand and picked up her phone. She glanced at the screen and frowned. She'd missed a call from Ben. Despite the anger and disappointment that still sat heavily in her belly, her heart skipped a beat. *Was he calling to apologize, or was this an official break-up call?* Needing to know for sure, she dialed into her voicemail and listened to his message.

The message was succinct: He wanted her to call him. That was it. There was no hint of his state of mind or whether she should be nervous that her fleeting romance with him was about to come to an abrupt end, or whether he'd come to his senses and wanted to apologize for being so quick to pass judgement on her and jumping to the wrong conclusion. Until she spoke to him, she'd be none the wiser. It was time to wrestle control back of her life and find out where she stood. She dialed his number. He answered on the second ring.

"Where are you?" he asked, getting straight to the point.

"I'm at home. I... I had a late start. What about you?"

"Me, too. I mean, I'm not at home, but I left late. I'm just heading over the harbor bridge on my way to work."

"I see." She paused and an awkward silence fell between them. She broke it by saying, "So, you want to talk."

"Yes, but not like this. Can I come over?"

"I thought you were heading in to work?"

"I am. I was. Perhaps we can both call in sick?"

Her heart leaped. She frowned and forced herself to calm down. He wanted to talk. And then... Who knew what might come after that? Whatever he had in mind was going to take some time. Either that, or he didn't think either of them would be in a state to face the office afterwards. Damn it! She still wasn't any closer to knowing whether things were going to work out for them or not.

"Abby? What do you think? Can you take the day off?"

Ben's voice broke into her tumultuous thoughts. She hurried to answer him. "Yes, I... I think so. I'll call my secretary and let her know."

"I'll do the same," he replied.

Abby ended the call and tried hard to get her pulse back under control. Despite what she told herself, even that Ben might very well be coming over to break things off, her heart was having none of it. He'd told her to take the day off, like they'd need all those hours to sort out the misunderstanding. If he truly believed the drugs were hers, it was more likely she wouldn't hear from him again. It was a life he'd left behind a long time ago. It was a life he never wanted to return to. She understood. She felt the same way. All she had to do was convince him of it.

Hurriedly throwing on a long-sleeved T-shirt and a pair of jeans, she pulled a brush through her wet hair and twisted it into a knot on the top of her head. She hung the wet towels in the bathroom, collected her phone off the bed and headed back to the kitchen. Jeff had showered in the main bathroom and though he still wore the clothes he'd arrived in the night before, he looked and smelled a lot fresher. As she entered the small room, he looked up from where he sat at the breakfast table and smiled softly.

"Hey."

"How are you doing?" she asked.

"Better. Much better. Just so you know, I got rid of all the gear. I should never have touched the stuff. Oh, and I called Ben. I told him it was all mine and that you had nothing to do with it."

She nodded and wondered if it was Jeff's telephone call that had changed Ben's mind. All of a sudden, she wanted him to have come to that conclusion all on his own. She was determined to ask Ben that question. Her belly fluttered with nerves.

"Well, I guess I'd better get going," Jeff said, pushing away from the table. "I have a lot to do at the office. It's not like the lawsuit's going to go away and those subpoenas aren't going to get answered on their own." He grimaced and Abby felt a tug of sympathy.

"Are you sure you're okay?" she asked, gazing at him in concern.

"Yes. I'm fine. I'm sorry about last night, but I'm grateful for your understanding and for your offer to help." He paused and then added, "Ben told me he's stepped aside, that someone else from his firm will take over the case. I really appreciate it, sis."

She moved closer and put her arms around him and gave him a hug. "I love you, little brother."

He smiled and his eyes shone with tears. "I love you, too."

"Call me, okay? We'll do dinner," Abby said as Jeff headed toward the front door.

He turned and nodded, his expression solemn. "I will. And thank you. Take care."

Abby had barely cleaned up the breakfast things and called her secretary to tell her she wasn't feeling well when there was a knock at the door. Her belly took a nosedive and butterflies swarmed, flooding her with nerves.

Ben. It had to be.

Drying her hands, she smoothed out her hair and then opened the door. He stood on the landing in a dark gray suit that hugged his broad shoulders and emphasized his narrow hips. His white shirt dazzled against a maroon-and-white tie. He looked delicious.

"Hi," he said.

"Hi," she said, feeling unaccountably shy.

"Jeff called me," he said.

"Yes," she replied. "He told me."

"That's not the reason I'm here," he said hurriedly. "I… I'd already made up my mind to come and talk to you, to ask you to explain. This time, I was prepared to listen." A crooked smile tilted up the corners of his lips. She smiled back at him.

"Do I detect the note of an apology?" she asked.

"More than that," he replied. "I'm here to grovel."

Her smiled got wider and her heart leaped with joy. It definitely didn't sound like he was here to break up with her. She stepped back to allow him to enter. "Then I guess you'd better come in."

She led him into the kitchen and picked up the coffee pot. "Would you like some? It was made fresh not long ago."

"Thank you that would be great. I overslept my alarm and I haven't had time for a cup, yet."

She quirked an eyebrow at him. "You overslept?"

"Yes. I don't know what time it was when I finally stopped going over and over what had happened in my head. I don't even remember lying down, but I woke up in my bed. I had less than ten minutes to shower and get on the road."

"I know the feeling. I didn't sleep much, either."

She handed him a mug of coffee and then poured herself a cup. He murmured his thanks and looked around the kitchen. "Where's your brother?"

"He already left."

Ben acknowledged her announcement with a nod and a slight raising of one of his eyebrows. Abby's belly continued to churn with a mixture of nerves and anticipation. She took a seat at the table and a moment later, Ben joined her.

Clasping his hands around his coffee, he looked up at her. "I'm sorry, Abby." His voice was quiet and somber, the expression in his eyes was sincere. "I shouldn't have jumped to such a wild conclusion. I should have let you explain."

She stared at him and bit her lip. "Yes, you're right. You should have, but I understand. Who's to say I wouldn't have jumped to the same conclusion if I saw booze at your place? You knew I lived alone. I'd mentioned that my brother was coming over, but that was probably the last thing on your mind and you didn't know about his past habit. You had no reason to suspect the drugs belonged to him. I was the one who used to be a drug user. You knew that, too." She shrugged. "I get it."

"But you're nothing like that girl you used to be," he protested. "You told me you'd changed. I should have given you the benefit of the doubt. I should have trusted you."

"Yes," she said, nodding slowly. "You should

have trusted me. Then again, we haven't seen each other since we were teenagers. We hardly know the people we are now." She paused and then added, "Your grandmother told me how you don't like the water. That makes two of us."

He looked at her in surprise. "You don't like the water? I never knew that."

She shrugged. "I can't swim."

He nodded slowly. "I'm sure you know why I hate the water."

"The accident," Abby said simply.

"Yes. The accident. The accident that changed my life forever."

"And the life of your father. He hadn't intended to lose his wife and daughter that night," she said quietly.

Ben's expression turned hard. "No doubt he had plenty of time to regret his actions and replay every last detail of the way his wife and daughter died. Then again, he was drunk. Unlike me, he might not have a single memory of the nightmare that destroyed my life."

The bitterness in his tone tore at Abby's heartstrings. She understood his anger, his animosity—she'd once felt the same way about her dad—but bitterness and hate had a way of eating up one's soul and a person without a soul was the saddest tragedy of all.

She reached across the small table and took his hand and brought it up to her lips. She brushed kisses across his knuckles. "I'm so sorry, Ben. No one should have to go through such a terrible ordeal. It just goes to show what kind of man you are that you managed to overcome it. I want to help you forget the past, to let the anger go. If you don't, it will destroy you and you've worked too hard and sacrificed too much to let that happen. *I* won't let that happen to you!"

Her breath was coming fast and her chest was tight before she finished. She stared at him, trying to make him see.

"I love you, Ben! I always have. I loved you then as a wild, angry teenager and I love the man you've become. Fill your heart with love and all the good things in your life. Give those things oxygen, let them live. Your bitterness needs to die. Only you can lay that to rest, but I'll be here by your side to love and support you if you'll let me."

Ben stared at her in confusion, bewilderment, disbelief, as if he wasn't sure if he could trust what she was saying. He'd been alone on this journey of hate and resentment for half of his entire life. Apart from his grandmother, he'd had no one. He'd fought his battles on his own. Abby understood. Though she had a family, apart from her little brother, they were no family she would claim.

"How can you be so forgiving?" he asked her.

Tears pricked the back of her eyes. "You asked me that once before and this time, I'll give you an answer. Hate has a way of destroying you, of eating away at you from the inside out. For so long, I let those feelings take over me. They dictated my every waking thought. I lashed out at everyone around me. I let drugs take away the pain. You were the only bright light in that blackest of times and then you left and I realized I had to do something about taking back my life.

"I'm not going to say it was easy—far from it. I don't have to tell you how hard fighting an addiction can be. But, with the help of my aunt and uncle and the priest at my local church, I learned to forgive my parents for what they had done, or failed to do. You might think my father was the monster, and he was, but my mother knew it was going on. She turned a blind eye to it, scolded me for mentioning it. As far as I was concerned, she was just as much to blame."

Abby drew in a ragged breath. Her fingers were tight against Ben's. Becoming aware of the death grip she had on his hand, she forced herself to relax. Remembering those years of learning to let go, she blew her breath out on a sad sigh and continued.

"In turn, I learned to forgive my parents, like I told you and I reclaimed my life. I went to college, I graduated from law school, I landed my dream job. It could never have happened if I hadn't let go of the hate and though you've come this far and achieved so much without doing that, I want you to think about how much better your life could be if those dark clouds were no longer hanging over you and the heavy burden of bitterness no longer weighed you down."

Ben stared at her and tears filled his eyes. Her heart clenched at the raw emotion that filled his face. "I don't know if I can do that," he croaked, his voice hoarse. "How do I let it go? How do I forgive the man who destroyed my family, my life?"

She leaned forward and framed his beloved face in her hands. "You don't have to do it on your own, Ben. That's the best thing. I'm here. So is your grandmother and there are many excellent professionals who know how to help."

Ben blinked hard and looked like he was trying to keep back the tears. Abby pushed away from the table and came around to where he sat. Taking both of his hands in hers, she pulled him upright and then stepped into his arms. She dragged his head down to hers and pressed her lips against his. She kissed him softly, tenderly, hoping to impart all the love she felt for him, had always felt for him. His arms tightened around her and with a groan, he participated fully in the kiss.

His lips moved over hers with increasing passion. He pressed her as close against him as she could be. His hard body against hers drove her wild. She longed to be skin to skin. As if he read her mind, he tugged at her shirt. It came free from her Levis and was soon whisked over her head.

She reached for his tie and loosened it and a moment later, tossed it away. His shirt buttons were next and her nimble fingers made short work of those. She spread the fabric wide and palmed the firm flesh of his pectorals. Her fingers skimmed over his chest hair. It was soft and springy and warm. She found his nipples and thumbed them until they were hard. His breath hissed between his teeth.

"Do you like that?" she whispered.

"*Mm*, it feels good."

She continued to stroke him. He gazed down at

her, his eyes glinting green fire. The power she had to turn him on sent heat rushing through her veins. It centered in her core and spread liquid need through every part of her, weakening her knees. Coming to a sudden decision, she took his hand and led him down the hallway to the main bathroom. When she pulled him inside, he shot her a quizzical look.

"The bathroom? I already took a shower today and you smell mighty fresh. Do we really need to take another? I'm really not that fond of the water."

Abby reached up and put a finger to his lips. "*Shh*. Do you trust me?"

He held her gaze. His eyes burned with sincerity. "Yes, I do."

"Good. Because I trust you. We're going to take a bath."

His eyes widened in surprise. He looked around and spied the large hot tub that filled one corner of the room. It was big enough to hold two people comfortably. It had been in the place when she'd bought it. This would be the first time she'd used it.

Ben pulled back and began shaking his head. "Oh, no, no, no. I don't do baths and *definitely* not hot tubs."

Once again, she reached for his hand. "Do you trust me?" she repeated.

He winced and tried to pull away, but she tightened her grip. "Ben, trust me. I can't even swim! I'm hardly going to let us drown! I promise. We're going to enjoy a nice warm bath. You and me. I'm going to soap you all over. I'm going to drive you wild. Your only thought about being in the water will be how good it feels. Trust me. You can do this. We both can."

She spoke to him calmly, quietly, like she'd speak to a frightened child and in some ways, he was. Somehow she knew he hadn't been in deep water since the accident. She also knew that by doing this, he was on his way to letting go of the final hurts from his past. She was also overcoming her fears.

He continued to look at her doubtfully and once again, she ran her hands over his naked chest. Her fingernails raked his biceps. She stood on tiptoe and licked his nipples. He groaned and the sound was a mixture of want and anguish. Her heart felt for him, but she refused to show him mercy. He needed this. And so did she.

Stepping away, she turned on the faucets and poured half a bottle of shampoo into the bath. Swishing the water with her hand, she smiled when it foamed up into piles of white bubbles. She turned back to the man she loved. Reaching around, she undid her bra clasp and tossed the garment on the floor. Next she undid the top button on her jeans and slid the zipper down. She shimmied out of the denim and then stepped out of her underwear.

Once upon a time, she'd never have dreamed she'd have the confidence to strip naked before a man, but Ben was different and when she was with him, *she* was different. There wasn't anything she wouldn't do for him. It seemed like he felt the same way.

To her relief, Ben's hands went to the top of his pants and in short order, he was as naked as she. A look of grim determination came over his face and she could tell he just wanted to get this over with. She suppressed a grin and stepped into the tub. The poor man had no clue what he was in for. One thing she could guarantee was that it wouldn't be over with quickly.

She held her hand out to him in silent encouragement and reluctantly he put one foot in. The warm water came up to his knee. The tub was only deep enough for it go slightly higher. She tugged on his hand and he set the other foot in and then stood rigid. It was almost like he was unable to move another step. And perhaps that was the case.

Willing to do whatever it took to get him to sit down in the water, Abby went down on her knees and then came up high enough so that her face was at the level of his groin. His cock was only half erect. His attention had been stolen. Still, she was nothing if not determined and she encircled him with her fingers. With slow sure movements, she stroked him back to hardness.

Bending her head, she took his cock all the way into her mouth. She sucked and licked and stroked in the ways she knew would drive him wild. His hands spanned either side of her head, his fingers buried in her hair. She looked up and his head was thrown back, his eyes closed, his jaw clenched.

She turned off the faucets and then renewed her efforts on his cock. She found his balls and fondled them with her hand. Weighing them, squeezing them, she learned their shape and texture. They were soft and warm and pliant. Next, she let her hand slide around his taut ass and in between his crack. He tensed slightly, but she stroked the soft skin over and over and finally, he relaxed. She eased her finger into his butthole and once again, he clenched his cheeks. But the cock in her mouth twitched and hardened even more and he didn't pull away.

Slowly, she pushed her finger in further and continued to suck on his cock. He moaned and clung to her more tightly. He thrust his hips and his cock moved in and out of her mouth. She looked up at him and noticed the tension had gone from around his mouth. It was time to put the next step of her plan into action.

Still on her knees, she grasped his hips and pulled him down toward her. He resisted momentarily, but finally gave in and lowered himself into the water. It sloshed around his waist and fear flashed across his face. She was there immediately, taking his cock back in her mouth and stroking him with her hand. She sucked and licked and stroked until he relaxed and the tension around his mouth once again eased.

"Lie back against the tub," she murmured and was pleased when he did as she asked.

She moved until she was straddling his hips and pressed herself down on his lap. His cock was hard and huge beneath her. It was all she could do not to mount him. But this wasn't about her and she was determined to see it through right to the end, if it killed her.

She suppressed a grin at the thought. She didn't think anybody had died from not finding release from pent-up desire. Besides, she intended to find her release just as soon as she'd brought Ben to a climax.

With that thought in mind, she dipped her hands into the foamy bubbles and spread them over his chest. She found his nipples and scraped her fingers over them, pleased when they pebbled under her touch.

His hard cock pressed against her soft lips and she ached to have him inside her. Instead, she swiveled her hips and teased both of them until they were both breathless and panting.

"Abby! You're killing me!" Ben gasped. She knew exactly how he felt.

Her body was on fire. She tingled from her head to her toes. Blood pulsed in her core, heating the inferno between her legs. She moved against him, up and down and couldn't suppress a moan. He leaned forward and caught it in her mouth, kissing her with wildness and passion.

She matched him, kiss for kiss, until she couldn't stand it and it appeared Ben couldn't take it, either.

"Do it, Abby. Fuck me," he said, his voice so low and husky.

Her heart skipped a beat and then took flight, galloping out of her chest. She found his cock beneath the water and positioned herself over the tip. Guiding it inside her, she sighed when he slid all the way in.

Too late, she remembered protection, but there

was no way she was backtracking now. He felt thick and hard and fantastic. He felt like the man she loved. Clinging to his shoulders, she rode him for all she was worth. Up and down, she pounded onto his cock. His hands tightened on her hips.

He guided her pace and rhythm and within moments, they were hanging on the edge. They stared at each other, breathing hard and then toppled right over the cliff. With her fingernails clawing at his back, she bucked her hips and cried out. His own shouts of triumph and relief mingled with hers until finally they both quieted.

When at last she could speak again, she opened her eyes and stared at him. He gazed at her in disbelief and wonder. "Did we just make love in a hot tub?"

CHAPTER 19

Ben greeted his secretary with a smile and almost skipped into his office, like he did most mornings these days. He'd spent yet another glorious night with the woman of his dreams. Life couldn't get any better. Though they still had to work through some obstacles—contacting his father was at the top of the list—he was certain the love he'd found with Abby was strong enough to withstand the strongest of hurricanes. With her by his side, there was nothing he couldn't achieve. Starting with winning the case against Richmond University and the Lady of Lourdes Nursing Home.

He and Abby had talked it over again and she'd been the one to suggest he stay on the case. She'd been giving the matter more thought and while she appreciated his offer to withdraw from it, she was mature enough to concede that the outcome wouldn't change for her brother no matter who was at the helm. She was confident Jeff would agree. She urged Ben to proceed and assured him that after all the work he'd put into the case, it was only right that he be given the opportunity to see it through to the end. He'd been grateful for her professional attitude and looked forward to once again digging his teeth into the matter.

Today was the last day the defendants had to file and serve their defense. It was also the date the subpoenas were returnable. By this afternoon, Ben should have the written evidence he needed to properly prove his case. With the addition of the oral testimony from Jiao Zheng, Wang Xiu Ying, Li Min and the half dozen other nurses he'd interviewed, he was confident of a win.

The media was already all over it and a trial date hadn't even been set. The death of Dulcie Eveleigh and the way she'd died at the hand of Jiao Zheng was once again front page news. Ben could only imagine the panic at the nursing home and the anarchy over in the dean's office. He hoped Abby's brother was keeping his head down.

Abby.

She'd turned his life around. While he'd been thankful for the blessings he'd been given and the achievements he'd made, it wasn't until she came back into his life, so warm, so loving, so giving and forgiving that he realized how lonely he'd been and how much he needed that special kind of someone in his life.

He now approached each day with a smile on his face and a hope that the day would turn out bright. He had someone to call and share his day with; he had a loving woman to fill his nights. Things had even worked out with his grandmother. He and Abby had packed her up and moved her into the nursing home in Lane Cove a week ago, and though it was still early days, she appeared to be settling in well. He'd spoken to her the night before and she'd sounded happy. She'd even cut their conversation short by telling him she had to be at Bingo. It was so good to know she was safe and protected and wasn't missing her home. There was still a lot of rubbish to clean out and bags and bags of things to be donated to Goodwill, but they'd made a start and Abby had helped him. Together, they'd do what needed to be done.

His thoughts returned to his father and the way Abby had urged him to make his peace. Sorting through the boxes of old photos and other memorabilia at his grandmother's place, he'd remembered how it used to be, recalled the good times he'd shared with his family before the accident. Now that he'd had more time to think about it and about the future he wanted for him and Abby, he knew she was right. It was time to wipe the slate clean and put the past behind him. He wanted to repair his relationship with his father and move forward into the future, reconnected to his family.

Abby had been overjoyed when he'd told her of his decision. She'd even agreed to meet her own parents after years apart. Though she'd forgiven them from a distance, she hadn't seen either of them since she'd left home as a teen.

Ben knew the difficulty of the decision she was making and how hard it would be for her to tell them to their face that she bore no ill will. It just went to show how remarkable she was and it made him want to be the best man he could be. Abby Brown deserved the best. It was as simple as that.

With his mind made up, he drew in a deep breath and reached across his desk for the phone. Before he could pick it up, it rang, startling him. After a second or two, he answered it.

"Hello?"

"Ben, I have Anthony McDougall of Harris Botham and Marshall on line three," Cheryl said. "He's calling about the Richmond University case."

Ben recovered his surprise and took the call. "Anthony, it's Ben Fitzgerald. What can I do for you?"

The man on the other end of the line cleared his throat. "Ben. We need to talk."

Ben frowned. "About the defense? It's meant to be filed and served by the end of the day. Are you requesting an extension?"

"No. See, the thing is, the university has instructed me to make you an offer. They want to settle this thing. The negative publicity has infiltrated the foreign news networks. Indicators show that enrollments will be down thirty-five percent. If that comes to fruition, the college will be hemorrhaging money. They can't afford for this to go to trial. Any further bad press would just about ruin them, no matter what the ultimate outcome."

Ben sat back in his chair in surprise. Right from the outset, he'd been confident he had a strong case, but he'd never expected the university to go down without a fight. Still, what McDougall said about the negative media reports was true. Even that day, on his way to work, Ben had heard the case being discussed on morning radio. It seemed everyone had an opinion on who was responsible for the fact there seemed to be an infinite number of university graduates who were unable to properly read English and who were putting the community at risk. The mood out on the street was tense and angry. They were looking for someone to blame.

"What kind of money are they talking?" Ben asked.

"One million for each beneficiary, plus legal costs. Of course, you'd have to drop the case against Jeffery Brown and the terms of settlement would be strictly confidential. My client has had enough of talking to the media or fending off allegations that might or might not be true. I've been speaking to Richard Halliwell. The nursing home feels the same way. His client is also keen to see this matter settled. Take the money and your clients never say a word about this again."

"That sounds fair enough," Ben agreed, "but I wouldn't be too confident about keeping this under wraps. There are a lot more nurses out there who can't read English well and who are putting the community at risk. And it's not just Richmond University. If you ask me, it's only a matter of time before someone else stuffs up. The question is, how many more lives are going to be taken unnecessarily before the government steps in and fixes the problem?"

McDougall sighed. "If what you say is correct, this thing is a whole lot bigger than either of us thought, but that's not my problem. I'm representing Richmond University. We'll deal with this, one case at a time. Let's hope there aren't any more."

Ben didn't like the man's chances, but refrained from referring to it again. Instead, he said, "I'll put your offer to my clients. I'll come back to you later today."

"Thank you," McDougall replied. "I look forward to your call."

Ben hung up the receiver and once again leaned back in his chair. He stacked his hands behind his head and contemplated the phone call. The settlement offer was a good one and he was prepared to recommend it to his clients. Even if the court found the university responsible for Dulcie Eveleigh's death, the woman was in her nineties. Her life expectancy was short. She also had very little in the way of an estate. Her premature death brought about pain and suffering before its time, but there was very little else in the way of damages that could be claimed.

As for exposing the dubious practises of the universities when it came to their foreign students, the lawsuit had already achieved this aim: the spotlight had been well and truly switched on. He hoped the excessive attention from the media would bring pressure on the government to open an inquiry and investigate more fully what was going on. Only then could the problem and the potential for more deaths be resolved.

Sitting forward, he picked up the phone again and called the executor of Dulcie Eveleigh's estate and outlined the offer on the table. The man was the spokesman for the beneficiaries. He promised to speak to them and relay the offer and get back to Ben as soon as he could.

While he was still in the mood for conversation, Ben dragged his keyboard toward him and opened up the online telephone directory to the name he'd found a week earlier.

CM Fitzgerald. 1 Whiting Drive, Mount Druitt. A telephone number was listed beside the address. Ben had no way of knowing if it was his father, but the initials "CM" matched Christopher Martin, his father's name. It was also in the same suburb where Ben had grown up, although the street address was no longer the same.

The only thing to do was to pick up the phone and call the number. Then he'd know for sure. *Did he still have the courage to go through with it? What if his father answered the call?*

Ben's chest went tight at the thought of speaking to the man after all these years of silence. He thought of his mother and sister and the nightmares he still sometimes had. He hadn't had one for years, but that wasn't to say they'd stopped for good. *Did he really want to dredge up all those old memories? Did he really want to go back down that path?*

And then he thought of Abby and the sacrifices

she'd made. She intended to meet with her parents, to speak with them face to face. She was the bravest, most resilient, kindest woman he knew and she was his. She loved him just as much as he loved her.

He had to do it. He had to make the call. He wanted to be the man Abby deserved. He wanted her to feel proud. No matter how much he dreaded the thought of calling his father, he refused to let her down.

With a surge of courage and determination, he reached for the phone.

Abby absently twirled a lock of hair around her finger and stared at the only picture frame on her desk. It was a photo of her and Jeff. It had been taken around the same time as the one that hung on the wall in her condo. Visitors to her house or office often expressed surprise that there were no pictures of her parents. She dismissed their curious questions and glances with a tight smile and would often tell them her parents were dead.

And to her, it was true. They'd been dead to her for years, since the time she'd packed up a small bundle of possessions and escaped the house of horrors and disappeared into the night. She could still remember the smell of orange blossoms and the moisture on the air. It was meant to rain that night, but she didn't care. She couldn't spend another moment living there.

She hated to leave her little brother, but she knew he was safe—at least safe from the horrors she'd been forced to endure. Her father's sick tastes only ran to young girls. She thought of all he stole from her and tears ran down her cheeks. Even the smaller things, like having friends over to spend the night. She'd never invited a single girl to a sleepover at her place. She'd been terrified they'd end up a victim, just like she had. She'd refused to take the chance.

And so, she'd suffered in silence after that single fateful time when she'd found the courage to tell her mother and found out in no uncertain terms that she'd find no support there. The discovery had horrified her and almost done her in, but she'd found the courage from somewhere to bury the hurt and pain deep inside her and continue to soldier on.

And now she'd promised Ben she'd call her parents and make arrangements to meet them face to face. It was one thing to forgive them from a distance, in the comfort and security of her church. But to see them, get close to them... Tell them she'd let go her hate... She wanted to do it for Ben's sake as well as her own, but the more she thought about it, the more she knew she couldn't go through with it.

Her chest went tight and she stifled a gasp, but then her emotions overwhelmed her. With her head in her hands, she leaned her elbows on her desk and sobbed. The sound of the door opening registered in the back of her mind, but she was too distraught to care. It wasn't until Ben knelt at her side, his face creased in concern that she realized he'd entered the room.

"Abby! What's the matter? What happened?"

She shook her head, beyond words, and tried to control her sobs. In silence, Ben stood and took her in his arms. With a ragged sigh, she leaned against him and rested her head against his broad chest. Taking comfort from his presence, her sobs gradually quieted. At last, she pulled out a tissue, wiped her eyes and nose and then lifted her head to look at him.

"Are you all right?" he asked softly, his eyes still filled with concern.

She shook her head.

Tenderly, he scraped her hair out of her eyes and tucked it behind her ear. "What happened?"

"I… I can't do it. I know I said I would, but I… I can't." Her voice broke on the last word and fresh tears welled up in her eyes.

Ben frowned. "What are you talking about, honey? What can't you do?"

"I can't face them!" she cried. "I thought I could. I thought I was strong enough, but I'm not. The thought of coming face to face with my mother and father sends terror through my heart."

His eyes widened with comprehension. He nodded. "I understand and guess what, honey? It doesn't matter. You don't have to meet them. You never have to see them again. I won't think any less of you. I'll love you just the same."

She stared up at him, her lashes still wet with tears. "You won't be disappointed?"

He shook his head adamantly. "Hell, no! Why

the hell would I be disappointed? This is between you and them. I don't have anything to do with it and I sure as hell am not in a position to judge. I haven't seen my father for seventeen years. Nearly half of my life. Do you think I'm going to judge you for not having contact with yours?"

"But what about all those things I said about you needing to let your hurt go, forgive your father, reconnect with him? I feel like such a hypocrite!"

He took her by the shoulders, his gaze burning into hers, like he wanted to make sure she understood what he was saying. "Don't be silly. I'd never think that way about you. What your father did to you was far worse than anything that happened to me. You were a baby! An innocent child! Your father acted deliberately. My father might have been reckless, but he didn't mean to cause those deaths. He was probably devastated by the loss of my sister and mother, as much as I was. Worse, because he was at the wheel. It was an accident that he contributed to. Nothing more, nothing less."

Ben's eyes widened as he said the words, like the realization had just occurred to him. It was true. His mother and sister had died in a tragic accident. All right, so his father was too drunk to be behind the wheel and should never have driven them home, but there was no pre-meditation, no evil plan to bring about the end of his family. It was like Ben said: an accident. No more, no less.

With a soft sigh, Abby leaned back against him

and tightened her arms about his waist. He felt so good, so strong and dependable. He was her rock, her anchor in life's stormy seas. He had been that for her all those years ago and he still was. She said a quiet prayer of thanks that he was back in her life.

"Are you sure you're not disappointed?" she asked again, her voice muffled against his shirt.

He set her a little away from him and frowned down at her. "Abby Brown! How many times do I have to tell you? Of *course* I'm not disappointed. You're the bravest, kindest, sweetest, most beautiful girl I know. Nothing you could do or say would disappoint me. Not now, not ever."

He softened his words with a gentle kiss placed against her lips. She kissed him back, just as softly, grateful all over again for this special gift. The gift of love, the gift of safety, the gift of understanding. The gift of Ben.

When Ben finally dropped his arms and set her away from him, she was feeling so much better. Though the thought of meeting her parents still filled her with dread, she could think about it now without being overcome with terror. He had helped her through her crisis, had helped her get through her fear and she loved him for it.

"I love you," she said simply, needing to let him know.

He bent his head and pressed another sweet kiss on her mouth. "I love you, too."

"What are you doing tonight?" she asked. Though he'd spent just as many nights at her place as she had at his, she didn't want to assume he kept every night open for her. Though they'd freely shared the 'L' word, there had been no talk of anything more permanent. She didn't want to spoil things by pre-empting something that he might not be ready for, like moving in together, and with the court case against her brother about to kick up a gear, now probably wasn't the best time.

"I don't have any plans. In fact, I just received an offer of settlement from Anthony McDougall."

Abby frowned. The name was familiar. "Anthony McDougall? Isn't he representing Richmond University?"

"Yes."

It took a moment for the news to set in. When it did, a smile broke out across her face. "They've offered to settle?"

"Yes."

"That's great news." She paused and thought about it. "Wait a minute. What about the lawyers representing the nursing home? Halliwell and Westman, wasn't it?"

"Yes. McDougall assured me he had authority from Richard Halliwell to put the offer to me on behalf of both the first and second defendants."

"Was it a good offer?"

"Yes, I think so. I've told my clients as much and advised them to take it. I'm waiting to hear back from the executor of the estate. Part of the deal is that we drop the case against your brother."

"If they accept the offer, the case comes to an end. Jeff won't be forced to testify. In fact, he'll be in the clear. He'll be able to get on with the rest of his life."

"Yes, although he might not want to get too complacent. In the course of my investigations, I uncovered some pretty alarming evidence that this kind of thing is happening a lot. International students with a poor grasp of English, particularly in written form, are being graduated from Australian universities and nobody seems to care. Something needs to be done about it. The government needs to step in. There should be an inquiry."

Abby nodded slowly. "If what you say is true, then I agree. We don't want any more unnecessary deaths."

"No. The fact that the majority of these nurses take up positions in nursing homes is no comfort. The elderly are among our most vulnerable. They deserve to be protected and shouldn't have to wonder if they face the risk of premature death because a nurse wasn't properly educated."

"You're right." She thought of Ben's grandmother, recently settled into the very kind of facility they were talking about. She glanced at Ben and could tell he was thinking of his grandmother, too.

"How is she?" Abby asked quietly.

"Grandma? She's fine. At least, she seems happy enough. She regales me with stories of what she's been up to and the new friends she's made. Repeats them over and over..." He laughed, shaking his head.

Abby reached out and touched his arm. "You did the right thing, Ben. She's in a much better place, now. She's safe and with people around her to look out for her."

"Yes."

He said the word, but his grim expression told her he wasn't sure if he truly believed it. She only hoped Evie would be fine and that neither of them had anything to worry about.

"Would you like to come over tonight?" she asked.

He looked down at her and smiled. "Thank you. That would be nice."

"I'll cook your favorite meal," she promised.

He quirked an eyebrow. "Oh, yes? And what would that be?"

She shrugged and laughed. "I don't know. Anything with chilli."

He chuckled and pulled her close for another hug. "Already you know me so well."

Chapter 20

Ben glanced at his watch and muttered a curse. It was already twenty minutes past the time he'd agreed to meet his father. He'd set up the appointment to coincide with his lunch hour. They were supposed to meet at the northern end of Hyde Park, near the fountain. Now he was going to be late getting back to work. It was a good thing he didn't have any clients expected that afternoon. Even so, this suddenly seemed like such a bad idea.

His father had seemed so enthusiastic when they'd spoken over the phone. Though taken off guard, after his initial shock had worn off, Christopher Fitzgerald had sounded eager to reconnect. In stilted sentences, they'd shared a little about each other and had eventually agreed to meet. And here he was. Still waiting.

With another look around him, he spun on his heel and started off toward his building. This had all been such a waste of time. He should never have come.

"Ben?"

The cautious question reached his ears and he halted mid-stride. Turning around, he spotted a man coming toward him. As he got closer, Ben recognized the unmistakable features of his father. It was like looking into a mirror in thirty years. A stab of emotion went through him.

"Dad?"

"Ben! It really *is* you! I don't believe it!"

His father closed the distance between them at a half-run and launched himself at his son. Taken aback by his father's enthusiasm, Ben stood stiffly with his arms at his sides.

"Oh, Ben! I can't believe it's you! I never thought I'd see you again! For so many years, I've dreamed of this moment and now that it's here..." He shook his head back and forth and tears glinted in his green eyes. Eyes just like Ben's. A lump clogged Ben's throat.

"I just don't believe it," his father said again. He stepped away and looked Ben up and down. "You look good, son. And you're a lawyer! Imagine that! My son is a lawyer!"

Once again, Ben fought against emotions that threatened to undo him. He didn't know how he'd feel about meeting his father after all this time, but he'd imagined their meeting would be far more formal and stilted than this. He'd only agreed to make contact because he knew it would make Abby happy and yet, his heart was clenching with pain *and elation* now that his father was here.

"Perhaps we could get a drink somewhere?" his

father asked, filling the silence. "Do you have time for that?"

Ben flushed. "I... I don't drink, Dad. I... Actually, I'm a recovering alcoholic."

His father's eyes widened momentarily in shock and then an awful look of understanding filled his face. "It was because of me, wasn't it? Because of the terrible mistake I made that took so much away from us..."

He sounded so forlorn and dejected, Ben wanted to reassure him he was wrong, but the truth was, Ben *had* turned to alcohol as a way to hide from the pain—pain caused by the actions of his father.

"I'm sorry, Dad. I wish I could tell you different. After..." He cleared his throat and tried again. "After Mom and Jennifer died, I went right off the rails. My family, as I'd known it, had suddenly been ripped apart. Mom and Jennifer were dead. You were serving ten years in jail. It was so hard to have lost so much. I didn't know how to handle it. I was angry and wanted to be left alone. I lived on the streets for a year and a half. It was there I became dependent on alcohol."

Christopher Fitzgerald's complexion paled a bit more with each sentence Ben uttered. His father's eyes filled with fresh tears. He shook his head sadly. "What about my mother? Your grandmother?" he said brokenly. "Didn't she take you in?"

"She offered, but I refused to go with her then. I was sixteen. No court was going to force me to live somewhere I didn't want to."

His father stared at him in confusion. "Why wouldn't you want to? Your grandmother loved you so much."

"It wasn't that, Dad. I was in no fit state to live with anyone. I was angry all the time. I lashed out, always looking for someone to blame. I think the time I spent on the streets helped me to heal and helped me to come to the realization I needed to try and get my life back together again. That's when I turned up at Grandma's. She embraced me with open arms. No harsh words, no recriminations, no judgements. She might drive me crazy at times, but I'll love that old woman until I die."

"So, she's still alive?"

"Yes, although she's not as good as you might think. She's battling dementia. It's taken hold. In fact, I had to move her into a nursing home only a week ago."

His father nodded slowly, his expression sad. "I'm sorry to hear she's been unwell. She was a good mom and a remarkable woman. She tried to visit me a couple of times while I was in prison. I refused to see her."

Ben was filled with surprise. "Grandma went to the jail?"

"Yes. I wasn't sure if she came to rail against me or to sympathize with my cause. As I said, I didn't have the courage to face her and find out."

Ben absorbed the information and slowly shook his head in disbelief. "Well, you were certainly right about her being a remarkable woman. And you know, she's never said as much to me, but I think she forgave you a long time ago. Like I now have."

Ben frowned. *Had* he forgiven his father? *Is that what this was all about?* Pondering the questions, he decided that he had. Somewhere between Ben's arguments to and fro, and his decision to call his dad, he'd opened the door to forgiveness for what had happened—and had relegated the tragedy to the past, where it belonged. From his grandmother's recent suggestions, he was sure she'd done the same.

He looked at his dad and felt only sadness that they'd lost so much time. His father was in his sixties, now well past his prime. In fact, he looked at least a decade older. It was obvious life hadn't been easy. Ben couldn't imagine that ten years behind bars would be good for anyone.

"You should talk to her, Dad," he said softly. "Better still, go and see her. I think she'd like that. While she remembers a lot about the past, and of course, the accident, her memory isn't what it used to be. I think you might find she loves you as much now as she ever did."

His father's face filled with hope and the sight of it tore at Ben's heart. All this time, he'd never given any thought to how his father was feeling. Christopher Fitzgerald had also lost his family that night. Ben wasn't the only one who'd suffered. He understood that now.

Glancing at his watch, he reluctantly made his farewells but made plans for them to meet up again soon. Ben wanted to introduce his father to Abby and he wanted to tell his grandmother about the meeting, too. Though they'd never talked about the accident, Ben was sure she'd be glad to see her son again. A lot of time and pain had passed. It was time to move on.

Abby spooned a generous portion of chilli con carne onto Ben's plate. She added boiled rice and two disk-shaped pappadums and placed it all in front of him.

"*Mm*, this looks delicious!" he said and tilted his head up for a kiss. She giggled and obliged him.

After filling her plate, she returned to the table and took a seat opposite him. Before she could pick up her fork, Ben picked up his glass of Sprite and raised it in a toast.

"I want to propose a toast to the cook for her splendiferous meal."

Abby giggled again and clinked her glass of Diet Coke to his. She put the drink down and picked up her fork, but Ben wasn't finished.

"I'd also like to propose a toast to my father. May he live a long and happy life."

As his words sunk in, Abby stared at Ben in amazement. "Your father? You called him?"

Ben nodded. "I went to see him. We met today in Hyde Park."

Still blown away by his announcement, Abby shook her head. "Wow! That's amazing! Why didn't you tell me about it?"

"I'm telling you now."

"Yes, but earlier, before you met him. Surely you called him first?"

"Yes, I did. I called him this morning. It was right after I took the call from McDougall, offering a settlement."

Abby thought back and realized he'd already spoken to his father when he came into her office and found her blubbering all over her desk. All at once, she understood why he hadn't said anything. She'd spent the entire time upset about the fact she couldn't bear to face her parents. He was hardly going to tell her he'd just arranged to meet his father.

She reached across the table and took his hand. "I get it," she said softly.

"I didn't think you'd want to hear about me and my dad," he replied just as softly.

Tears welled up in her eyes. "It's all right, Ben. I understand and I'm happy for you! I'm so happy things are working out between the two of you. They are, aren't they? I could tell something good had happened, from the look on your face when you mentioned his name."

Ben nodded. "Yes, I think things are going to work out. You were right. I needed to let go of my hate and resentment, my bitterness at what he did. And understand his pain and guilt over what happened. He lost his family, too, and spent a decade in jail as punishment. It's enough. We've both suffered enough. Now it's time to get on with living."

Abby was filled with so much love and admiration for the man who sat across from her she thought she might burst from it. Pushing away from the table, she came around to where he sat and plastered his face with kisses.

"I love you, Ben Fitzgerald. I love you with everything that I am."

"And I love you, too, Abby Brown. Without you, my life wouldn't be the same."

––––––––––

Ben was swimming in the ocean, like he used to when he was a kid. The salt burned his eyes, but the waves were soft and foamy, breaking around his legs. He swam in lazy circles, enjoying the water and sand and then, without warning, the water turned darker, danker. The taste of salt was overcome by the sour smell of slime.

He was in the river and it was dark and cold and he couldn't catch his breath. Something was holding him back. Something was holding him down. He screamed, but his cries for help were drowned out by the water. It bore down upon him, filling his lungs, terrifying him.

His world narrowed to the viscous water. There was barely a speck of light. The darkness crowded in around him and then he heard another scream. It was coming from somewhere close beside him. He reached out and touched an arm. *His sister!* She was there, too! Trapped by the seatbelt. He needed to get to her, to set her free, only he couldn't move. Thrashing around, he renewed his efforts and at last, the ties that bound him in place broke free.

"Benjamin! Help me!" Jennifer screamed, her face a picture of terror.

"I'm coming, Jenny! I'm coming! Hang on!"

He swam as hard as he could, but something kept holding him back. It was as if a giant elastic band let him go only so far forward and then snapped him all the way back. Jennifer's screams echoed in his head. His lungs were desperate for air. Her beloved face, pale and terrified, swam in front of him.

"Jenny! I'm coming! Hang on! I'll be there as soon as I can." Once again, he struggled against the pressure that held him back.

Then his mother's face floated into view and she already looked dead. Her eyes gazed at him vacantly. Fish had already begun to nibble on her lips. He screamed again and terror so awful seized his heart until it pounded right out of his chest. He gasped and screamed and fought to get closer, but nothing seemed to work.

And then his father appeared and he was beckoning him closer. "Come on, Ben! Over here! We need to get out of here."

His father reached for him. A moment later, the pressure that held him back was released. He saw the slackened seatbelt and realized what had happened. Before he could speak, his father took hold of Ben's shirt and wrenched him up from the darkness.

All of a sudden, Ben's head broke the surface and he gasped and filled his lungs with air. His father dove into the water one more time. An eternity later he broke the surface, empty handed. His face was ravaged with grief, tears poured down his cheeks. Then he saw his son.

"Ben! Oh, thank God! You're alive! Oh, thank God, you're okay!"

His father cradled him in his arms, kissing him over and over again. Ben coughed and spluttered and gasped again. His mouth tasted of the river. Pushing away from his father, he stood and bent over and vomited. Brackish, dark water flew out of his nose and mouth and landed all over the grassy bank. Unable to stand, he fell to his knees and cried.

"Ben?"

The tears streamed down his cheeks and dripped onto the ground. He cried for his mom and his sister and for the fact he was alive.

"Ben?"

A gentle hand was at his shoulder. He tried to ignore it. He didn't want to talk to anyone.

"Ben? Are you all right?"

The same voice came again, soft and insistent, but still he ignored it.

"Ben, wake up! It's Abby. Wake up!"

Ben came awake with a start, his heart pounding. He stared at Abby. Her face was pale in the darkness. She rested on her elbow, staring down at him. Her gaze was filled with concern.

"Abby?" he asked, his head still full of fog.

"It's all right, Ben. You were dreaming."

He closed his eyes and remembered the nightmare and then reached up and touched his cheeks. They were damp from his tears.

"My dad," he said.

Abby frowned. "What about your dad?"

"He saved me and he tried to get the others."

"He saved you? I thought you said—?"

"I know what I said, but I was wrong! All these years, I thought I was the one who got me out of that car wreck. But it was Dad. He saved me! I was caught in the seatbelt. I couldn't get it free. Dad saved me, Abby. He saved me!"

The realization overwhelmed him and sobs overcame him again. Burying his face in the softness of Abby's breasts, he cried his heart out. All this time, he'd blamed his dad and hadn't once considered the part his dad had played in his own fate. Okay, so they would never have been in the situation if his dad hadn't climbed behind the wheel drunk, but Ben could have drowned just as easily as his mom and his sister if it hadn't been for his dad.

He was just so relieved he'd made his peace with him and that it wasn't too late to build a relationship. He wanted to get to know his father again, man to man and do his best to make up for the lost years. They could never be the family they'd once been, but his dad and his grandmother were the only family he had. And Abby. Of course, there was Abby. She would be part of his family until the day he died.

With a sudden surge of determination and feeling like he was running out of time, Ben sat up and stared at the woman he loved with all his life.

"I love you, Abby Brown. I always have and I always will. You're mine for all eternity. Will you marry me?"

CHAPTER 21

Abby came awake slowly. A faint light glimmered through the crack in her bedroom curtains, where they didn't quite meet in the middle, heralding the arrival of a new day. She smiled, not even fully conscious, but aware that today was the first day of the best times of her life.

Ben had proposed and she'd accepted! She still couldn't believe it. Even a few short months ago, she couldn't have imagined her life would turn out so well. She rolled on her side, careful not to wake the man who breathed softly and deeply beside her. Over the weeks they'd been together, his dark hair had grown a little longer and it now curled gently around his ears. She found she liked it that way.

Just as she liked his beard. She'd never been into beards or moustaches and Ben now sported both, but somehow, they suited him. It was a part of him and therefore, she loved it like she loved the rest of him.

She thought back to the nightmare that had

disturbed him the night before and frowned. She'd guessed that he was dreaming about the car accident that had claimed the lives of his mother and sister even before he woke and began speaking about his dad. He kept telling her his dad had saved him. She wondered if it were true or if their recent reconciliation was the real reason his father had been given a more positive role in Ben's dreams.

She didn't know and it didn't matter. What mattered was that Ben and his father had set aside their differences, had agreed to forgive and forget and move forward, together. It was what she wanted to do with her parents, if she could only find the courage...

Her hands clenched into fists and her breath came faster. The thought of approaching her parents, coming face to face with her dad again... That terrified her. But, if she wanted to make things work with Ben, she needed to find the nerve to do it. Though she'd found peace through her church, she wanted to come to him cleansed and whole and ready to face life head on, without the nightmare of her past holding her back. She wanted to feel free of all that.

Decision made, she was impatient to share it with him. He still snored quietly beside her. She leaned over and pressed a kiss against his lips and then gently nibbled her way to his ear. He stirred and lifted his hand to bat her away. She increased her efforts by sliding her hand across his chest and pinching one of his nipples.

His hand moved fast and stilled her fingers,

holding them against his chest. She gasped and looked up at him and met his green-eyed gaze. His eyes twinkled.

"Good morning, Ms Brown. You seem mighty keen to see me awake. What time is it?"

She glanced at the clock on her nightstand. "It's half-past six."

He groaned and pulled the pillow over his head. "Way too early to be up," he complained good naturedly, his voice muffled.

"I'm sorry, but there's something I have to tell you," she replied.

Something in the tone of her voice caught his attention. He pulled the pillow away and came up on an elbow. The teasing light in his eyes faded. "What is it?"

"Don't worry. It's nothing serious," she hurried to reassure him and then corrected herself. "What I mean is, it's serious, but not in a life-or-death kind of way."

He frowned. "Abby, what are you talking about? It's kind of early for riddles."

"I'm sorry," she said. "I'm not making sense. See, the thing is…I'm going to call my parents. I want to meet them face to face, too."

The surprise and delight on Ben's face was everything she needed to reassure her she was doing the right thing. But then, his expression faded and became solemn. "Are you sure? I mean, don't feel like you have to just because I met with my dad. Your situation was different. Your father's abuse was intentional and cruel. I don't expect you to—"

She leaned forward and pressed a finger against his lips. "*Shh,*" she whispered. "I know. And it doesn't have anything to do with that. I've needed to do this for a long time. Part of my recovery, I guess. A closure, if you like. Yesterday, I lost my courage, but being with you, loving you, knowing that you want to spend the rest of your life with me by your side, clarifies all this. I *want* to do this! For me and for us. So we can really step past all this. I hope you understand."

He moved until he was pressed against her side and then reached up and tenderly brushed a wayward strand of her hair off her face. The love in his eyes took her breath away. Her chest went tight and she blinked back tears. He leaned forward and kissed her.

"I'm so proud of you," he whispered, his voice hoarse with emotion. "I'm so, so *proud* of you."

The sob she'd been trying hard to hold inside, escaped her and tears flowed down her cheeks. Ben was immediately concerned.

"Abby! What is it? What did I say?"

She shook her head, unable to speak and when she finally managed it, she spoke between her sobs. "I'm c-crying because I'm h-happy. I c-can't believe you're m-mine, that you l-love me."

"Of course I love you! I've loved you from almost the first moment I saw you and nothing has changed in all this time. In fact, I love you even more for your strength and courage and for the amazing person you've become. You had all the reasons in the world to become an addict and to stay that way for the rest of your life. But you didn't. You dug deep, found the courage to get away from that life. And here you are. You're an amazing, special woman, Abby Brown, and I will love you until I die."

She threw her arms around his neck. Their lips touched and melded and heat ignited inside her. Her arms crept around his shoulders and she pulled him down, sighing at the feel of his weight on top of her.

Ben buried his face in the crook of her neck and nuzzled her ear. "How much time do we have?" he mumbled.

She twisted until she could look at the clock and then turned back to him and smiled. "It's not even seven. Plenty of time."

Ben carefully read over the settlement documents that had been prepared by Anthony McDougall and Richard Halliwell on behalf of their respective clients and sent over to Ben that morning. He'd also received a telephone call from Paul Mosely who advised him he'd been retained by Jeffery Brown. Mosely assured him his client was happy with the terms of settlement. Everything appeared to be in order and Ben was certain there wouldn't be any last-minute hitches. The beneficiaries had been brought up to speed and all of them had agreed to accept the offer. It was simply a matter of having it signed by the executor and then filed and approved by the court. Not bad for what had been shaping up to be an all-out fight.

He'd scheduled a visit with Jiao Zheng at the prison. In fact, he'd better get a move on if he wanted to get there in time. It would be the first time he'd seen her since her incarceration. He wanted to tell her in person about the settlement. He hoped she'd take some comfort from the fact the university and her former employer were going to make reparation to her victim's family and that because of the media attention, the problem of underqualified nurses would be scrutinized more closely at higher levels of government. It was all Ben could hope for and he hoped she agreed they were making steps forward.

Pushing away from his desk, he grabbed his jacket and keys. He was halfway out of his office when his phone rang. Tugging it out of his pocket, he glanced at the screen.

Abby. His heart smiled.

"Hey, you," he said.

"How are you doing?" she asked.

"Great. Just going over the settlement papers for the university case. Everything's coming along."

"Good. Have you had lunch?"

"No, I'm on way out to visit Jiao Zheng at Long Bay. I wanted to tell her the good news in person."

"How do you think she'll take it?" Abby asked.

"I'm not sure, but I'm guessing she'll be relieved and pleased. I interviewed her before she was sentenced. Five years is tough. I mean, I get that she should be punished, but it was an accident that she was only partly responsible for. Soon, all the world will know the university and the nursing home were the real ones at fault."

"You mean the defendants didn't insist that the terms of the settlement be sealed?" Abby asked.

"Of course they did. But trust me, this case won't end here. I interviewed over a dozen nurses whose English skills left a lot to be desired and yet they were all fully qualified university graduates. Not all of them studied at Richmond. We're going to be busy over the next few months."

"Wow! That's unbelievable!" Abby exclaimed. "I'm so glad it's come to light before any other innocent people lose their lives."

"Yes. Anyway, honey, I'd better go. I'm about to head into the underground parking lot and I'll probably lose service."

"Okay, I'll talk to you soon. Oh, I just wanted to let you know, I called my parents. I spoke to my mom."

Ben came to a sudden halt, filling with surprise. They'd talked about it early that morning, but he had no idea she was going to do it so quickly. "You called them already?"

"Yes. I wanted to do it before I lost my nerve."

"Good for you," he said and meant it. "How did you do?"

She sighed on the other end of the phone. "Okay, I guess. Mom didn't sound overjoyed to hear from me. In fact, I had to repeat my name. Three times. I nearly hung up there and then. But then I thought of you—of us—and I held on to my nerve. Anyway, they've agreed to meet with me. I... I'm going to see them this afternoon."

"This afternoon?" he repeated in surprise.

"Yes, like I said, I wanted to get it over with before I lost my nerve."

Ben nodded. He understood. "Would you like me to come with you?" he asked. "I should be back from the jail by then."

"Would you?" Her voice was barely a whisper, but he heard her quiet plea.

"Of course! I want to be there for you, now and forever. They're not just words, Abby. I mean them."

"I know you do and I love you for it. We're meeting at three near the white water rafting area at Penrith Lakes," she said, referring to a man-made recreational lake with surrounding parkland, complete with bike trails, barbeques and rapids.

Ben frowned. "That's an odd place to meet."

"Yes, well, apparently it's close to where my parents live now and my father finds the sound of the water soothing. At least, that's what my mother said. It will take at least an hour to get there. Can you spare the time?"

"I can spare the time, Abby, but I might have to go straight from the jail. Can I meet you there?"

"Yes, of course. Do you need directions?"

"No. I know where it is. I'll see you there."

After bidding Abby goodbye, he ended the call and climbed into his Ferrari. Heading out of the parking lot, he turned toward the eastern suburbs and Long Bay Correctional Center. Traffic was light and he made it with ten minutes to spare. After signing in at the front desk and handing his briefcase over for scanning, he walked through the security area and finally came out the other side.

"I'm here to see Jiao Zheng. I'm her lawyer," he told the corrections officer when the man demanded to know his business at the jail.

A buzzer sounded and the steel gate barring his way, opened, allowing him entry. He walked through the visitors' lounge and into a vacant interview room used by lawyers during scheduled visits and there he waited for the nurse.

It seemed to take forever. Twice, he walked out and found a guard and asked what the holdup was and twice he was told to be patient; that his client would be out in good time. Throwing himself down at the table, he opened his briefcase and flicked through the notes he'd made on another case he'd taken on only that morning.

A woman was suing her employer for damages after she slipped on a wet floor and damaged two vertebrae in her back. It wasn't a particularly meaty case and no doubt the insurance company fronting for the employer would offer some paltry amount. They'd negotiate back and forth for a while until everyone walked away happy.

The door to the room opened and Ben looked up as Jiao Zheng was brought in. Handcuffed and in prison greens, she looked small and young and defeated. He felt a stab of sympathy.

"Do you want me to leave the handcuffs on?" the corrections officer asked him.

"No. Take them off, please," he replied and received a grateful glance from his client.

When the handcuffs were removed, the guard let himself out and then positioned himself right outside the door. Ben wasn't sure what the man thought Zheng might do to her lawyer. He outweighed her by more than a hundred pounds.

"How are you?" he asked.

The woman shrugged. "Okay."

"I wanted to tell you about the case I was working on. The one involving Richmond University and your former employer."

She sat forward. "Yes?"

"Yes. We've settled it out of court. They made a generous multimillion-dollar offer, one my clients couldn't refuse."

Her eyes flashed with anger. "What about the fact that my bosses are guilty of not taking enough care? Did you get them to admit that? They're the ones who should be in here! Not me!"

Ben regarded her solemnly. He understood her anger. He'd be angry, too. "The terms of settlement required that there would be no admission of guilt, but don't worry, this doesn't finish here."

He told her about the other nurses who'd come forward to speak with him, nurses she'd contacted on his behalf.

"I really appreciate your help with that. Without them, we'd have nothing. Now we have enough evidence to really bring some pressure on the government to do something about this. It's wrong and if it continues, it's going to end up costing more innocent lives."

"Yes, you're right," Jiao said in a calmer voice. She glanced idly toward his open briefcase. "I thought you told me your birthday was in June, just before mine?"

He frowned at the sudden change of topic. "It is. June seventh. Why?"

She indicated the briefcase. "That looks like a birthday card."

He followed the direction of her gaze and saw the card peeking out of its envelope. He'd received it in the mail that morning. It had come from his grandmother. She always sent him a card for his birthday, but sometimes she remembered well after the date. This one was more than a month old, but it didn't matter to him. He was just glad she cared enough to send him one at all.

He pulled the envelope out of the briefcase and smiled. "It is. It came from my grandmother this morning. She's got dementia. She gets a little confused. In fact, I had to put her in a nursing home a week ago."

Zheng smiled and reached for the envelope. Curious, Ben passed it to her. She turned the envelope over and looked down at the return address.

"Ah, St Patrick's at Lane Cove. It's a nice place. She'll like it there."

"Yes, she seems to have settled in well. It makes it easier, somehow."

"I know what you mean. I saw many relatives struggle with the decision to remove their loved ones from their home, but sometimes, it's for the best, right?"

Ben nodded in agreement. He'd come there to give the nurse some good news and she'd ended up cheering him up. He'd never expected that.

A little while later, their visit was over and Ben wished the woman the best of luck. "If there's anything you need, just give me a call," he said, giving her his card.

"Thank you, Mr Fitzgerald. I appreciate you saying that," she replied and tucked the card inside her bra.

The guard opened the door and secured the handcuffs back around Jiao's wrists. Within moments, she'd disappeared down the same corridor she'd come. Ben gathered his things together and tossed the birthday card back in his briefcase. It landed facedown. He looked at the return address and smiled.

Sender: Evelyn Fitzgerald
St Patrick's Residential Aged Care
3 Wilson Ave,
Lane Cove, New South Wales 2066

The words had been written in his grandmother's neat and elegant script and reinforced that she now thought of the place as home. It was good. He was glad. As he'd told Jiao, it made it easier knowing his grandmother was happy to be there.

He was halfway across the prison parking lot when it hit him. Jiao Zheng had commented on his grandmother's nursing home. She said it was a nice place. *How did she know where his grandmother was living?* She must have been able to read the return address...

No, that couldn't be right. The nurse couldn't read. She couldn't read the label on a medicine bottle or a medication chart. If that were true, there was no way she would have been able to decipher his grandmother's fancy script. He must have made some mistake.

Maybe he'd mentioned St Patrick's at some stage during their conversation? He replayed it in his head... No, he was sure he hadn't said anything about where he'd put her, just that she'd been settled into a home.

His heart pounded. Thoughts raced through his head, but he refused to dwell on them. It couldn't be... It wasn't possible... And yet, it was the only thing that made sense. Jiao Zheng *could* read. She hadn't made a mistake based on her lack of English reading skills at all. Were her actions purely negligent, or had the lethal dose of hydrogen peroxide been intentional?

Fuck! Had she *meant* to murder Dulcie Eveleigh? The idea was almost too much to comprehend. He dug out his phone and punched in Blake's number at the same time he reversed his direction and headed back into the jail.

Blake's phone went through to voicemail and Ben left a short message for him to call. The security guard started in surprise when he saw him again.

"Back so soon? You must enjoy it here," the man joked.

Ben didn't so much as crack a smile. He stared

at the guard, his thoughts still in turmoil. "I need to see Jiao Zheng again. Can you have her brought back in?"

"I'll have to phone down to her cell block. She's only just been returned. The guards aren't going to like having to bring her back up here again so soon."

"I'm sorry. I... I forgot to tell her something," Ben said, forcing himself to remain calm. It wouldn't do for the guard to realize how hard Ben was fighting to hold on to his anger.

With a shrug, the guard turned away and Ben saw him pick up a phone. A short while later, the man returned.

"It's your lucky day, Counselor. She's on her way back up."

"Thank you." Ben breathed deeply and prepared himself. He'd have to be careful...

Hurriedly divesting himself of his jacket and shoes and briefcase and setting them in a container to be scanned, he once again walked through the jail's security screening and waited on the other side.

This time, Jiao appeared with a guard only minutes after he entered the interview room and he wondered if she'd even made it all the way back to her cell. Chafing silently at the bit, he waited while the guard released her handcuffs and then left the room. Ben stood and closed the door and just like that, his fury returned.

"You played us all so well, didn't you?" he snarled.

Jiao blinked in surprise and sat back in her

chair. "Played you? I don't know what you mean."

Ben strode over to where the woman sat and put his hands flat on the table. He leaned toward her menacingly.

"Oh, yes you do. You told Blake and me and anyone else who would listen that your English skills were so poor that you couldn't even properly decipher the words on a medicine bottle. You poured hydrogen peroxide down that poor woman's throat and made us all believe you thought it was cough medicine. But you were playing us all for fools and we fell for it without a murmur. You knew exactly what you were doing! Didn't you?"

The last words were shouted and Jiao jumped in her seat. The color left her face. She stared down at her hands.

"I don't know what you are—"

"Don't lie to me!" Ben shouted, slamming his hand against the Formica. "You know exactly what I'm talking about! It was all an act, all a way to get away with murder and guess what? It worked! Well, almost. You managed to convince Blake to get the charges reduced to manslaughter and even then he was beating himself up about the length of your sentence. He's one of the best criminal lawyers in this town and he was feeling bad that you were given five years."

Ben shook his head in disgust. "Five years! Ha! What a joke. You must laugh at us all every night—how we fell for your ruse; how we believed your sad story that you were a victim of a tertiary education system that only had its eye on the pot of gold. Even now, you're still blaming your employer, when all the time you knew *you* were the only one at fault." She shifted uncomfortably in her chair and lost eye contact.

"How *could* you?" he cried, his breath coming fast.

Jiao Zheng regarded him calmly. "Have you ever been to China, Mr Fitzgerald?"

Ben stared at her and shook his head. "No."

"I didn't think so. There are many millions of people in China living below the poverty line. Most live on less than one dollar a day. Hundreds of thousands don't have electricity or other basic services. That number includes members of my family. When I was offered the opportunity to earn a college degree in Australia, I jumped at the chance. It took many months and much hardship, but finally, my family arranged the money.

"I applied and got accepted. I graduated and got a job. My wages have been supporting thirty-five of my closest relatives living in China. Their lives have never been better."

Some of the tension went out of Ben. He stood upright and moved away. With his hands on his hips, he paced the small confines of the interview room, still trying to get his head around everything.

"I still don't understand," he said. "Why would you murder Dulcie Eveleigh?"

Jiao's lips twisted up into a bitter smile. "I loved my new life in Australia. I loved my job. But I missed my family. I wanted them to come out here, to live with me. At least, my parents. They were making preparations. They'd submitted applications through the immigration department. Everything was looking good and then they found out about my mother's illness."

"What was wrong with your mother?" Ben asked.

"She had tuberculosis. It was only in the early stages, but they rejected her visa application on that basis. They said she was too ill to come to Australia; that once she was here, they'd be obligated to treat her. She'd be a burden on their health system. They don't look kindly upon people who will become a drain on the public purse."

Ben frowned and once again struggled to make the connection. "What did any of that have to do with Dulcie Eveleigh?"

Jiao stared at him. "My mother died, still trying desperately to come to Australia. Heartbroken, my father's decided to stay where he is. Mrs Eveleigh was the mother of the minister for immigration. I feel he was responsible for the loss of my mother. I never got to see her again. He took my mother; I took his. It's really very simple."

Her statement was followed by a smile so sweet and innocent, Ben stared at her aghast. The woman was crazy. Totally off her rocker. And yet, she looked so normal, so sane.

He shivered.

"The only thing that infuriates me now is that you've succeeded with your case and the bastard immigration minister will benefit financially from my actions. And a multimillion-dollar settlement, no less! The very thought makes my head feel like it might explode." She glanced down at her hands where they were clenched together in her lap. "Tell me, I'm curious," she added. "How did you guess?"

Ben found his voice. "The birthday card. You read my grandmother's address."

Jiao nodded. "Ah, the envelope. It was careless of me. Still, it doesn't matter. My case is closed. I'll do my time and that will be the end of it."

Anger at her casual attitude poured through Ben's veins. The fact that she was right made it even worse. She'd pleaded guilty to manslaughter and had been sentenced to five years. With good behavior, she could be out in half that time.

Anger and disgust flooded through him. *How could they have been so blind?* First Blake and then him. No one had seen through her ruse or even guessed at the motivation behind it. She'd given the perfect explanation and she knew very well there were other nurses in that position she'd presented, genuinely struggling to read English, who could verify her claim. And they had.

Jiao had led them straight to him and one by one, they'd backed up her assertion: Nurses were being graduated from Richmond University when they couldn't read properly. They were a danger to the patients under their care. It was only a matter of time...

He'd fallen for it hook, line and sinker and all the time, Zheng had successfully carried out her plot for revenge, had been laughing at them. And then another thought occurred to him and it filled him with a feral kind of satisfaction. He narrowed his eyes at the woman who sat across from him.

"You think you're so clever, don't you? You've managed to get away with murder. What you don't know is that this doesn't end with the completion of your sentence."

Jiao stared at him and frowned. "What do you mean?"

"I mean, that as soon as your time here is up, you'll be deported back to China. To your poverty-stricken homeland. And I'll make sure you don't slip under their radar. You can't be tried again, but our government doesn't want to harbor criminals, especially those who don't belong here. You'll go back to your life of poverty and your family will continue to struggle—all because of some petty need for revenge. It looks like the immigration minister will have the last laugh."

Twin spots of fury colored the nurse's cheeks. Her eyes blazed with anger. She opened her mouth to speak, but Ben was through listening. Striding over to the door, he tore it open and brushed past the guard on his way out.

"She's all yours," he tossed over his shoulder and stormed away without another word.

With his shoulders weighed down in defeat, he climbed into his car and headed away from the jail. Blake still hadn't returned the call and now that Ben knew everything, the thought of telling his colleague what had been disclosed by their client filled him with dread. Blake would blame himself for not seeing through the ruse and there would be nothing Ben could say to convince him otherwise. It was going to be a difficult conversation and one he looked forward to like a hole in the head.

He glanced at his watch and noted the time. He was going to be late for his meeting with Abby and her parents. He wanted to tell her about his meeting with Jiao and the shocking discovery that Nurse Jiao Zheng could read English just fine and had intentionally administered the lethal dose, but most of all, he needed to hear her voice. To reassure himself that there was still some goodness in the world. To shake off the feeling that he'd just come up close and personal with evil.

Tugging out his phone, he dialed her number.

CHAPTER 22

With a bright yellow highlighter in one hand, Abby read through the transcript of the interview fifteen-year-old Luke Forrest had given to the police when he was arrested and ultimately charged with malicious damage. His first court appearance was in the morning and he was currently outside her office, waiting to see her. As soon as her meeting with the child was over, she planned to head out to meet her parents.

The thought kicked her heart rate into overdrive and nerves swarmed in a flurry in her stomach. She forced herself to take a deep breath and calm down. She was the one who'd instigated this. She needed to see it through to the end. She never had to see her parents again after this, if that's what she wanted. She'd reserve that decision for later.

Ben had called her outside the jail and filled her in on his visit with Jiao Zheng. She still couldn't believe the woman had intentionally killed her patient and had then lied about not being able to read English in an attempt to cover it up. It never failed to astound her, the depths some people would go to to seek revenge.

And it had worked. No one had been the wiser. It was truly a travesty of justice. Abby didn't blame Ben. How could he have known? He hadn't even represented Zheng during the criminal matter. Still, there was nothing anybody could do about it now. She could only hope word would somehow leak out around the jail and Zheng's time in prison was anything but comfortable.

With a sigh, Abby pulled the record of interview toward her and as quickly as she could, took in the details of the child's offense and highlighted the important parts. The boy had been at home with his mother and step-father. An argument had developed. Luke had gone outside with a baseball bat and had destroyed his step-father's car. The police were called. Charges were laid. The boy was currently on bail. It was an all-too-familiar story and one that got to her every single time. With a soft sigh, she pushed away from her desk and went out to meet him.

He was smaller than the average fifteen-year-old and looked scrawny and underfed. His blond hair was limp and greasy and he had terrible acne on his cheeks. Without hesitation, she went up to him and stuck out her hand.

"Hi, I'm Abby. You must be Luke."

The boy barely acknowledged her. His eyes cut in her direction and then returned to stare at the floor. The middle-aged woman beside him sighed. Abby turned to her.

"Hi, I'm Abby Brown. I'm the lawyer looking after Luke's case. Are you his guardian?"

"No, I'm his aunt. He's spent the last week, since it happened, with me. I'm Megan Morris," the woman added and Abby shook her hand.

"Nice to meet you, Megan, and thank you for bringing Luke in. I don't always get to meet with my young clients and their family members before their court appearance. This is a real treat."

Her comment didn't appear to register with the boy and the woman barely nodded, and then looked away. Abby ushered them both into her office. Luke immediately strode over to the window and stared out at the street far below. Abby wondered what he was thinking. She cleared her throat to get his attention.

"Luke, if you wouldn't mind taking a seat over here. I'll get your aunt to sit beside you. That way, we can talk better about what happened and what's going to happen tomorrow. All right?"

The boy glanced at her and offered a non-committal shrug, but sauntered over to her desk and threw himself down in one of the chairs that were reserved for clients. Megan followed suit. Abby regained her seat behind her desk and dragged the record of interview toward her.

"Okay, so the police facts state that you got into an argument with your step-father. Is that right?"

The boy stared at his feet. "Yeah."

"What were you arguing about?" Abby asked.

"What does it matter? We argue all the time," came the surly response.

Abby held onto her patience. She was used to belligerent kids. "It matters. It goes to your state of mind when the offense occurred—when you took a baseball bat to your father's—"

"He's not my father!" Luke's eyes blazed into hers.

"I'm sorry, your step-father's car," Abby corrected. She picked up the statement and scanned it. "I have a copy of the record of interview you gave to the police." She showed it to him. "Is that your signature down the bottom?"

The boy gave the document a cursory glance. "Yeah."

"You told the police you smashed your step-father's car with a baseball bat. Is that correct?"

"Yeah. I smashed it as hard as I could and I'm not one bit sorry!" The angry words burst from Luke's mouth. Abby didn't react.

"Okay, so you admit to causing the damage. What I need to know is why. There's no question we'll have to plead guilty, but we can reduce the sentence if we offer mitigating circumstances to the judge."

The boy's eyes narrowed on hers in suspicion. "What does that mean?"

"It means that if we provide the judge with an explanation—an excuse, if you like—as to why you behaved the way you did, it might help keep you out of jail."

His aunt sat forward in alarm, a look of consternation on her face. "Surely he won't go to jail for this?"

Abby's gaze remained steady on Luke's aunt. "It depends. Luke caused a lot of damage. There isn't a single panel that wasn't destroyed. The car will likely be written off. It was a sixty-thousand-dollar motor vehicle. That puts the offense in a more serious category. Coupled with Luke's confession to the police and his age—the court is entitled to assume Luke knew that what he was doing was wrong... If so, we're in a spot of trouble." She turned her attention back to her client. "So, Luke, I'd like you to tell me what happened and how you came to take a baseball bat to that car."

The boy stared at the floor in silence.

"Come on, Lukey. You need to tell the lawyer. She can't help you if you don't talk to her."

He glanced briefly at his aunt and then stared at the carpet once more. Finally, he shook his head. "It was nothing. A stupid argument over nothing. I did it because I felt like it."

Abby stared at her client, disappointed. There was no way the argument had been about nothing. Nobody took a baseball bat to someone else's vehicle so badly that it had to be written off, over nothing. But if he wasn't going to tell her the real reason, there wasn't much she could do. She glanced at Megan and then back at Luke and then back at Megan again.

Where Luke was all blond with fair skin and freckles, Megan had the dark, exotic look of a Pacific Islander. Abby wondered which side of the family she was from. She turned to Luke's aunt.

"Megan, how are you related to Luke?"

"I already told you. I'm his aunt," the woman replied.

"Yes, but are you related to his mom or his dad?"

"His step-dad, actually. I'm Jackson's sister."

"Jackson's your step-father, is he, Luke?" Abby asked, looking at the boy. He gave her the slightest of nods.

Abby thought for a moment. It was standard practice to have a parent or guardian in the room during an interview with a minor, but she wondered if the presence of Luke's aunt was holding him back from telling her the truth. She decided to find out.

"Luke, would it be all right if your aunt waited outside for a moment?"

He glanced up at her and then back to the floor, but in those few seconds, she glimpsed a flash of surprise in his eyes.

Abby turned to Megan. "Would you mind giving Luke and I a few moments?"

Megan looked at her nephew. "Do you want me to leave the room, Lukey?"

Luke remained silent. Abby watched his thin shoulders rise and fall on a heavy sigh. Finally, he nodded.

His aunt raised her eyebrows in surprise, but got to her feet. "All right, I'll leave you to it." She patted Luke on the shoulder. "I'll be right outside."

The boy watched her go and then returned his gaze to the floor. Abby tried again. "I don't believe that argument was about nothing, Luke," she said quietly. "You said it yourself: You argue with Jackson all the time. But you don't go and destroy his property every time you have an argument, do you?"

Luke slowly shook his head. "No."

"Then what was it about this particular argument that set you off like that?"

She waited what seemed like an eternity and tried not to look at her watch. This appointment was going on longer than she'd guessed. If Luke didn't start talking, she'd be late for her meeting with her parents. Once again, her belly took a nosedive at the thought. She forced her mind elsewhere.

"I want you to tell me the truth, Luke. I can't help you if I don't know."

"Nobody can help me." The words were barely a whisper, but they clutched at Abby's heart.

"What do you mean?"

"I mean, that it doesn't matter what I say. Nobody can make it go away."

"Make what go away?" she asked gently.

"The photos! The videos! All that other sick stuff!"

Abby stilled. At the same time, her heart accelerated. She didn't like the sound of this. "What photos, Luke?"

"The ones Jackson took of me when I was younger. He sells them now online. I thought it was fun at first. He used to tell me to pose for him, show him my muscles. First he wanted me to take my shirt off and then it was my pants. Pretty soon, he was taking photos of me naked and then he started taking videos."

She stared at the young boy and was filled with

shock. Straight on the heels of that was white hot anger. She could barely hear what he was saying over the noise in her head.

"I was only nine or ten when he started taking pictures. I didn't think anything of it. He'd give me ten bucks to buy lollies. The only thing I had to do was keep quiet. That was easy to do. There was no one to tell. Only my mom and why would she want to know? It was only as I got older that I worked out what was going on. I went to him and asked for more money. I figured he must be getting paid a lot for shit like that. You hear it all over the news. It's big business."

Abby did her best to keep her expression from revealing the turmoil she felt inside. She wanted to call the police and have them go around and arrest the step-father immediately. Men like him made her sick. It brought back the awful nightmares of her past and though she hadn't brought criminal charges against her father, she was all for other victims making their perpetrators pay.

At the time she'd been molested, she'd been young and vulnerable and helpless. She had no voice and no confidence anyone would believe her. Now she was an adult and it was still possible to go down that path, but she didn't want to. She'd closed that door behind her, buried those memories forever. She didn't want to trawl through them all over again. No, as soon as she saw her father and let him know she'd forgiven him for what he'd done, it would be over between them. She'd have the closure she needed and could put it behind her, once and for all.

Couldn't she? What if it didn't work out like that? What then? She pushed that thought away, unwilling to think about it.

"Is that what the two of you were arguing about?" she asked quietly.

"Yes. I wanted five thousand dollars. He laughed in my face. I told him I was going to report him to the police and it would cost him a lot more than five thousand bucks to get out of kiddie fiddler charges. That's when he threatened to kill me if I ever opened my mouth. I believed him. I stormed off, so pissed. He was going to win. That's when I spied the baseball bat in my room." He shrugged. "You know what happened after that."

It was all Abby could do not to rant and rave and scream at the step-father she'd never met. But that wouldn't help the boy in front of her. No, first she needed to assure him she believed him and she was going to see that the judge heard the truth. Once his criminal matter had been dispensed with, she'd call a cop friend of hers and get him to pay a visit to Luke's step-father. She was confident the police would do their job and the man would be arrested. Luke would receive justice for the crimes committed against him, whether he saw it that way now, or not.

Sitting forward, she clasped her hands in front of her in an effort to stop clenching them into fists. She gave the boy a smile of reassurance. "Okay, Luke. Here's what we're going to do."

In a straightforward manner, she set out her

plan of action, including having his step-father charged. The boy listened, a solemn expression on his face. At one stage, he became alarmed at the thought of how his mother might react.

"What if she doesn't believe me? What if she thinks I made the whole thing up?"

Abby tried to breathe through the lump of dread that blocked her airway. She knew exactly how Luke felt. With a deep breath, she forced herself to answer and reassured him that wouldn't happen. Besides, there were the photos, the videos. He had proof.

At last, the boy appeared convinced and even gave Abby a shaky smile.

"Thanks for believing me, Abby," he said and tears welled in his eyes.

Abby blinked back tears of her own and came around and gave him a quick hug. "Is it all right if I bring your aunt back in?" she asked. "I think she needs to know."

Luke nodded and with a quiet sigh of relief, Abby went to fetch her.

It was going on for three when Abby pulled into the parking lot reserved for visitors to Penrith Lakes and climbed out of her car. The afternoon was pleasantly warm, although a cool breeze drifted up from the water. Abby shivered, but she couldn't tell if it was because of her reasons for being there, or the temperature.

There were a handful of other cars in the lot, but none of them were Ben's. When he'd called her earlier to tell her about Jiao Zheng, he'd warned her he'd be late. She pulled out her phone to call him and ask him how far away he was and had barely dialed his number when she spied the red Ferrari coming around the corner. She ended the call and waited for him.

"Hi," she said as he climbed out of the car.

He came over and kissed her. "Hi, yourself." He looked around the parking lot. "Are they here, yet?"

"I don't know. I'm not sure what kind of vehicle they're driving. I'm supposed to meet them over there." She pointed in the direction of the white water rafting area. A few people could be seen in the vicinity, but from this distance, it was hard to tell who they were. A couple of rowers were canoeing through the water, their paddles flailing.

"Are you okay with that?" she asked.

He grimaced, but offered her a nod. "Just don't get too close to the water, all right?"

"You don't have to remind me," she said and gave him a wry smile. "I'm the one who doesn't know how to swim."

"I guess there's only one way to know if they're over there," Ben said and then looked at her, his brow creased in concern. "Are you sure you want to do this?"

A wave of nervousness and dread washed through her and all of a sudden, she felt sick. "No, I'm not sure, but I have to do this. I'll never get any peace until I do."

She reached out and squeezed his arm, grateful for his presence. "Thank you for coming with me. I couldn't have done this without you."

Ben pulled her in close against him and pressed a kiss against her hair. "That's nonsense and you know it," he said without heat. "You're the strongest, bravest woman I know. But if it makes you feel any better, then I'm glad I'm here. Do you want me to come with you while you speak with them?"

She looked at him and tried not to sound too desperate. "Would you? I know how much you hate the water."

He hugged her again. "It's okay. For you, I'll cope."

Going over to his Ferrari, he reached inside and pulled out a jacket. He slipped it on and then turned back to her. "Are you ready?"

Abby closed her eyes and drew in a deep fortifying breath. She opened her eyes and stared at Ben with determination. "Yes."

Hand in hand, they strode across the parking lot, over thick soft green grass and eventually found the paved path that led to the white water rafting area. The water was loud beside them, roaring and rushing over the manmade rocks and boulders.

As they drew closer, Abby noticed an elderly couple standing off to one side, not far from the water's edge. The woman was small and shriveled. The man sat in a wheelchair. They turned toward her and Ben as they approached them and Abby's heart skipped a beat.

Her parents.

They'd both aged considerably since she'd last seen them, with snowy white hair and a myriad of wrinkles replacing what had been there before, but their features were familiar and that reassured Abby it was indeed her parents who were now mere feet away.

Her mother nodded in greeting, but made no move to come closer. Though her face showed outward signs of aging, her figure remained as taut and shapely as ever. Beryl Brown had always been petite, with a tiny face to complement her tiny frame. Abby had taken after her father. Even at sixteen, she'd been as tall as him. Not that it was possible to see that now. Wallace Brown was in a wheelchair.

The man that had haunted her nightmares stared at her balefully from his seat. His jowls were loose and fleshy and his hard eyes were beady and red. He'd put on more than fifty pounds since she'd last seen him and now looked bloated and sick. She remembered Jeff telling her their father had bowel cancer, with only weeks to live.

Hmph! She scoffed silently in her head. He didn't look like he was dying. She didn't care if he was. She'd come there to make her peace, to find closure, to slam the door shut on that part of her life, once and for all.

"Hello, Dad," she said and stared him in the eye.

Her mother stepped forward, a sneer marring the still-attractive features of her face. "Why now, Abigail? Why now, after all these years?"

Abby was taken aback. Whatever she'd expected from her parents at this reunion, it hadn't been that. She should have known her mother would still feel bitter. As far as Beryl Brown was concerned, Abby was a recalcitrant teenager who deserved everything she got. Beryl had been well rid of the girl.

Ben squeezed her hand and Abby was grateful for the silent show of support. She'd have her say and get out of here before she regretted coming in the first place. She drew in a surreptitious breath and braced herself for what was to come.

"I came to see you, Dad, to tell you I've forgiven you for what you did."

The lump in the chair came alive. "Ha! That's rich! You've forgiven *me*? I'm the one who put up with you all those years. You were a little slut. You always thought you were better than us. You were always looking down your nose, too good for your own family. Well, I showed you, didn't I? You have no one else to blame but yourself. It was your fault it happened. You were always parading yourself around half-naked. What was a man to do?"

Ben tensed beside her. She felt it in every line of his taut body. He squeezed her hand so tightly it hurt, but the pain in her fingers was nothing to the agony that tore through her heart.

She stared at her father in horror and took a couple of steps back. He was red in the face, puffed up with self-righteousness. Her mother merely smirked.

"No! No! No!" she cried, gasping for breath, trying her best to get her father's awful words out of her head. She took another few steps back.

Ben let go of her hand and stepped forward, his expression one of cold fury. "Enough!" he shouted. "The two of you make me sick. I don't care that you gave birth to her, you're not fit to carry her name on your lips. Stay the hell away from her or I'll—"

"You'll what?" her father goaded from the security of his chair. "What are you going to do? Take on an old man in his wheelchair?" He smirked at Ben. "I think not."

"Who are you, anyway?" her mother demanded, joining in the fray.

"Can't you see, Beryl?" her father crowed. "They're fucking each other. It's written all over their faces."

"No! Dad! *Please!*" Abby gasped and fresh horror flooded through her. She looked at Ben. His face had gone white. She needed to get them out of there before he did something stupid. She wouldn't blame him if he hit her father, but it wouldn't end well for Ben. Besides, she refused to give her father the satisfaction of knowing he'd gotten to the man she loved.

"Come on, Ben, let's get out of here." Without waiting for his reply, she spun around on her heel.

The sound of her father's motorized wheelchair reached her seconds before he did. "Come back here, you little slut! I haven't finished talking to you!" he screamed.

She stopped and turned back toward him, but he kept coming at her. She backed up and tried to get out of his way, but still, he came closer.

"Dad! What are you doing?" She put her hands out in front of her. "Stop! I'm going to fall—"

Her three-inch sandal caught in the soft grass. A moment later, she toppled over as she lost her balance. Crying out, her ankle twisted and then she was falling, falling, falling into the foaming water down below.

"*Help!*" she cried just seconds before she hit the water. It was icy cold and rushed straight over her head. She gulped and sputtered and tried to keep her head above the water. She'd fallen into the white-water rapids and the current was swift.

Within moments, she was carried away downstream and the nightmares from her near-drowning all those years ago bombarded her. She gasped and struggled and fought to breathe. Her chest grew tight with fear. Ben and her parents were still on the shore. Ben was racing along the riverbank shouting at her to stay calm. He was frantic. She tried to lift her arm in an awkward attempt to swim, but her form-fitting jacket had tightened around her in the water and she could barely move a limb.

The water rushed once again over her head and she swallowed what felt like half the lake. Choking and spluttering, she gasped for breath. She needed to try and conserve some of her energy. There was no way she was making it out of the rapids otherwise. The current was just too strong. Her best bet was to try and keep her head above water and let the water take her along. Eventually, she'd come to the end of it and someone would be able to help her out.

With that thought in mind, she tried to manoeuver herself so that she was lying on her back. With her narrow skirt hampering her movements, it was easier said than done. Coupled with that was the rushing water, dunking her more times than she could count. Choking from yet another lungful, she had flashbacks to the swimming pool and began to wonder if she'd survive.

Just then, she heard a shout from the shoreline and looked up in time to see Ben. He was close, still running beside her. She tried once again to reach out to him, flailing with increasing panic. A wave washed over her head, drowning her temporarily. She gasped. A stab of pain caught her in the side—a stitch had made itself known. Her arms felt heavier, her breathing more labored. She was suddenly overcome with a terrible dread. *What if she didn't make it to the end? What if she drowned before she got there? She'd never see Ben again. Ben...*

CHAPTER 23

en saw Abby disappear under the foam-covered water and his heart stopped dead. One minute she'd been standing beside him, being subjected to the most awful things he'd ever heard and the next, her father was charging toward her and she was toppling into the water. Ben had stood in stunned silence for a couple of seconds, frozen in shock until the enormity of what had happened hit him up the side of the head.

Abby had fallen into the water! She was being carried away and she couldn't swim! He could see her bobbing up and down like a cork in stormy seas. He'd see her face for a moment and then she'd be gone again, only to reappear further downstream. Ignoring her parents, he'd taken off at a run. He ran until he was out of breath and still she was being swept along. He needed to get ahead of her and somehow slow her down.

Spying a man on a bicycle, he shouted for him

to hand it over and quickly climbed on board. Peddling as fast as his legs would go, he gradually drew in front of Abby as she was swept along by the current. Once he was far enough ahead, he tossed the bike down and pulled off his jacket. His shirt and boots quickly followed. He stripped right down to his boxers. Knowing what he was about to do sent icy dread shivering down his spine, yet he would do it.

He stared at the tumultuous water and could only see his father. "Ben! It's all right! I've got you!" The words reverberated in his head.

Knowing it was now or never and that he didn't have a choice, he dove into the cold water and began to swim. The current was strong—it wasn't any wonder Abby was being tossed about—but Ben was fit and strong, too, and he had adrenaline and a fierce love on his side. It had taken him fifteen years to realize Abby was the love of his life. He wasn't about to let her drown now.

"Ben!"

He heard her scream and turned his head to peer over the foaming white water. She was only yards away. Swimming with strong, sure strokes, he tried desperately to cut her off. Reaching out he snagged a piece of her jacket and relief poured through him, but the jacket tore in half and she was once again out of his reach.

"Abby! Hold on!" *Please, honey, hold on.* The words echoed around and around in his head as he struck out once again. This time, with better luck.

His hand came in contact with her leg and he held on for dear life. Quickly, he took hold of her shoulder and then lifted her head. She gasped and choked, but then relaxed against him and he was able to turn her onto her back. Holding her with his fingers on her chin, he towed her to safety.

When he felt the bottom of the lake beneath his feet he'd never been so grateful to reach land. Taking Abby in his arms, he carried her from the water and set her gently on the grass. She was still coughing and spluttering and at one point, she rolled over and vomited, but she was alive and she was going to be fine. He fell to his knees in gratitude and thanked God for having spared her. And him.

"Th-thank you for saving me," she managed through chattering teeth.

He hurried over and helped remove her soaking jacket. She refused to let him remove her skirt. A crowd of onlookers had gathered and some had their phones out, no doubt trying to capture the moment to upload to their social media sites.

"W-where are my parents?" she asked, her voice dull.

"I don't know," he replied. "I left them way back there."

He looked in the direction from which he'd come, but could no longer see any sign of Beryl or Wallace. He couldn't imagine they'd left without finding out if Abby were all right, but perhaps they had.

Regardless, she was better off without them.

She had him and she had Jeff. It would have to be enough.

Her gaze hardened and he wondered if she were in pain. "Are you okay, honey?" he asked.

"Yes. I'm fine. I've decided to press charges against my father."

Ben reeled back in shock. After all she'd just been through, it was the last thing he expected to hear. Besides, they'd talked about this already. She'd told him she didn't want to dredge it all up again. This meeting was supposed to be part of her closure, an end to the nightmares of her past.

"Are you... Are you sure?" he asked.

The hard expression in her eyes didn't lessen. If anything, she looked more determined. "Yes. I'm sure."

"Look, you know I'll support you in whatever you want to do, but... What made you change your mind?"

"It wasn't just what happened back there, although that reinforced what I've always known. The thing is, I had a client today. A fifteen-year-old boy. His step-father had been taking photos of him since he was a little kid. There were videos, too. The sicko was selling them on the black-market, no doubt to pedophiles willing to pay a good price."

She shook her head in disgust and he understood how she felt. His guts roiled with anger at the thought.

"Do you know what the worst part of it all was?" she asked, her voice barely above a whisper.

Ben shook his head. "Tell me."

"The reason that poor kid was in my office was

because he'd been charged with malicious damage. He'd argued with his step-father over the payment he should get. After all, they were pictures of him. It was only fair he get a cut."

She looked up at Ben and her eyes burned with a ferocity he'd never seen. "The only reason that bastard got caught was because his step-son took a baseball bat to his car," she hissed and then a sob caught in her throat. "He has to pay, Ben! That bastard has to pay!"

Ben wasn't sure if she was still referring to her client's step-father or if it was Wallace in her sights. As if the enormity of the past few hours had just hit her, her eyes filled with tears. She cried out and collapsed in a heap on the ground.

Ben leaped to her side and cradled her against him, soothing her with quiet murmurs against her hair. The pair of them were still sopping wet, but neither of them seemed to care. He held her tightly and let her cry, knowing her response was residual shock as well as anger. Eventually, her sobs subsided to the occasional sniffle and he set her gently away.

"I'd offer you a handkerchief, but mine's a soaking mess," he said and smiled.

She smiled back at him, a watery, hesitant smile, but a smile just the same. His heart lightened. She would be fine. They were going to be fine.

Now that the drama was over, he had time to think about what he'd done. He'd gone into the water! And not just any water—he'd dived into a raging torrent! He still couldn't believe it. He hadn't been in the water since the night of the accident. He was convinced he'd never go into the water again. It had been tough enough to endure the hot tub. He'd only done it because Abby had been there, too. And yet, now he'd swum in a river full of rushing water and had managed to survive to tell the tale.

He stared at Abby where she lay on the grass looking wet and bedraggled and pale. She'd turned his life upside down, but every minute of it had been worth it. She'd helped him through his most difficult times and he'd helped her through hers. They were meant to be. They were soulmates. They would be until the end of time.

Epilogue

Three months later

The day couldn't be more amazing. The beautiful spring afternoon on one of Sydney's iconic beaches was the perfect spot for a wedding, even if Ben said so himself. When Abby had first suggested it, he'd been slightly taken aback, but then he remembered he wasn't afraid of the water anymore and if she wanted a beach wedding, she'd have it. He'd given the idea his wholehearted support. Now the day had finally arrived and he couldn't wait to see his bride. Fiddling with the cuffs of his white shirt, he checked his watch.

"Don't tell me you're nervous?" his best man joked.

Ben turned to Jeff and laughed. "Nervous? Why would I be nervous? I've waited for this day my whole life."

Jeff smiled back at him, obviously pleased with his response. And so he should be. Ben was a respected lawyer with a good job and even better prospects. Along with his friend Dimitri Gianopoulos, he'd just been named junior partner. Besides that, he loved Jeff's sister more than he ever thought possible. He'd love her until he died.

And then she was there, coming toward him, barefoot in the sand. Her long white veil streamed out behind her, blowing gently in the breeze. She reached his side and smiled at him and his breath caught in his throat. She glowed with happiness. She emanated love. She was the most beautiful woman he'd ever seen and best of all, she was his.

They said their vows before a small crowd of family and friends. Dani and Jett, Dimitri and Cornelius, Blake Harton and a few other colleagues from work. His father was there, of course and the sight of him filled Ben with conflicting emotions. They had a long way to go, but they were slowly mending their fences. He was sure one day they'd be good friends.

Seated beside his father was his beloved grandmother, Evie, who'd been given a day pass from her facility. They had reconciled too. Ben gave her a big smile. She smiled back at him and then turned to the woman who sat on her other side and said something. Ben's gaze wandered to his grandmother's companion and he frowned. The woman was of Asian appearance and looked like she was in her early twenties. Her short dark hair looked like a cap. She was dressed in a nurse's uniform.

"Do you know that woman sitting over there next to Grandma?" he asked Abby quietly.

She turned to look in the direction he indicated

and nodded. "Yes. She introduced herself as Chen Wu. She's a nurse from the aged care facility. They were a little concerned your grandma might become unruly. Apparently, her memory's been getting worse. She's even shouted at the staff a few times."

"Really? Why didn't they say anything?"

Abby shrugged. "You've had a lot on your plate lately, darling. What with that class action against three of Sydney's universities and helping me draft an affidavit in support of the charges against my father. On top of that, we've been busy with the preparations for the wedding..."

Ben heaved a sad sigh and drew his new wife into his arms. His grandmother's illness was progressing and the reality of that was difficult to accept. Still, this was his wedding day. He refused to let anything dampen their special celebration. With a determined effort, he pushed his uneasy thoughts back to the edge of his consciousness and asked his bride for a dance.

It was going on for two in the morning and Chen Wu was tired. She still had a medication round to get through before she could return to the comfort of the daybed and the late night TV shows. Digging in her uniform pocket for her flashlight, she finally located it and made her way into the rooms. One patient after another was given their tablets.

She came into the room housing Evie Fitzgerald. The old woman was snoring gently in her sleep.

"Evie, it's Nurse Wu. I have your tablets. You need to wake up."

She shone the light at the woman's face and then gave her a bit of a shove. Finally, the old woman stirred.

"What is it, Nurse?"

"I have your tablets."

"What tablets? I don't take any tablets."

The nurse sighed with impatience. She was way too tired to put up with this. "You need to take your tablets," she said sharply. "Now open your mouth. I don't want this to take all night."

"I told you, I don't take any tablets," the old woman said again, her jaw thrust out at an obstinate angle.

"And I told you, you do! Now open up before I have to force them down your throat!"

Some of the bravado went out of the old woman at the nurse's tone, and she shrank back against the bed. "I don't want any tablets," she said in a small voice.

Thoroughly sick of the confrontation and impatient to get back to her TV show, the nurse shot a cursory look at the medication chart and then put the tablets in Evie's hand. She gave her a glass of water and watched while the woman swallowed them.

"There! That wasn't too bad, was it?" she snapped. And with that, the nurse walked away.

NOTE TO READERS

I do hope you have enjoyed reading Ben and Abby's story. If you've enjoyed this book, please feel free to leave a review for An Accidental Murderer at Goodreads and your favorite digital retailer. Every review is very much appreciated.

Receive a free book when you sign up for my newsletter if you would like to receive news on upcoming stories, release dates, book launches and other snippets. I love to receive feedback from my readers. Please feel free to contact me at chris@christaylorauthor.com.au

At the Hand of her Father is the next book in The Sydney Legal Series.

Turn the page for a sneak peek:

PROLOGUE

The faintest sliver of pale moonlight leaked in through a gap in the curtain and gilded Lacey Johnson's cheek in gold. Ian Johnson stared down at his young daughter and his heart clenched with pain. She was so small, so perfect, so beautiful, asleep and unaware of the danger that lurked all around her. At three years of age, what did he expect? It wasn't as if the child had spent much time in the outside world. No, most of Lacey's short life had been spent closeted and protected by her loving parents. That was, until their love ran out.

He squeezed his eyes shut tightly against the surge of pain and pushed a fist up to his mouth in an effort to keep the agony from spilling out and waking his children. Even still, small whimpers of torture escaped him. He gazed across the room to the double bed that held his twin sons and was relieved to discover that Bailey and Darby continued to sleep soundly beside their little sister, equally oblivious to their father's dark thoughts.

A kaleidoscope of memories rushed through Ian's mind and he shook his head slowly back and forth. *How had it happened?* He couldn't even pinpoint the time. He'd vowed to love Natalie until death did they part and he'd meant every word. Little did he know their love would dwindle slowly but surely, like fine sand through an hourglass, until there was nothing left.

He'd thought they'd last forever. They'd been in love since they were kids. In the end, it had taken less than seven years. Seven years and they'd gone from being passionately in love to spitting out hate at the sight of each other. The speed of the demise of his relationship with the mother of his kids still put his head into a spin.

Lacey murmured in her sleep. Her forehead creased in a frown. One of her tiny hands curled into a fist. He stared at her and wondered what she was dreaming about. Did she have an inkling that her world had been turned upside down? Did she know what it meant for her and her brothers to come from a broken home?

Broken. That's what they were. All of them. Into a million pieces. Him, Natalie, and the kids and nobody could pick up the pieces and put them together again. Life didn't work like that.

Chapter 1

Natalie Johnson spooned the last of her cereal into her mouth and still chewing, pushed away from the kitchen table and took her bowl to the sink. Rinsing out the residual milk, she left the bowl on the dish rack to dry. She glanced at the clock on the wall above the fridge and frowned. Ian should be here by now. If he didn't hurry up, the boys would be late for school and she'd be late for work. It was just like her ex-husband to not care about things like that. Things that were important to her.

With a grimace, she picked up a stray hairbrush and ran it through her shoulder length hair. Finding a scrunchie on the counter beside a basket of fruit, she secured her hair into a loose ponytail and then continued down the hallway to the bathroom. Brushing and flossing her teeth, she peered at her reflection in the mirror and sighed at the woman who stared back at her.

It had been a rough couple of years. She'd lost

more than twenty pounds since the divorce, weight she couldn't afford to lose. Stress had a way of making her appetite disappear. Eyes that looked too big in her gaunt face stared back at her. There were dark circles beneath her eyes, evidence of another night where she'd tossed and turned and watched every hour come and go on the clock. It was always that way when the kids were at their dad's. Thanks to the judge, it happened every other weekend. At least he'd seen it her way the last time.

The Friday just gone had seen her and Ian and their legal representatives come before the family court yet again. The battle over who should have residence of their children had been a bitter one. There was no way Natalie was going to let her babies live permanently with their father. Uh, uh. No way. Never going to happen. It was the reason she kept pouring every cent she had into the coffers of her lawyer's firm. She needed all the help she could get.

And it had finally all been worthwhile. The judge had found in her favor. He'd agreed that she was the best person to have residence of their kids. She was their mother! They were babies! The twins were only five and Lacey—at three, she really was still a baby. Okay, a toddler.

Ian hadn't taken the judge's decision well. He'd screamed abuse at the man from his seat at the bar table and had then turned it on his lawyer. Nat thought the corrections officers would step in and escort him from the building, but at the last minute, Ian closed his mouth and chose to depart the building unassisted. Natalie had breathed a sigh of relief.

It was over. After two long years, the court had made final orders. She was still coming to terms with the fact that she need never step foot inside a courtroom again. Of course, it didn't mean her ex-husband was finally out of her life—he'd been given fortnightly contact with their children, after all—but brief contact while he collected or dropped them back off was something she could handle. To know her children were finally legally able to live with her on a day to day basis brought nothing but relief.

Returning to the kitchen, she glanced at the clock again and cursed. *Where was he?* Even if he arrived in the next couple of minutes, she was going to be late. She went to the front room and peered through the window. The driveway was empty. She swallowed another curse.

Dammit! Anger surged through her veins. It was at times like these that she was reminded of how rude and arrogant and aggravating her ex-husband could be. He thought only of himself. He always had.

Heading back to the kitchen, she grabbed her handbag and riffled inside it for her phone. It wasn't there. No, it had to be there. She felt around again and came up empty. With a groan of impatience, she upended the handbag onto the counter.

A couple of tubes of lipstick, a packet of tissues, a pile of bills she'd meant to pay last week in her lunchbreak. A wallet, three pens, two packets of gum, a pacifier in case Lacey lost her usual one. A spare disposable nappy and a packet of baby wipes, a Snickers that had been in there more days than she could count. It all ended up in a pile on the counter, but it was clear there was no phone.

"Shit!" she muttered and wondered where it could be.

She went back into her bedroom and checked the nightstand. It wasn't there. She walked into the bathroom, but it wasn't on the sink. Finally, she returned to the kitchen and spied it across the room, poking out from under one of the seat cushions of the couch.

The night came crashing back in on her and she remembered spending the previous evening curled up on the sofa with a glass of wine, watching old movies and trying not to think about her kids.

She'd called them earlier and had spoken to each of them, asking about their day. She'd blown them kisses down the phone and bid them a good night. She wished them all sweet dreams and assured them all she'd see them in the morning. She'd fallen asleep holding a cushion pressed tightly against her chest, tears drying on her cheeks.

Shaking her head impatiently, she pushed the sad thoughts from her mind and snatched up the phone. Dialing Ian's number, she waited for him to pick up, relieved when he did.

"Ian! Where the hell are you? It's way past the drop off time. We're going to be late!"

"For fuck's sake, Natalie! Back off, won't you! I'm

fifteen minutes past the appointed time. Big deal."

"Don't swear in front of my babies, Ian. I won't stand for it! And for your information, you're twenty-five minutes late. The boys are going to be late for school and I'm going to be late for work. You promised the last time it wouldn't happen again, Ian. You promised."

"Jesus Christ, Natalie! You're always going on about something, aren't you? You just can't help yourself! No wonder I walked out on you! I can't believe I once thought you were hot. I mean—"

"Shut up, Ian! Shut up!"

Natalie started shaking. She didn't want to fight with her ex, but somehow, they always ended up in an argument. Mostly because Ian broke the rules. The court had set strict pick up and drop off times and Ian barely paid them heed. It was the same every time it was his turn to have the kids. It drove her crazy.

"I'm on my way, Natalie, so just quit with your whining. Leave me alone!"

She saw red. "Don't put this on me! You're the one who didn't leave home on time! You know you're supposed to have them back here by eight and you know how traffic can be on a Monday morning. There's nothing new about any of this, Ian. You're doing this out of spite."

"Bullshit! I slept in, all right. The alarm didn't go off. I—"

"I don't believe you. You're just—"

"Yeah, that's right, call me a liar. Good on you, Natalie. That's what I am," Ian snarled.

She opened her mouth to retaliate in kind and

then closed it again. No doubt Ian had the phone on speaker and her babies were in the car. They might not be old enough to understand what was being said, but they sure could sense the anger. It wasn't fair on them. They didn't ask to be caught up in the middle of this. Taking a deep breath, she forced herself to calm down and then opened her mouth to speak again. Ian beat her to it.

"Look, I'll drop them off, okay? That way you won't be too late for work. I'll take the boys to school and Lacey to daycare. That's where she's going, right?"

His voice was thick with sarcasm. It took a gargantuan effort to ignore it. Ian hated knowing his daughter was in daycare when she could have been with him. The truth was, she couldn't be with him. He was a self-employed plumber. Sometimes he was called out on a job. He couldn't take a three-year-old with him, no matter how much he argued against that. It was another bugbear between them. Lacey was safer where she was. She'd go to daycare and that was that.

"What about their school bags?" she asked, changing the subject. "The boys need morning tea and lunch. I've already packed sandwiches and fruit."

"I'll give them some money. They can buy something from the cafeteria," Ian replied.

"What about Lacey?"

"I'll stop by the store. Yoghurt and museli bars are her thing right now, aren't they?"

Nat nodded. "Yes. Make sure you get those Kelloggs ones. She doesn't like the other brands.

And strawberry yoghurt. It's her favorite. And a couple of cheese sticks. And a banana. She loves bananas."

"I got it, all right. I'm her father. I think I know how to feed my own child."

Nat bit back a retort and held onto her temper with an effort. She was grateful for Ian's offer and grudgingly told him as much. With him doing the school run, she might even make it to work on time.

"Tell them I love them and that I'll see them this afternoon," she said.

"Tell them yourself. You're on speaker."

Nat had guessed as much. She smiled into the phone. "Hi Bailey! Hi Darby! Hi sweet baby girl!"

"Hi, Mommy!" came a chorus of high-pitched voices.

They sounded so happy, she couldn't help but widen her smile. They were fine. They were with their dad. For all his faults and failings, he truly loved his kids. She couldn't fault him there."

"I'll see you this afternoon, okay?" she said.

"Okay, Mommy," one of the boys replied. She couldn't tell who.

"Have a good day, babies. I love you!" she cried.

The call came to an end.

Ian hit the end button and canceled the call. It had gone on for long enough. His ex-wife already had his kids for way more days than he did and now that the judge had made a final decision that was unlikely to change for a long time. It infuriated him that someone else got to decide where and when and for how long. They were his kids as much as Natalie's. Why should she get them for most of the time? It wasn't fair. It fucking wasn't fair.

A familiar surge of rage flooded through him and he thumped the steering wheel with his fist. Pain shot up his arm, but he ignored it, in fact, he welcomed it. After all his ex-wife and the family law courts had put him through over the past couple of years, a sore arm was the least of his concerns.

At the thought of the past tumultuous years, he ground his teeth and growled low in his throat. Even after all this time, after the court had found in her favor, his bitch of an ex was busting his balls about being late. Didn't she get it? She'd won the fight! The judge had sided with her and her nancy pansty lawyer. The prick who sat so high and mighty, lording it over them on the bench, had taken Natalie's side over his. The knowledge sent a fresh wave of fury surging through him.

And now he was on his way to drop his baby girl at daycare. He'd been given two measly days with his kids and now they were going to be left in institutions to while away the day. It was bullshit. Lacey should be home with him. He could work around her; schedule call outs on another day. It only got tricky when he had to attend an emergency—like the other day when old Mrs

Flaherty's toilet pipe had bust. What a fucking mess!

Still, it didn't mean Lacey should be in daycare. He could look after her. He was a great Dad. It was bullshit the courts had seen things differently. They'd made orders that his little girl spend her days in care while her parents were at work. He was perfectly capable of looking after her. He'd argued as much in court, but the sanctimonious bastard seated on the bench ignored him. The crack of the gavel had sealed Ian's fate. The whole thing was bullshit.

Another surge of anger washed over him, flooding him with heat. His face and ears burned. It was like he was combusting from the inside out. His head pounded, the residual effects of the bottle of rum and the joints he'd smoked last night. He shouldn't have hit the bottle so hard, but the alcohol helped calm him, kept him from thinking about the court orders and the effect they would have on him and his kids.

One weekend a fortnight. That was it. Fifty-two days a year. Fifty-two fucking measly days out of three hundred and sixty-five. It was total bullshit. He ought to buy a gun and blow that judge's fucking brains out. That would show him. That would show him Ian Johnson wasn't a man to be fucked with.

The idea appealed immensely, but a few minutes later, he dismissed it. Who was he kidding? The gun laws in Australia prevented purchases like that. He couldn't just walk into a gun shop and buy a weapon. There were all sorts of paperwork and red tape to plow through before they'd hand him a gun. He needed a permit to own one and they took weeks to be approved and there was a good chance he'd be turned down, rejected once again.

Rejected by his wife of seven years, rejected by the courts. Nobody loved Ian Johnson and it was really pissing him off. The noise in his head increased to a roar. The traffic around him receded. He glanced in his rearview mirror and saw his kids. The twins, identical in nearly every way, sat either side of their sister. They were unusually quiet and subdued, as if sensing their father's dark mood.

The memory of his ex-wife smiling broadly as the judge handed down his decision ate into his gut. When her lawyer had hugged her in triumph, she'd even teared up. The stupid bitch had been crying, as if the decision meant so much to her. Would it have been so hard if the judge had found against her, given Ian residence of his kids?

He was their father, he deserved more than a stingy fifty-two days a year. It wasn't fucking right that Natalie got them the rest of the time. He loved them as much as she did. He took care of them just as well. They'd had a great weekend together. They'd gone fishing on the pier. They'd eaten ice cream and donuts and soda. Lacey had fallen over and skinned her little knee, but he'd stuck a plaster over it and wiped away her tears. He'd stopped by a department store and had bought them all some toys. His little girl had fallen asleep with her new teddy bear tucked under her arm. She still had the stupid thing with her now, stuffed beside her car seat.

They were on the Harbour Bridge, heading east of the city toward Randwick, where his kids went to school. Lacey's daycare center was nearby. The sun glinted off the water, turning it golden. It looked like it was going to be another great spring day, but what did he care about things like that when his life was in free fall? When some fucking stranger had believed the lies of his ex-wife and had passed him over as the primary care giver of his kids.

He punched the steering wheel again and this time cursed aloud.

"Is everything okay, Daddy?"

Ian glanced again in the rearview mirror and narrowed his eyes at Bailey. "No, son. Everything's gone to shit. The judge said I could only see you on the weekend every fortnight. You have to stay with your mother the rest of the time. It's bullshit, Bailey! That's what it is and I'm not going to stand for it!"

Bailey's expression became pinched and frightened. Darby had also paled. Oblivious to the harsh words that he'd spoken, Lacey chattered quietly to her bear. Ian glanced from one child to the other and an idea formed in his mind. He couldn't buy a gun and blow the judge's head off, but there were other ways to make his protests known.

His gaze fell on Lacey and his gut tightened in anticipation. Yes, she'd do. She was exactly the right size. His lip curled up in a sneer. He'd show them not to fuck with Ian Johnson. He'd show them once and for all and his hoity-toity ex-wife who'd always thought she was better than him and the judge who'd stared down his nose at him and had stolen away his kids could both go to hell.

With his mind made up, he switched on his indicator and abruptly changed lanes. A car horn blasted behind him, but he pause. With his foot planted on the accelerator, he steered the vehicle through the heavy morning traffic. For his plan to work, he needed to be in the lane furthest to the left.

Spying an emergency parking bay, he flicked on his indicator once again, headed straight for it and braked. Flinging off his seat belt, he opened the car door and then opened the rear passenger side door on his side. Bailey stared up at him in alarm.

"What are you doing, Daddy? Why are we pulled up?"

Ignoring the questions, Ian reached over his son and unstrapped Lacey from her seat.

"Wait, Daddy! My bear!" she squealed, but he hardly heard her over the noise in his head.

Pulling her across her brother's lap, he tugged her harder until she came free of the car. Holding her on his hip, he strode over to the barricade and without pause, stepped over it. Lacey clung to him with her small hands, her face turned up to his. Sweet and trusting, it tugged at his heart, but then the anger took over once again.

He cleared the steel barricades that stood

between him and the pedestrian lane and then walked the short distance to the high wire fence that served as a barricade between the pedestrians and the water far below. The roar in his head grew louder. It thundered through his ears. Lacey's eyes widened in confusion and then they filled with sudden fear. He held her high and braced himself and then threw her over the fence with all his might. Up, up, up she went and cleared it with a foot to spare. And then began free falling over the other side, all the way to the bottom.

There, it was done. That would show them. Now he could get on with his day. Calmer now, he returned to the car and climbed back behind the wheel. Flicking on his indicator, he once again headed out into the traffic.

"Daddy! Daddy! We have to go back!" Bailey cried, his eyes huge and dark in his pale face.

Ian looked at his sons through the rearview mirror. Tears poured down both of their cheeks.

"Daddy! We have to go back." Darby repeated his brother's words. "Please, Daddy! Please! Lacey can't swim!"

"Lacey's fine," Ian muttered, his anger still raw and fresh. "Don't worry. The water's not deep."

"It looks deep," Bailey whispered, staring out the window.

"How will Mommy find her?" Darby asked, his voice cracking on a fresh sob.

"She doesn't finish work until late," Bailey added, fear stark on his pale face.

"Lacey's fine. I told you," Ian snapped, his patience wearing thin. "Now, shut the fuck up about it. I don't want to hear another word out of either of you until I drop you off at school."

The harsh reprimand did its job. Both boys fell deathly silent. Tears continued to roll down their cheeks, but Ian resolutely ignored them. He'd done what he had to do. It wasn't his fault. They'd pushed him into taking drastic action. It was too bad Lacey had borne the brunt.

But that was the way it was.

CHAPTER 2

Nat frowned at the computer screen in front of her and once again tried to find the error in the figures that covered the page. She'd been entering the pile of invoices into the excel spreadsheet open on her screen, but something wasn't right. She made a sound of exasperation. Computers were all very good when the data entered into their programs was accurate, but they still didn't compensate for human error.

The truth was, she'd entered the wrong data in somewhere, but she couldn't work it out. She blamed her unaccustomed ineptitude on the sleepless couple of nights she'd endured over the weekend. Coupled with the stress of the morning that had come to a head in another argument with her ex and the week had begun just dandy.

She grimaced and rubbed her forehead. A headache was already beginning to form behind her eyes and it was barely half-past nine. The day stretched out in front of her, long and unrelenting.

The only good thing about it was that the end would bring a reunion with her children. It seemed like a lifetime had passed since she'd seen them.

She sighed sadly. Now that the family law orders had been finalized, she faced more than a decade of missing every other weekend with her kids. She'd wanted to protest any time they spent with their father, but her lawyer had explained gently that such a thing was unrealistic and she knew it was true. Ian was their daddy. Nothing was going to change that. He was entitled to spend time with them, even a couple of days a fortnight. She shouldn't begrudge him. He'd been a good father. It was only as a husband he'd fallen down.

Still, that was all behind her and now that they'd finally finished with the courts, she could look to the future and start getting on with her life. Her children deserved the best mother she could be. It wasn't their fault their parents had fallen out of love.

The phone at her elbow peeled and she absently reached over to pick it up, her gaze still focused on the computer monitor.

"Baker and Carr Construction. This is Natalie. May I help you?"

"Oh, Natalie. It's Janice Bourke from Caring Kids Daycare Center. I noticed Lacey hasn't come in today. Is she sick?"

Nat started in surprise and frowned in confusion. "What do you mean, she hasn't come in? My ex-husband said he would drop her off. He had the kids for the weekend. She should have been there an hour ago."

"Well, I'm not sure if he stopped in. I didn't see him and Lacey isn't here."

A swift burst of anger surged through Nat. *The bastard! He'd taken her to work!* She should have known she couldn't trust him. He hated having Lacey in daycare. Barely holding onto her temper, she thanked Janice for her call and hung up. She immediately picked up the receiver again and dialed her ex-husband's number, fury pouring through her veins.

"Ian!" she shouted when he answered. "Where's Lacey? Why didn't you drop her off at daycare, like you promised? That's the last time I'm going to fall for that! What about the boys? Did they make it to school, or have you given all of them the day off?"

"*Tut, tut*, Natalie. You're always so angry. Of course the boys are at school. What do you think I am?"

His condescending tone grated on her nerves. She gritted her teeth and did her best to get ahold on her temper.

"What about Lacey? The daycare center just called me. You didn't drop her off. Where is she?"

"She's gone."

"What the hell do you mean, she's gone?"

"Like I said. She's gone."

Something in the calmness of his words sent a chill down her spine. Icy dread formed a pool in her stomach.

"Ian, stop playing games. I mean it. Where's Lacey?" She hated that her voice trembled with fear, but there was nothing she could do about it.

"Are you *stupid?*" he yelled. "I already told you! She's fucking gone!"

Nat tried and failed to stem her panic. "Gone *where?*"

"I threw her off the fucking bridge. She's gone."

A tightness started low in Nat's belly and worked its way across her chest. She couldn't breathe. This couldn't be happening... Not to her baby... Not to Lacey... Nat opened her mouth and screamed.

Work colleagues stared at her in shock. She barely registered their reaction. Out of control, she screamed and screamed again.

"My baby! He's killed my baby! Please! Somebody help me! Somebody call the police!" Devastated by sobs of terror, she collapsed on the floor. People gathered around her. Someone reached for her and tried to help her to her feet, but her legs wouldn't support her and she collapsed back against the floor.

"Somebody call an ambulance! This woman needs help!"

"No! No! The police," Nat cried. Her voice seemed to come from a long way away. "Please, he's killed my baby. I need the police." Once again, her sobs overwhelmed her and she bent over, gasping.

"Natalie, look at me."

The stern voice of her boss broke through the terror that had overtaken her mind. She stared up at Jason Gregson and did her best to control the panic that held her in a vice-like grip.

"J-Jason. He has my baby! He has Lacey!"

Jason knew all about the drawn out battle she'd had with her ex over the kids. "Ian, right?" he asked.

"Yes! He just called me! He told me he'd thrown Lacey over the side of the bridge! He was supposed to take her to daycare. Please, we need to call the police!"

Jason held out his hand and helped her to her feet. This time, with his support, she managed to stay upright.

"The police have been called," Jason assured her. "An ambulance is also on its way." He looked at her pointedly.

"No! I don't need an ambulance! I'm fine! I need to find my baby!"

"The police will be here shortly. You can tell them all about it. What exactly did Ian say?"

"He-he told me Lacey was gone. That he'd thrown her over the side of the bridge."

Jason frowned. "He couldn't have possibly meant that literally. He's just playing games with you, Nat. Like he's done so many times."

"But the woman from the daycare center said Lacey wasn't there! He must have her somewhere!"

"Yes. We need to find her. Oh, good. Here are the police."

Jason led her over to an empty desk and helped her into a chair. He greeted the officers that stood in the doorway of the open concept office and brought them over to where she sat.

"Natalie." Jason's voice was gentle, soothing. "These officers are here to help you. Tell them what you know."

In a voice that trembled with fear and confusion, Nat relayed the conversation she'd had with her ex. The police looked disconcertingly concerned, particularly when they were made aware that she and Ian had been in the middle of a messy custody battle that had been finalized in her favor only the week before.

"What do you think your ex-husband meant when he said he'd thrown Lacey off the bridge?" the older of the two officers asked, his expression somber.

Nat shook her head in bewilderment. Now that she'd had time to calm down, she realized that what Jason had said was true. Ian couldn't possibly have meant his words literally. No one in their right mind tossed their child over the side of a bridge. No, he must have meant...

She shook her head and desperate tears once again spilled down over her cheeks. She bit back a sob. She didn't *know* what he meant. All she knew was that she wanted her baby back. *Now.* She needed to pull her little girl into her arms and know that she was safe. She needed to hold her close and never let her go. She needed to tell her she loved her. She looked up at the police officer.

"Please," she sobbed. "You need to find her. You need to find my baby!"

"We'll do everything we can, ma'am. We need to get some more information. Can you give us your ex-husband's full name?"

Nat gave him the information.

"What about his address?"

Once again, she gave him what he asked.

"Where does he work?"

"He works from home!" she cried, her patience exhausted. "Please, officer. I understand you need information, but my baby's out there! She needs me! You have to find her."

The officer regarded her with a sympathetic look on his face and Nat tried hard to get herself under control. He was only doing his job. He couldn't find Lacey without her help. She took in a fortifying breath and tried again.

"I'm sorry. I... I'm a little overwrought. The phone call from Ian... It sent chills down my spine. I actually believed him when he told me he'd thrown Lacey off the bridge. It sounds ridiculous. I mean, who would do such a thing? He's her father! He loves her! He must have said it to upset me."

The officer looked at her curiously and waited for her to continue.

She dragged in another deep breath. "We... We had an argument this morning. Ian and I. He was late returning the kids. They spent the weekend with him, but he was supposed to bring them home by eight. He told me he'd overslept and that he'd drop the boys at school and take Lacey to daycare. Even though I was mad at him, I was grateful for his offer. It meant I wouldn't be late for work."

"How did he sound over the phone?" the second officer asked.

"He sounded okay this morning. Annoyed that I was mad that he hadn't brought the kids home at the allotted time, but not anything over the top.

He sounded quite reasonable when he offered to do the school run. When I found out Lacey hadn't arrived at daycare and I called him a second time, he sounded quite different. He ended up screaming at me, saying over and over that Lacey was gone. When I questioned him, he told me he'd thrown her off the bridge."

The second officer scribbled notes in a notebook. The older officer looked grim. "What kind of car was your ex-husband driving?" he asked.

"An early model Toyota HiLux ute. A four door. It's white."

"Do you know the plate number?"

"Yes. He has personalized plates. IJ 1987."

"I take it he's thirty?" the first officer asked.

"Yes. We're the same age."

The second officer made a few more notes and then looked at his superior. "I'll call the station. Have them put out a BOLO on the car."

Nat frowned. The officer noticed her confusion. "It means 'be on the lookout'," he explained.

"I'll have a patrol car attend your ex-husband's address. See if we can find him home. With a bit of luck, he'll have your daughter with him," the older officer said.

"Th-thank you," Nat managed and then another thought struck her. "I need to call the school. I need to make sure my boys are there."

"We can do that for you, Ms Johnson," the same officer offered.

"No, it's all right. It will be quicker coming from me. Besides, I don't want to alarm anyone unnecessarily. As you say, hopefully Lacey's safe and sound at home with her dad." Nat heard the tremor in her voice, but forced herself keep her thoughts positive.

With something else to focus on, she felt stronger and quickly made the call to her boys' school. Her voice almost sounded normal when she asked the office lady if Darby and Bailey were there.

"Yes, I believe your ex-husband dropped them off earlier. I saw them running into the school a little while after the bell went. He really should sign them in at the office if he's going to be late. That's the correct procedure."

Nat couldn't hide her relief. After asking the woman to keep an eye on her boys, she assured her she'd pass the request onto Ian and ended the call. She looked up at the officers standing nearby and gave them the news.

"So, the boys are where they should be," the senior officer replied. "That's a good sign. Let's hope he was only playing games with you about Lacey. We'd best get going."

The officers made their farewells and Nat accompanied them to the door that led from the office out to the elevators.

Nat grabbed the sleeve of the older officer. "You'll call me, won't you? As soon as you know anything?" she asked.

"Yes, of course. We'll keep you informed," he replied.

"Don't worry, Ms Johnson," the younger officer added. "We'll find her."

Nat watched them disappear behind the sliding doors of the elevator and hoped he was right.

In the end, it took the police two days to find Lacey's little body. She'd been swept along with the tide and was discovered by a fisherman washed up near a rocky outcrop several miles away. Nat could still see the officer's face, pale and drawn, as he brought her the grave news. She'd see his face and hear his words until the day she died.

"I'm sorry, Ms Johnson. We've found your daughter. I'm so very sorry. There was nothing we could do."

Chapter 3

Blake Harton Junior ran a hand through his short blond hair and thought about the weekend ahead. It was hump day and that was the perfect day to start planning some Friday and Saturday night revelry. It was one of the reasons he steered away from long term girlfriends. They always ended up expecting something from him. He liked the freedom of choosing what he did with his time, including his weekends. Of course, that wasn't the only reason he was still footloose and fancy free at the ripe old age of thirty-two. His brother was most of it.

With a grimace, he forced the thought from his mind. Perhaps he'd take his boat out this weekend? The weather was supposed to be fine and sunny. There was nothing like the feeling of pushing his boat full throttle across Sydney Harbour, with the sound of the waves crashing across the bow and the wind lifting his hair. It had been months since he'd been on the water. This weekend might be the time. He'd call his work colleague and buddy, Ben Fitzgerald and his new wife, Abby. They'd been married a month now. Long enough to want to come up for some air and touch base with the real world.

Reaching across his desk, he picked up the phone, intent on making the call. Now that Ben was a junior partner like him, they both worked on the same floor, but it was easier to buzz his workmate's office than to walk the gamut of female secretaries and young associates who would vie for his attention as he went passed. It happened every time.

Before he could get Ben on the phone, there was a knock on his door and his secretary, Esther Otieno appeared in the opening.

"Blake, I have a man by the name of Ian Johnson on the phone," she announced.

He frowned. "Ian Johnson? Why's that name familiar?"

"That's why I came in here instead of using the intercom. You have a client waiting out there. I didn't want her to overhear me."

Blake's frown deepened. "What would that matter?"

Esther huffed an impatient sigh. Her fat cheeks wobbled with the effort. Blake had seen all the TV shows where the lawyers worked in glitzy offices with hot young secretaries hanging on their every word. Esther was as tall as she was round and was black and shiny like freshly washed coal. She'd emigrated from Kenya and had been at Sydney Legal for more than ten years.

When Blake had made junior partner a few

years earlier, he'd inherited Esther, along with a much nicer office. While he couldn't complain about the view out his window, Esther had been another story, but it hadn't taken him long to realize that there was nothing going on both inside the office and out that Esther didn't know about or could get access to the information. She was worth her weight in gold.

"Don't you ever watch television?" she asked, placing her hands on her hips. "It's been all over the news. The man on the phone—Ian Johnson—he's the one who dropped his baby over the side of the bridge."

Blake started in shock. Fragments of sound bites and film clips came back to him in a rush. He'd heard something about the awful tragedy. Most everyone in Sydney had. He couldn't believe the man who was supposed to have done it was calling him.

"Tell him I'm unavailable and I'll be that way for the best part of the year."

Esther raised her eyebrows. "You don't want to do it?"

Blake shook his head, impatient and bewildered. "Why would I want to represent a man who tossed his child over the side of the Sydney Harbour Bridge?"

"Allegedly, Counselor. Don't forget whose side you're on."

Blake cursed beneath his breath. "I'm not on anyone's side and I sure as hell aren't going to represent a man who could be capable of something like that. Tell him I'm not interested."

To his consternation, Esther stood her ground. "I agree, it's a nasty one, but I think you should take his call."

Blake narrowed his gaze at her. "Why?"

"The thing is, this man was in the middle of a bitter custody battle. He was at his wit's end. He told me he didn't mean for it to happen. It just did."

Blake stared blindly at the papers on his desk, his mind in a turmoil. Esther was one of the few people who knew the truth about his brother, David. After a long moment of silence, Blake raised his head.

"Where is he?"

"At home. He was released on bail earlier today. He said he can be here within the hour."

Blake sighed in resignation. No doubt he'd regret his decision, but right now, he didn't have a choice. "Tell him to make an appointment."

Esther nodded soberly. Blake's capitulation didn't appear to bring her any joy. "There's one other thing," she said.

Blake groaned and threw her a death stare. "What is it?"

"Johnson can't afford to pay a lawyer. He's spent all his money in the family court."

Blake seized upon the excuse he'd been hoping for. "That's too bad. Give him the number for Legal Aid."

Esther just stood there and continued to look at him, a questioning look upon her face. Blake cursed again.

"Dammit, Esther! What do you want me to do?"

She shrugged. "It isn't like you don't do pro bono cases every now and then. Why would this one be any different?"

Blake glared at her. "You know why. Do I have to spell it out?"

Her expression gentled and her eyes filled with compassion. "No, you don't have to spell it out, but I think we both know you need to do this. This man has been through hell and it isn't over, yet. He needs you."

Blake clenched his jaw and ground his back teeth. He counted silently to ten, but the tension that had him coiled tight didn't ease. Esther had him over a barrel and she knew it. She knew he was going to say yes. His head screamed out all the reasons why he shouldn't do it, but his heart wouldn't have a bar of it.

"All right, you win. I'll take the case on for free. But you'd better tell him to get his butt over here as quickly as he can, before I change my mind."

Esther's face broke out into a smile. Her teeth shone white against her dark skin. "Thank you, Blake. You won't regret it."

She shut the door behind her and Blake sat back in his chair with a sigh. It wasn't often his secretary was wrong, but this time at least, she was. She'd barely cleared the doorway and already he was regretting what he'd done.

It was almost two hours' later that Blake escorted Ian Johnson into his office. The man looked nothing like he'd expected. Of medium height and average build, Ian Johnson was quiet and softly spoken. His nondescript, light-brown hair was a little long for the current fashion and he was in need of a shave, but he answered Blake's questions respectfully and what Blake believed was the truth.

"You've been charged with the murder of your daughter," Blake stated once they had the preliminaries out of the way.

Johnson stared at the carpet. "Yes."

Blake kept his gaze fixed on his client. He'd already read the police facts. Now he wanted to hear it from the man who'd allegedly tossed his daughter over the side of a bridge. "Tell me what happened."

With his head downcast and his elbows resting on his knees, Blake's client began to relay the events that had culminated in the terrible tragedy. He talked about the divorce and bitter custody battle and how he'd lost the right to see his kids.

"Two days every fortnight, that's all the judge gave me. Two days! How are they supposed to get to know me, to love me when I don't see them for most of every month? It's bullshit!" Ian's voice cracked on a huge sob that seemed to start from the bottom of his chest. He gasped and held his head in his hands. Blake sat silently and let the man cry.

"They're my kids as much as hers!" he cried. "That judge didn't know anything! He took my kids away from me! My kids! My fucking kids!"

Blake understood the man's pain. While he wasn't a father, he'd done his fair share of family law work. It was never easy dividing up the assets. When it came to the children and the orders to be made, tough didn't begin to describe it. There were never any winners in a family law dispute. It was one of the main reasons he'd turned his back on practicing that kind of law. He preferred to concentrate on criminal matters. Less heartache involved, most of the time.

"What happened on the day Lacey died, Ian?" he asked quietly.

The man took a moment to gather himself. When he started talking again, his voice was low and quiet.

"The day started out badly, right from the start. I overslept and was running late. I was supposed to have the kids back at my ex-wife's house at eight and it was already nearly that when I woke. She rang me, busting my balls over the fact I hadn't returned them on time. We argued. I eventually offered to do the school run myself."

"You had all three children with you?"

"Yes."

Blake absorbed the information and his gut filled with dread. If he were right, his client had tossed the young child over the side of the bridge with his other children witnessing it. He forced himself to ask the question.

"Yes, all three kids were sitting on the back seat."

"What happened after you ended the phone call to your ex-wife? I take it she agreed to let you drop the kids off at school and at the daycare center?"

"Yes. She was happy. It meant she wouldn't be late for work. It was always about Natalie.

Then, and now." His lip curled upwards in a sneer.

Ben didn't react. He'd seen it all before. In his experience, people who'd fought long and bitter custody battles didn't usually have good things to say about the other person. He let the comment slide.

"What happened after you ended the call to—Natalie, is it?"

"Yes. Natalie. I was still so mad about her giving me grief about being late and I couldn't stop thinking about the court decision. It was a final decision. It had been handed down the Friday before. The judge found in favor of my ex."

He spat the word and Blake caught the glint of anger in his eyes. Once again, he didn't judge the man for his reaction. It was an unfortunately normal attitude most divorced couples had toward each other.

"Let's go back to the weekend before," Blake suggested. "It was your weekend with your children, right?"

"Right. I picked them up at six from Natalie's. She doesn't get home from work until then."

"Where are the boys in between time?" Blake asked, curious.

"After school care," Ian snarled.

Once again, Blake didn't react. "So, you took them back to your place and you had a nice weekend."

Ian smiled softly. "Yes, we did. We played football in the park across from my apartment and I pushed Lacey on the swings. We watched TV, went to the shops and on Sunday, we went fishing off the pier. We did the usual things—ice cream and stuff—we had fun."

"Did anything else happen?"

Ian stared at the floor and his hands clenched into fists. "Their mother called a few times to speak with them throughout the course of the weekend, including right before they went to bed. She reminded me to have them back on time, so they wouldn't be late for school. That's why she was so pissed when I overslept. Anyway, after I hung up the phone, I kept thinking about her and how the judge had given her my kids. I guess it got to me, knowing that it was finally all over and she'd won."

He dragged in a ragged breath and continued. "I found a bottle of rum in the cupboard and I smoked a couple of joints. The kids had gone to bed and I needed to do something to relax. I felt like going around to Natalie's and punching her in the face. I knew that wouldn't be good for anyone, least of all my kids."

Blake stilled. "Was there violence in your marriage?"

Ian looked affronted. "Hell, no!"

Blake held up his hands. "I'm sorry. I have to ask."

"It's all right. I understand," Ian muttered.

"So, you'd been drinking pretty heavily and smoking marijuana the night before this happened, right?" Blake asked.

"Right. I woke up in the morning with a pounding headache and the kids screaming for me to get them breakfast. I realized I'd overslept and I knew Natalie would be mad. I was mad at myself for giving her the opportunity. Then she phoned and called me out and everything went downhill from there." He shrugged. "You already know what happened after that."

Blake pursed his lips and watched his client closely. So far, the man appeared to be telling the truth. "Yes, you pulled over into the emergency lane halfway across the Sydney Harbour Bridge. You removed your three-year-old daughter from her car seat and tossed her over the side, all while your young sons watched on. Did I miss anything?"

Ian's face turned red with embarrassment. He looked at Blake and anger glinted in his eyes. "I guess that's about it."

Blake held the man's gaze, trying to get his head around the enormity of what had happened. "Why did you do it, Ian? What made you throw your little girl over the side of the bridge?"

Ian's hands clenched and unclenched and his breath came hard and fast. He stared at the carpet and Blake wondered if his client was going to answer. Ian had already told him he'd refused to participate in a record of interview with the police. Would he be prepared to talk to his lawyer? Blake was about to find out.

"I was off my head," Ian started, his voice low and rough. "I was furious about the court decision. I was mad at Natalie for chewing my ass. I was still half-drunk and hungover, foggy from the joints. I wasn't thinking straight. I wasn't thinking at all."

He fell silent. Blake continued to watch him steadily. "Why Lacey?" he asked finally. "The boys were in the car, too. Why not one of them?"

Ian compressed his lips and continued to stare down at the floor. "She was small enough to lift over the fence. It's probably the best part of seven feet high. The boys would have been too heavy to toss."

The words were uttered quietly and without inflection. To Blake, seated across from him, their effect was devastating. Shock reverberated in his head and sent chills running up and down his spine. His gut twisted. He thought he might be sick. Fighting back the nausea, he distracted himself by scrawling some notes down on the blank legal pad in front of him. When he felt more in control of himself, he looked up at his client.

"I'm going to arrange for you to see a psychiatrist. I'll organize an appointment for as soon as possible. I'm hoping the medical diagnoses will support a defense that when you acted the way you did, you were in a dissociative state. There's no denying you tossed your child over the side of the Harbour Bridge. Claiming dissociation is our only hope."

"What the hell is a dissociate state?" Ian muttered.

"There are a few different types of dissociation, but generally it's defined as disruptions in aspects of consciousness, identity, memory, physical actions and/or the environment. The most common causes typically include some form of prolonged trauma such as sexual or physical abuse. The stress of war can also cause dissociation. I'm willing to argue that the prolonged stress of your divorce and bitter custody battle triggered the condition."

Ian nodded uncertainly. Blake continued.

"One of the signs of dissociation is a sense of detachment from oneself; seeing one's life as if it's a movie. From what you've described, I think that's what you were experiencing out on the bridge, but in order to successfully argue it as a defense to the murder charge, I need to back my hypothesis with medical proof."

"Hence the visit to the shrink," Ian said dryly.

"Exactly. And that's why we're going to plead not guilty," Blake added.

Ian's face flooded with relief. "You believe me? You believe me when I tell you I didn't mean to do it?"

An image of David appeared before Blake and he hurriedly forced it away. This wasn't about his brother. It was about a client who desperately needed his help.

"I believe you were in a dissociative state and you didn't know what you were doing. I'm prepared to take that argument to court and fight my very hardest to get a jury to believe it."

Moisture appeared in Ian's eyes and Blake could tell the man was trying to hold back tears. It moved him to know how important it was to Ian that Blake believe he hadn't meant to murder his daughter and Blake suddenly realized it was important to him, too. Once again, his brother's image swam before his eyes. This time, David was smiling. Esther had been right, after all. Blake was glad he'd taken the case.

At the Hand of her Father will be released on 25 June, 2017 and is available for pre-order from your favorite digital retailer.

About the Author

Chris Taylor grew up on a farm in north-west New South Wales, Australia. She always had a thirst for stories and recalls writing her first book at the ripe old age of eight. Always a lover of romance and happily-ever-afters, a career in criminal law sparked her interest in intrigue and suspense. For Chris to be able to combine romance with suspense in her books is a dream come true.

Chris is married to Linden and is the mother of five children. If not behind her computer, you can find her doing the school run, taxiing children to swimming lessons, football, ballet and cricket. In her spare time, Chris loves to read her favorite authors who include Richard North Patterson, Sandra Brown, Kathleen E Woodiwiss and Jude Devereaux.

You can find out more about Chris and sign up for her newsletter at her website:

http://www.christaylorauthor.com.au